EMMA'S SECRET

EMMA'S SECRET

EMMA'S SECRET

Steena Holmes

amazon publishing

Text copyright © 2013 Steena Holmes

Printed in the United States of America.

Published by Amazon Publishing
P.O. Box 400818, Las Vegas, NV 89140
ISBN-13: 9781477800669
ISBN-10: 1477800662

This book is dedicated to all those who fell in love with Emma and wanted to know more. Without you, there would be no story.

CHAPTER ONE

June 20

I found her.

I was driving in a neighborhood that I'd never visited before. I had been headed somewhere else, but now I can't remember where. I'm not even sure how I got to be in that part of Kinrich—I rarely go there anymore unless it's to my special spot on the lake. Jack thinks I was there for groceries, but I prefer going to Hanton for my shopping, even though it is farther away.

Call it fate or divine intervention or just a deep awareness. If my mother were here, she'd say it was God's angels directing me, but God turned His back on me a long time ago. Or maybe it was the other way around. Either way, it was destined that I was to be there, at that time and place, for a specific reason.

My poor little girl was wandering all alone. I don't know how she got to be so far from home or why she was alone, but I'm so glad I saw her as I drove by.

My sweet little Mary has come home!

No, not Mary. Her daughter. My second chance.

Such a brave little girl to be out by herself. She kept telling me that she wasn't alone, that her small stuffed lion was watching over her. As I buckled her into the backseat, she introduced me to her little toy, which she called Tiger. What a sweet little girl.

She didn't talk much; only cried a little before she fell asleep. The poor thing must have been exhausted.

Jack was confused when I brought her home. She looked so much like Mary, almost her twin. Of course, we never knew Mary had a daughter; why would she tell us? Or rather, why would she tell me? But I can't believe she'd let her little girl be out on the streets by herself. Jack wanted to call Mary, to find out why she never told us about her daughter, but I stopped him.

No. She's now our little girl. Our second chance. God knew that she needed to be loved and that we were the perfect people. This is our gift.

She is our precious little Emmie.

⚜

Megan burrowed deeper under the covers, arms tucked tightly to her chest. She didn't want to open her eyes. Not yet. The desire to hold on to her dream a little longer was too strong.

Instead of another nightmare of Emma disappearing, last night's dream was as if her little girl had never been kidnapped. They'd gone for a picnic as a family; there was a cabin in the background and a field of flowers with butterflies flitting about. Emma was running among the flowers, her laughter filling the air as she and the butterflies danced. Peter sat beside her on the bright-red blanket—funny that she remembered its vibrant color. She could almost feel the soft wool beneath her legs and the gentle breeze upon her cheek.

Megan smiled to herself. She'd been so happy in her dream. Peter was with her, and Alexis and Hannah played off to the side.

But the part that held her eyes closed was the heavy feel in her arms and the soft cooing of a baby. Megan couldn't see the baby's face and didn't know if it was a boy or a girl, but she knew the child was hers.

Once upon a time, they'd been a happy family, and if Emma hadn't gone missing, maybe things would have turned out differently.

The sound of Emma's laughter still rang in her ears. Such a beautiful sound. One she no longer heard very often.

Megan rolled over and patted the sheets but found them empty. Again. Lately, Peter had been leaving earlier than normal, not even waking her up for her run. She splayed her fingers across the sheets and realized he must have woken up some time ago; his usual spot was cool.

With a sigh, she rolled over and rubbed her eyes. When she opened them, she saw a solemn Emma staring down at her.

For a very brief moment, Megan wished for that happy little girl from her dream instead of the quiet one in front of her. Just as quickly, Megan pushed that thought away.

"Emma, sweetheart, why are you up so early?"

Emma shrugged and held out the book she'd been holding to her chest.

Megan mustered a smile as she swung her legs out of the bed and sat up. She saw the new recipe book she had bought the night before and left on the kitchen table. She preferred to do her shopping at night, leaving the girls at home and away from prying eyes. She hated the stares and sweet words of encouragement from those who meant well. Emma always tensed up. Megan didn't like putting her daughter in situations like that.

With the kids on summer break, she thought it would be a good time to do some baking with them. Emma seemed to enjoy helping out in the kitchen, so when Megan had spotted the copy of *Kids Can Bake Too* while she had been out shopping, she didn't think twice about buying it, even though she had a cupboard full of cookbooks.

Megan glanced at the clock and groaned. She'd slept in and probably already missed Laurie for their morning run.

"It's a little early to be baking, isn't it?"

Emma shook her head and tendrils of hair escaped the braid Megan had plaited the night before. Her daughter's brows furrowed, and Megan caught the way her fingers tightened around the book.

"Let me shower and have some coffee first, okay?"

A sparkle shone in Emma's eyes, and a glimmer of the girl from Megan's dream peeked through. Maybe it wasn't too late to have that girl back.

To see the smile on Emma's face was all it took for Megan to give in. It was a rare treat. The counselor said it would take time for Emma to readjust to her new life, but Megan hadn't thought it would take this long. Emma needed time, the counselor kept saying. Time to grieve, time to accept the change in her life, and time to accept her new family.

That last bit was what hurt the most. They weren't her *new* family. They were her *only* family. If Megan could, she would erase the last two years when Emma lived in that country farmhouse with an old couple who could barely take care of themselves. But if time was what Emma needed, then time was what she would get.

"Why don't you pick out a recipe and wait for me downstairs?"

Emma turned on her heels and skipped toward the door. She paused before tilting her head and then gave Megan a questioning look.

"Promise, Mommy?"

Megan smiled. She couldn't help it. Even though it had only been a month since Emma's return, she still cherished every time her baby called her Mommy.

"Of course. I'll be right down."

She picked up the towel Peter had left on the floor of their bathroom. A month ago, her goal had been to find her daughter and heal the rift in her marriage. Now it was to help her daughter heal while continuing to look for a way to stop her marriage from crumbling.

❧

Setting his cup of tea on the coffee table, Jack sat down in Dottie's old chair and reached for the multitude of bags she kept to the side of it. Last week, he'd found a box full of knitted scarves, mittens, and hats tucked away at the back of the guest-room closet. He'd taken them into town and dropped them off at the Catholic church. The priest promised that they would find use in wintertime. It was hard getting rid of Dottie's things, but he felt like he didn't have much time left, and the last thing he wanted was someone else going through her things when he wasn't around anymore.

The first bag he grabbed held balls of yarn. Pink, white, and yellow. Jack dug his fingers into the yarn and knew right away that these had been meant for Emmie. Dottie was forever knitting that girl homemade dresses and doll clothes. He considered tossing it all in the donation box, but something stopped him. He wondered whether Emmie's mom knitted? Maybe she would appreciate the yarn. He could mail it to her and explain . . . what? That Dottie bought it to make Emmie things? That would not go over well.

He set the bag off to the side. The next bag he grabbed was heavier. Jack lifted it over the arm of the chair and dropped it into his lap. He pulled out a long brown-and-blue scarf, its soft wool caressing his calloused hands. He remembered the day Dottie bought this yarn. She'd come home excited to have found the perfect color for him. He'd shaken his head at her enthusiasm while she held the ball of wool up to his face. Complemented his eyes, she said. He wasn't sure that he needed a scarf that matched his eyes. Yet here it was, ready for him to wear. Jack wound it around his neck, disregarding the warm summer air. Dottie had spent hours knitting this for him, and he was going to wear it.

Jack pulled out the remaining item. It was a book with a creased, untitled black leather cover. Even without opening it, he knew it was Dottie's journal. It had been a long time since he'd seen this particular one.

She had called this journal a record of her "darkest time." When she'd first said that, Jack didn't understand. It was around the same time Emmie came to live with them, a time Jack thought of as the best years of his recent past. But now he knew what she'd meant. Now he understood why it was her darkest time.

In their bedroom was a bookshelf lined with Dottie's journals. Each cover was a different color, with each hue symbolizing her feelings. The years he had been off at war were all black. Every one of them, except for the first and last. Jack had bought the first journal for her before he left. He chose one with a soft yellow cover because he thought it would make her smile. He'd asked her to write letters to him in that journal. He never thought he'd be gone for so long. The last journal—which Dottie had written in after Jack was listed as MIA—was one he was never tempted to read. The white daisies dotting the soft pink cover symbolized new hope. But the hope she'd then held in her heart wasn't for his return. She'd thought he was dead. The hope was instead of future love. Dottie later confessed that Doug had given her that journal for her birthday.

Even now, Jack hated that cover.

The day he'd returned from war, Jack had brought his Dottie a gift from the shop on base. It was another journal for the love of his life. His return was the start of their new life. He'd even bought

Mary one, sure that Dottie had passed along her journal-writing passion to their daughter. The journal he'd bought for Dottie was bound in a pretty baby-blue material with small yellow flowers. He still remembered his first night back home. They sat on the bed, both a little shy to immediately rekindle the intimacy they'd had.

"What are you doing, Dottie-mine?" Jack had asked when she laid a pink journal in her lap. Dottie's eyes had filled as her fingers ran along the white daisies.

"Putting an end to the black days," she'd whispered.

Jack watched her as she slowly opened the baby-blue journal he'd bought her to the first page. She wrote the date at the top right-hand corner and then glanced over at him.

"What will you write?" he'd asked.

Dottie wrote three words on the page in the flowing script he'd grown to love.

Jack is home.

With a teary smile, she closed the cover. Jack reached for the journal and tossed it on the floor before gathering the woman he loved more than life into his arms.

After all their years together, all the nights they had shared a bed, that night was the most memorable. They'd created another baby that night, only to lose their son one month after he was born. Basil Jack Henry. They named him after Jack's father.

Jack glanced down at the black journal in his hands and knew he couldn't read it. Not yet. But when he rose to head for bed, his tea forgotten on the coffee table, his hold on the journal didn't loosen.

CHAPTER TWO

The smell of freshly baked chocolate-chip cookies wafted through the air as the oven timer dinged. Megan set down the picture in her hands and reached for her worn red oven mitts. She'd have to be careful she didn't burn herself through one of the many holes. She kept meaning to buy a new pair but always forgot.

"Is it my turn now?"

Megan turned and saw Emma standing in the kitchen doorway. Her hopeful tone made Megan smile. It wasn't quite the laughter from her dream, but it was close enough. She could hear the other two girls laughing at some cartoon they were watching in the family room. They'd already made their cookies.

After two years of searching, all Megan had wanted was to have Emma back home. Even when everyone told her she should move on, she'd never given up, never forgotten that her baby girl was out there somewhere. To find out that Emma had lived only twenty minutes away on a farm with the older couple who had kidnapped her . . . Megan wasn't sure she'd ever forgive herself for not looking hard enough.

Megan bent down as she opened the oven door and then turned her head as a heat wave engulfed her face. One day she'd learn to let that initial heat burst escape first. When Emma's unbound, curly golden hair swung out of her line of sight for a brief moment, Megan's breath hitched and held until her daughter's chubby cheek pressed against her arm.

"Careful, honey, this is hot," Megan cautioned as she pulled out the tray of cookies and set it on the cooling stand.

"Can I make my cookies now?" Emma pulled a stool over to the island counter and climbed on it. A new batch of dough sat in a bowl with an open bag of mixed candies beside it.

When Megan had come downstairs after her shower, the three girls were sitting at the kitchen table arguing over which cookie to make. Emma held firm to the cookbook and wouldn't let it go. Hannah wanted oatmeal raisin, Alexis went for chocolate chip, and Emma asked for monster cookies. Luckily, Megan had supplies for all three.

Megan opened a side drawer and searched for an apron that would fit Emma's small frame. She pulled out a pink flower apron her mother had sewn for Hannah when she was smaller and held it up for Emma to see.

"Here, kiddo, let's put this on you to keep your pretty dress clean." Emma had a fondness for dresses. She rarely wore the jeans or shorts Megan had bought for her after she came home. Actually, it was rare for Emma to wear anything Megan had bought for her. If Emma had her way, she'd always wear the clothes that had been packed in her suitcase. The clothes the *others* had provided for her.

Emma turned around on the stool and lifted her arms so Megan could tie the apron strings around her waist. She had to wrap the fabric twice before tying it in a knot.

"Grandma used to do that too," Emma whispered.

Megan froze at Emma's words. She forced herself to take in a deep breath, fighting past the tightness in her chest. Her teeth clenched as she reminded herself to count to five, nice and slow.

"She did, huh?" Megan lifted her gaze from the bow she'd just made to see Emma nod. Her daughter rarely spoke about the woman who had kidnapped her from their front yard.

One night, Emma had overheard Detective Riley Thompson, the man who'd been the one to locate Emma after Megan took that picture at the fair, when he'd dropped by to tell them of Dorothy's passing. Emma should have been in bed, but she'd been sitting at the top of the stairs waiting for Peter to give her a good-night hug. It was Megan who heard her small cry. But it had been too late. Megan knew Emma had heard her say "Thank God" when she learned that Dorothy was dead.

Ever since that night, Emma rarely smiled, unless she was playing with Daisy.

Megan made sure there was now a smile on her face. The hesitation in Emma's eyes slowly disappeared as she lowered her arms and leaned her elbows back down on the island counter. In the beginning, Emma would bring up Jack and Dorothy all the time, asking questions and telling stories. Eventually she stopped. Peter blamed Megan for that. He didn't mind the stories, saying that it helped them to get to know her again. But to know her daughter, Megan didn't need to hear stories of a life lived without her.

"Did you do a lot of baking with her?" She refused to call the woman *grandma*. Despite what Kathy Graham, their family counselor told her, Megan would never accept the relationship between the kidnapper and her daughter.

Emma smiled for a moment, and Megan winced. It bothered her that Emma would be free with her smiles for *that* woman. She straightened her shoulders and her thinking. Emma was *her* daughter. If anyone was going to earn Emma's smiles, it should be the one who loved her the most—Megan.

Emma jumped off the stool and washed her hands at the kitchen sink, holding her hands up high for Megan to see.

"Good job." Megan nodded. "We always need to make sure our hands are clean when we're baking." She moved to stand beside Emma and repeated the same motions. Emma dried her hands on the red dish towel draped over the oven door handle.

"Hey, do you remember when we used to make giant cookies and put faces on them with the candies?" Megan casually brought up a memory she was sure Emma would recall. Emma ignored her, just like she always did. And that bothered Megan more than she wanted to admit. Sure, Emma had been young, but she had to remember something from before she was kidnapped. Even Alexis could remember things they'd done before she was three years old.

Every day, Megan would ask her daughter questions about things from before—before she was taken and raised by another family. She knew she shouldn't, that Emma had been too young and that she might be putting too much pressure on her, but she couldn't help it.

When Emma returned to the chair, Megan handed her the bag of candies. "Okay, kiddo." She sighed. "These are your cookies, so put as much as you want in." Emma's eyes widened in delight as she reached for the bag and peered inside.

"All of them?"

Megan pretended to think about that. She pursed her lips and narrowed her eyes as she gazed at the bag. Emma slowly lowered the bag, the smile disappearing from her face. But when Megan finally nodded, she squealed.

Her daughter actually squealed. Megan couldn't stifle the laughter bubbling up inside her. For the first time in weeks, the heavy weight of sorrow had ever so briefly lifted from her daughter's small shoulders.

Megan wished Peter were home to see this. He'd been so worried about Emma, wondering whether they'd done the right thing by cutting off any ties she had with the older couple. But if he could see her now, he'd realize that all she needed was time. Time to realize this family—her real family—loved her even more.

Megan smiled. Contentment filled her soul, and it felt good. It had been so long. The last time had been only a month ago at the farmhouse when she had finally, after two long years of searching, held Emma in her arms again. Since then, the emotional roller coaster seemed to never end. She handed her daughter a wooden spoon to mix the candy into the cookie dough.

She caught sight of Emma's dog on the patio. The cute little yellow retriever that came home with Emma had grown into an awkward dog but still managed to worm its way into her heart despite her insistence that she hated dogs. Other than the suitcase full of clothes, a few books, and some dolls, Daisy was the only other connection Emma had to the people who had kidnapped her.

"Do you want to scoop the cookies or would you rather go outside to play with Daisy?" Megan dipped the cookie scoop in a cup of hot water while Emma glanced behind her where Daisy sat near the sliding door.

"Grandma said you always have to finish what you start." She bit her lip and looked back from the sliding door to the mixing bowl.

Megan moved to stand beside Emma and reached for the apron bow she'd tied earlier. "Tell you what: I'll finish the cookies while you go grab Daisy a treat from the cupboard. She's been waiting for you like a good little dog." It warmed her heart to watch Emma jump off the chair without hesitating and grab a dog treat from the cupboard. Little by little, she was going to erase that woman from Emma's mind.

She scooped cookie dough onto the pan as Emma stood in the doorway watching her. Daisy was jumping up on the glass wanting to be let in, and Megan was doing her best to ignore it.

"Mommy?"

She raised her gaze from the cookies and realized Emma was now standing next to her at the counter. In her hands was a drawing she'd made last night before bed. Megan had found it this morning on the kitchen table. It was a picture of Emma holding hands with her and Peter.

"Can we mail this today? To Papa?"

Megan tried to hide her sigh. "You didn't make that for me or Daddy?"

Emma shook her head. "This is for Papa. Can we send it to him today?"

It was impossible to say no while looking at her daughter's beaming face. Emma honestly thought she was going to mail the drawing. The sparkle was still in her eye. Megan wasn't about to take that away from her, not if it meant the smile would stay, but neither would she lie.

Instead, she kept quiet.

⚜

Soft giggles drifted in through the open window and wrapped around Megan's heart, squeezing it until she was sure it would break.

She placed the lid on the last Tupperware container full of freshly baked cookies and left it on the counter. She'd made sure to combine all the cookies so that there would be some of each kind in every batch. A few containers were now in her freezer, with one in her fridge. No doubt this one would soon be empty.

She glanced around her kitchen and realized she had nothing to do. She'd already cleaned up after the cookie fiasco this morning, lunch dishes were in the dishwasher, and the girls were outside playing. Her house was spotless—how could it not be when she was home every day with little to do but clean? Maybe she'd make some coffee and read through the stack of unread magazines sitting in the foyer. But the thought held little appeal.

When did her life screech to a halt? Normally, she'd be busy with meetings and errands. But then again, that would be during the school year, when the Safe Walks program was up and running.

As she watched through the kitchen window at her daughters playing, Megan rubbed at the knots in her neck. The scene felt surreal. She pinched herself to make sure she wasn't dreaming.

"Penny for your thoughts?"

Startled, Megan whirled around to find Laurie standing in the doorway to her kitchen holding two iced lattes.

"You scared me." Megan caught her breath and then reached for one of the drinks.

"Really? I couldn't tell." Laurie smiled before leaning over the island counter, pushing some papers out of the way.

Megan turned back toward the window to watch her daughters. The girls sat in a circle on the grass, picking the pesky yellow dandelions around them. Daisy's head was in Emma's lap, her tail thumping the grass.

"Poor kiddo. This must all be hard on her. Is she adjusting?"

Megan shook her head. She was beginning to wonder if she ever would adjust. Did Emma wish she were back at that farm, living with those *other* people? Megan wasn't sure she wanted to know the answer.

"I know you don't want to hear this, but will you ever let *him* see her?"

Megan clenched her fists when she saw Laurie holding Emma's latest drawing.

She snatched the drawing out of her friend's hand. "No." Of course she wasn't going to. Why did everyone assume she would? He might not have physically taken her daughter, but he kept her. For two years. He didn't deserve to see Emma.

There was a look in Laurie's gaze that Megan didn't like. A look she'd seen too often.

"He had her for two years. I only just got her back." Megan dared Laurie to disagree with her and was surprised to see her only shrug her shoulders.

"True." Laurie took a sip of her drink. "You should make him wait at least two years. An eye for an eye."

Megan nodded. That was her sentiment as well.

"Of course, you might as well tell Em that he's dead, since he probably will be by then." The edge in Laurie's voice was unmistakable. The smile disappeared from Megan's face.

"That was harsh."

Laurie took her drink and stood at the patio doors. "I know." A sad smile crossed her face. "We promised way back when that we'd always tell each other the truth, even if it hurts. Remember? I think you need to let go just a bit. It's eating you up inside."

Megan shook her head. She wasn't ready to let her fear and hatred go. Kathy had told her not to rush it, that it would come. Just like the day Emma would leave her sight and it wouldn't hurt so much. So she wasn't rushing; there was no reason to. Emma was home where she belonged: with her family. Her real family. And that was all that mattered.

"Are you going to mail that one?" Laurie nodded her head toward the picture Emma had drawn for Jack. It was a pathway lined with flowers, similar to the ones that Emma had helped Jack plant at his farmhouse.

"You're pushing me too hard." She thought about the letters she had mailed during that first week; Emma had written to Jack at least once a day. After the tenth one, Megan suggested they space out the mailings, especially when the first letter from Jack arrived for Emma. Megan had panicked and hidden it, only to have Peter find it and hand it to Emma who had lit up like a Christmas tree. She'd held on to that letter for days, even taking it with her to bed.

Laurie shook her head. "Someone has to. Honestly, Megan, I'm starting to get really worried about you. You rarely leave the house, and when you do, it's always with Emma by your side."

Megan crossed her arms. Emma was only five years old; it wasn't like she could leave her home alone. Besides, Megan went grocery shopping last night alone while Peter was home with the kids.

"Plus, you've canceled every girls' night we've scheduled in the past month."

Megan frowned. She didn't cancel every one. Just the last two, maybe three, times that Laurie had tried to plan one. Okay, so she had canceled every time. But it wasn't all her fault.

"Sorry. I have to work around Peter's schedule. If Hannah was a year older, I'd feel more comfortable with her babysitting." Megan shrugged, hoping Laurie would see past her weak excuse and accept her apology.

From the frown on Laurie's face, it didn't look like she had.

"She's eleven years old, Megan. She's old enough to stay at home alone for an hour with her sisters. And we're only ever just down the block at the coffee shop. It's not like we would be across town."

Megan shook her head. No way. "She's not twelve yet, though. I won't let her babysit any of the neighbors' kids until she's twelve, so why would I let her watch ours? I'm just not comfortable trusting her with . . ." She covered her mouth with her hand as her eyes widened. She did *not* just almost say that.

"Not with Emma." Laurie said for her. "That's what you meant to say, wasn't it?"

Megan sagged against the kitchen counter, her body weighed down by guilt. Life was slowly getting back to normal, so why couldn't she? Tears slid down her face, and when Laurie came to stand in front of her, she tried to smile, but when her friend's hands wrapped around her shoulders, she leaned in.

"What's wrong with me?" Her throat hurt from trying to hold back the emotion. The last thing she needed was for the girls to walk in and see her like this again.

Laurie rubbed Megan's back, a soothing circular motion that reminded Megan of how she'd calm her own girls when they were upset. Megan pulled away, wiping her cheeks before hugging herself.

"All I seem to do lately is cry. It's probably why Peter is hardly home anymore. He leaves early and comes home late. He's been putting in long hours, using the excuse that Samantha is overwhelmed with new deals. But he probably doesn't want to come home to an emotionally disturbed wife."

Laurie snorted as she reached into a drawer and pulled out a container they both knew held Megan's stash of emergency chocolate. "Emotional, yes. Who wouldn't be? But disturbed? Far from it. Give yourself and Peter a break, would you? Since the day Emma disappeared, your life has been a virtual roller-coaster ride."

Megan reached for the chocolate Laurie handed to her and put it down on the counter. As much as she wanted it, she wasn't about to waste the sweet morsel. It would taste like sawdust in her mouth.

She shrugged. "Maybe you're right."

Laurie checked her watch before reaching over to hug Megan. "Tonight is cheap night at the theater. I want to see that new chick flick that's out. Come with me."

Megan shook her head. "Peter's working late again. Some deal he's trying to close or something."

Laurie bit her lip. "I don't understand. Why isn't Sam helping more? She's the one who should be working late nights, not the husband with three children and a wife who rarely sees him." She crossed her arms and frowned.

Megan agreed. It made perfect sense to her. Unless Sam was the reason Peter was staying so late. "Not much I can do," she said.

Laurie shrugged her shoulder. "Then what about tomorrow night? Tell him you need him home, and don't give him a choice. We can even go to the late showing if that will help." She reached for her purse and slung it over her shoulder. "I won't take no for an answer, so don't even bother trying." She waved before walking out of the kitchen.

Megan shook her head as Laurie left. The door shut, but the alarm didn't go off. That bothered her. It meant Peter hadn't set it when he left or locked the door. It would also explain why she hadn't heard Laurie come in. With a quick check into the backyard to make sure all the girls were there, Megan headed to the door, locked it, and then entered the code into the panel. How could Peter not set the alarm? He knew how she felt about that. Especially with Emma back home.

A stack of mail on the table by the door caught her attention. Laurie must have grabbed it from the mailbox and set it down. She picked her way through the bills but stopped when she found an envelope addressed to Emma from Jack Henry.

There was no way in hell she was giving Emma this letter. How dare he write Emma again? Didn't he understand what his letters did to her daughter? After the first one, Emma would wait for the mailman to come to the door; if there wasn't a letter for her, she'd run up to her room. Megan found her once hiding in her closet, her face burrowed in her knees as her shoulders shook from the sobs she tried to keep quiet. It was easier after that to keep the letters from her. Kinder to Emma, Megan told herself.

She clenched the envelope in her hand and went upstairs to her bedroom. What if Emma had found the letter first? She laid the magazines and bills down on her bed but kept the offending piece of mail. Her fingertips were white from their tight hold. She opened the door to her walk-in closet and reached up for a box on the high shelf. She opened the lid and dropped the letter on top of the others.

When was he going to stop? What would it take? Last week, during one of her late-night grocery runs, she'd driven to his farm-house and dropped a note in his mailbox. Megan had sat in her parked car and stared at the dark house. She hadn't really looked at the place and its surroundings the day Detective Riley had asked her and Peter to meet him there. But in the evening, with the sun setting, Megan's heart ached. This was where her daughter grew up for two years, in the country, surrounded by flower gardens, trees, and open fields. She pictured her little girl playing in the front yard, chasing butterflies or picking dandelions. Now, when Emma told her stories of when she'd help Jack pick weeds and sing songs to his rosebushes, Megan could picture it.

She knew Emma had been happy in that run-down farmhouse—happier than she was at home now. She needed Emma to become settled back at home, to adjust, to smile, and to be willing to create new memories. She needed Jack to respect her wishes as Emma's mother. Apparently, he didn't.

He could write all the letters he wanted to her daughter, but she would guarantee that Emma never saw them.

He'd kept Emma from her for two long years. It didn't matter that her child had been happy and well cared for. It didn't matter that she had been loved by strangers. The fact of the matter was that he'd kept her daughter from her. She hadn't believed him when he'd said he had no idea; that he'd believed Emma was his granddaughter. Megan had listened to him try to explain how Emma had come to them and how he'd never thought to question his wife. How could he not? If Peter hadn't put his foot down after the investigation, Megan would have pressed charges.

No. Jack Henry would never be a part of their lives, and Megan would do everything she could to ensure that.

CHAPTER THREE

*E*mmie's First Year
July 25
It's my birthday today. Jack surprised me with fresh scones and tea. He took Emmie into town with him to the bakery, even though he'd promised me he wouldn't take her out in public. It's not safe. He knows how I feel about Emmie leaving the house. It's not often he goes against me like that. It's our responsibility to shelter her as much as possible. Her laughter, the way her eyes light up when she smiles—I don't want that to ever go away. Not like it did with Mary.

Jack understands. I know he does.

I've been told I need to spend some time today away from the house, and that there is going to be a special surprise for me, and I can't be home while they do it. Or make it. I hope Jack will bake me a cake. On our first date, we picnicked near the stream on his father's land, and he'd baked me the most delicious vanilla cake I've ever tasted. Even after all these years, he holds his mother's recipe close. I've tried to get him to write it down for me, but he refuses. Says it requires a magic touch. I'll be sure to leave the coconut out on the counter, though. I've got a hankering for a coconut cake today.

Emmie wanted to know what I would do, since I can't stay at home. I really have no idea. It's been a long time since I spent the day just by myself with nothing to do. Jack and Emmie are downstairs making a list for me. I already know what Emmie will suggest—a stop at the local bookstore. Jack handed me some money to buy myself a dress or two. But Emmie needs clothes more than I do. That child grows like a weed, just like Mary did.

I think the first thing I will do, though, is drive down to the lake. There's a place I like to go; it's special in some way . . . I wish I could remember how. The memory is there, I can feel it, but no matter how hard I try, it slips away from me.

There's a little tree that's been freshly planted in the wooded area just before you step onto the sand. I noticed it the last time. My mother used to tell me how important it is to plant a tree when a loved one has passed on. I think I planted it, but I'm not sure why. Maybe I was thinking of my mother that day, of how much she loved the water. But I have two trees in our yard—one for her and one for Daddy.

Maybe Jack will know.

The creak of the old wood rocker broke the silence. Jack knew he should turn on the radio for company, but there was something in the air tonight; a restlessness he couldn't quite understand.

It was a night for memories.

He sank his head back on the worn chair and closed his eyes. Fairies danced before him, their lights flickering as they twirled in the air, or so Emmie used to say. The fairy lights were just Christmas lights Dottie had unearthed from who knew where—lights that he had spent hours tacking onto the wall—but it made their little girl happy to have those lights in her room. He could almost feel the weight of her body snuggled in his lap, ready for a bedtime story. She'd curl up nice and close, her legs either tight underneath her or hanging loose over his knees as she rested in the crook of his arm. She'd help him turn the pages in the story, but first they had to close their eyes and wait for the fairies to dance—a silly game, but he indulged her all the same.

Jack still went upstairs every night to read Emmie a bedtime story. He didn't dare tell Doug or Kenny, men he considered almost brothers. He knew of course that she wasn't here anymore, but one moment he'd be down in the kitchen and the next he'd be opening her bedroom door to check on her. Seeing the empty bed covered with the stuffed animals she left behind nearly broke his heart every time.

He snuggled the floppy-eared bunny Emmie had given him on the day they'd packed her suitcase and sighed. He missed all three of his girls so much that it sometimes hurt physically. He never thought he could lose so much in such little time. He had just started to grieve for his Mary when Dottie had collapsed and was taken to the hospital. Then he'd had to give up Emmie, only to have Dottie pass away in her sleep, oblivious to his pain and the turmoil her actions had caused.

Or maybe she did know. Deep down, Jack suspected Dottie could no longer live with the guilt. That was why she never woke up from her coma. That was why, just moments before she breathed her last breath, she squeezed his hand three times in succession. The doctors said it was involuntary—a reflex. But Jack knew it had been her private good-bye, her final "I love you."

He just wished he'd had the chance to say good-bye back. To tell her he loved her and that he understood why she did what she did. Not that it was right, but that he understood.

With a groan, Jack pushed himself up from the chair, his old bones creaking from the exertion. He went to Emmie's bed and laid the bunny on the pillow, smoothing its fur. He knew it was silly, but he'd promised his little girl that he would take care of her bunny. He'd never broken a promise to Emmie, and he wasn't about to start.

He thought about the letter on the kitchen table, half-written. Did she know that he had planted a rosebush in his front garden just for her and that he'd cut the first bloom the other day? Did she even receive his letters?

Probably not. He knew if he was in her parents' shoes, the last thing he would do was allow his daughter to remain in contact with the people who took her away. The media labeled him and Dottie kidnappers, but if only they knew. Jack's hand trembled at the thought. It killed him to admit that kidnapping was exactly what Dottie had done, despite all her good intentions and her unstable state of mind. He and Dottie had been vilified in the media and had their life scrutinized, but no one really understood. How could they?

He thought back to that day in the hospital, shortly after Dottie's death, when he'd seen Emmie. He'd been there to bring flowers to one of the nurses, his way of saying thank-you. One moment his heart had been heavy, and the next a tiny pair of arms had wrapped around his waist. He knew then that it was his little girl. He didn't know how, but he thanked God anyway. He wished she had held on a little tighter, a little longer, just so he could savor the memory a little bit more. He wished he could take back the words he said, telling her that her grandma was gone. It wasn't fair of him to share his grief with his little girl. Not like that.

Jack went downstairs to make a cup of tea before bed. It was a heavy burden to carry, knowing that he'd been instrumental in tearing a family apart. He'd never forgive himself for that. He should have known when Emmie first came home with Dottie that something was wrong.

"Oh, Dottie-mine, you sure made a mess of things."

Jack didn't like to be alone. Lately, the silence bothered him. He'd confessed to his doctor that he had been talking to Dottie as if she were there with him, and he'd been ready for the doctor to say it was time for a nursing home. But the doctor only nodded and said it was normal—as though people talking to the dead was something he was used to hearing about. Jack shook his head at the thought. Back in the day, if his daddy had started to talk to his momma after she'd passed away, everyone would have said he'd lost it. But nowadays, it was "normal."

He pushed aside the dishes in the sink to make room for the kettle and filled it with water. If Dottie were here, she would have smacked his hand for leaving dirty dishes lying around. But then, if Dottie were here, there would be no dirty dishes.

As he waited for the kettle to boil, Jack tackled the dishes. Afterward, he made sure to wring the cloth dry, a lesson Dottie had taught him after finding too many smelly dishcloths in her sink. He cut a slice of store-bought apple pie, topping it with a piece of cheese and knew, even before he took a bite, that it wouldn't taste anything close to what Dottie used to make.

He missed her more than he thought possible. This house was never meant to be so empty, so void of laughter, of childish giggles, or even of companionable silence. He often thought that he would die with Dottie, together in their bed, when they were both much older. But not yet. Not now. He had never envisioned what life would be like alone.

God sure had a way of playing jokes on him. He'd promised Dottie the day he returned from the war that he'd never leave her alone again.

He guessed he had kept his promise.

CHAPTER FOUR

Megan shut off the vacuum. She popped her head up and scanned the family room. When she'd started cleaning, Emma was sitting in the big corner chair playing with her dolls. Now only Megan was in the room. She listened for Daisy's bark or the other girls playing, but heard nothing.

"Girls?" Her voice slightly squeaked. When there was no answer, she dropped the vacuum handle.

She checked to make sure the front door was locked and the alarm still set; then she ran into the kitchen and looked out the patio doors. Hannah and Alexis sat on the deck, their legs stretched out, soaking in the sun.

Megan scanned the yard. Where was Emma? Why couldn't she see her? Megan wrenched open the sliding doors.

"What's up?" Alexis sat up and raised her sunglasses.

"Where's your sister?"

"Right here." Alexis nudged Hannah's shoulder.

Hannah frowned. "Not me, you moron. Emma." She turned back. "I thought she was with you?" Hannah pushed herself up from her elbows, a panicked look on her face.

"She was, until I started vacuuming." Megan's heart raced, yet she struggled to keep her voice calm.

"She might be up in her room with the dog," Alexis volunteered before lying back down. "And don't call me a moron."

Hannah stood up, but not before giving her sister a disgusted look. "I'll take a look."

Megan shook her head. "No, it's okay. I've got it. Sit back and don't fight. I'll make you guys some lemonade in a few minutes." She closed the sliding door and pivoted on her heel.

"Emma?" she called out, unable to keep the frantic tone out of her voice. Where was she?

Megan ran to the stairs and flew up several steps when a rhythmic thumping against the carpet stopped her.

Emma must be in her room with Daisy.

She climbed the remaining stairs quietly and heard her daughter hum a familiar song. It worried her that Emma's first place to run to was her room, alone and away from her sisters. She should be blooming, like the roses in their backyard, instead of wilting now that she was back with her family.

Megan clenched her fists as she thought about the damage they had inflicted upon her daughter. She should be a loud, vibrant child full of energy and sass, not a quiet child who rarely spoke and found solace with her dog instead of her family.

Emma's door was slightly ajar, and she sat on the floor, her back against her bed and her feet propped up against the far wall. Daisy's tail was in view, thumping wildly on the floor. She couldn't completely see what they were doing, but Megan had a feeling Daisy's head lay on Emma's lap while she stroked her fur.

Nothing in Emma's room was out of place. Her bed was made, her stuffed bears lined up in a row against her pillows, the floor clear of any toys, and the lid of her laundry basket down. Peter had put together a little bookcase where she kept her toys, baskets, and books. Even those were organized.

Emma was the only neat freak in the house—a trait she must have picked up from living with those other people. Her sisters' rooms were a mess, and it was all Megan could do to get them to keep the floor clean. It wasn't normal for a five-year-old to be so tidy.

"I miss Papa, Daisy. Don't you? I bet you miss running around in the backyard the most."

Megan gripped the doorframe. Emma's soft voice walloped her heart into tiny pieces.

"I miss the fairy lights too. They were so pretty."

Fairy lights? This was the first time Emma had mentioned anything like that.

"Hey, Emma?" Megan whispered into the room.

"I miss Grandma's muffins and her bread and the way she smelled. I think it's 'cause she baked so much. I hope she's happy in heaven now and gets to bake bread all day long. Maybe Papa is going to go see her soon. Then I'll be sad, 'cause I'll be all alone." Emma's head disappeared from view.

Megan's heart hurt. How could she think she'd be alone?

"Emma?" Megan whispered again. She tried to make her voice louder but couldn't. Her daughter didn't hear her anyway. She seemed lost in her own little world.

Megan took a step into the room. She could have been a ghost, silent and unseen. Daisy didn't even notice her presence. On top of Emma's bed was a notebook, one of many Megan had bought for her to draw pictures in. It lay open, and there was an image of a small yellow dog and a girl sitting outside with round red circles floating above them.

As hard as she tried, Megan couldn't get Emma to admit she remembered much of the day when she was taken. But deep down, that memory had to be there. She just knew it. Otherwise, she wouldn't remember the red balloons they watched floating in the sky that day. They'd planned to take the girls to their town fair to celebrate Emma's birthday, and instead spent the day searching for their lost daughter.

Megan took in a deep breath. She was going to do something she'd thought of for a while now. She wasn't sure whether she was ready for the reaction, though.

"Hey, Emmie?" Megan kept her voice at the same low level as the previous times she'd called for her daughter. This time, Emma's head lifted in response.

As much as it hurt, Megan placed a smile on her face as her daughter smiled back at her.

"It's beautiful outside. Do you want to help me make some lemonade?"

Megan stepped into the room as Daisy lifted her head from Emma's lap. When Emma smoothed out her dress and wiped at the tears in her eyes, Megan knew that she couldn't pretend Emma's responding to her other name didn't happen. Even though she wanted to. So she sat down on Emma's bed, pushed the book out of the way, and held out her arms. When Emma crawled up into her lap, Megan rested her cheek against the top of her daughter's head and struggled to find words.

"What are fairy lights?"

Emma's body stiffened for a moment before she relaxed. "Grandpa put pretty lights in my room. They went from one corner to the next"—Emma pointed upward—"so I wouldn't feel lonely."

Megan wrapped a strand of Emma's hair around her fingers. She was talking about Christmas lights. "That was nice of him."

Emma nodded her head and sniffed. Daisy lay down across Megan's toes and whined for attention.

"You miss him, don't you?"

Emma nodded again.

Megan lifted her daughter's face so that she could look into her eyes. Teardrops hung from her long eyelashes.

"Would you like some fairy lights in your room? I think we have some extra ones in the basement. Maybe you could help me hang them up?"

Emma's eyes widened before a smile stretched across her face. Megan cherished the moment Emma wrapped her arms around her. Every gesture, every smile, every hug would never be taken for granted. Never again.

"It must be hard to have two names, isn't it?" Megan kept the tone of her voice light.

Emma's lips tightened and her brows knotted together for a brief moment before she shook her head.

"No? Are you sure?"

A frantic look crept into her little girl's face. Her eyes widened, her nose flared, and a tiny tremor swept through her body. "My name is Emma."

Daisy stood up and barked. Emma's panic was palpable, and Megan hated herself for doing this to her little girl.

"It's okay, honey. Your name is Emma. But sometimes it can be Emmie too." She paused for a few seconds. "Right?"

Emma's arms unwound themselves from around Megan's body. Her shoulders tensed under Megan's touch.

"Only to Papa," Emma whispered.

Megan swallowed. Papa. Of course. He had a piece of Emma's heart, and there was nothing Megan could do about it. No matter how hard she tried.

"Did you know, when you were just a baby, I used to call you Emmie?"

"You did?"

Megan nodded. "Late at night, when I would hold you close to my heart and rock you to sleep, I would call you Emmie and kiss your forehead." She held her breath as her daughter snuggled close to her again. "A special girl can have as many special names as she wants, just as long as she remembers one thing."

"What?" Emma whispered.

"That you'll always be mine." She kissed the soft skin of Emma's forehead, wishing for time to stand still.

"Always," Emma said.

Megan tightened her hold. "Always."

❧

Megan rinsed one last dish from dinner before placing it in the dishwasher. Peter sat at the kitchen table looking through the latest stack of grocery flyers, apparently oblivious to her at the moment.

Nerves made Megan's body feel like it was strung on a taut wire. Her chest was tight, and it hurt to take deep breaths. Since her talk with Emma, she'd been fighting against the doubts that kept creeping into her heart.

"All right, spill." Peter pushed his chair back, scraping the floor at the same time. Megan winced. She had meant to replace the little pads of fabric beneath the chair legs after washing them. They were probably still in the dryer from yesterday.

"What do you mean?" She wiped her hands on the towel hanging from the oven handle.

The look on Peter's face told her he knew something was wrong.

"You banged the dishwasher door shut, almost broke a glass earlier in the sink, and you've barely said two words since the kids went outside to play after dinner."

Megan turned her back, filled two mugs with coffee, and went to the table. She handed Peter his mug, reached for one of the grocery flyers, and prayed to God that Peter didn't notice that her hand shook.

"You're wound up as tight as my old yo-yo. What's going on?"

"I didn't think you'd be home so early tonight. Laurie had suggested going to the late show, but I told her you wouldn't be home." She wrapped her fingers around the mug.

"Well, I'm home."

She caught the slight shrug of his shoulders and knew it really didn't matter to him if she went out or not.

"I told her we'd go out tomorrow night instead. Will you be home?"

Peter tossed a flyer to the side and opened another one.

"Peter?" She glanced at what he was looking at. Golf clubs. Go figure.

"If you need me to be home early, all you have to do is ask. You know that." He laid down the paper and took a sip of his coffee. "Why don't you tell me the real reason you're on edge tonight."

Megan sighed. She bit her lip before standing up and glancing out the sliding doors. She drank in the sight of them, all together. She knew she was overreacting, that if she just took the time to really work her way through everything, she'd realize she was making a mountain out of a molehill.

"Have you ever noticed Emma not responding when you call her name?" She closed her eyes, not wanting to look at his reflection in the glass, afraid of what she'd see.

"No."

Maybe it was the tone of his voice or the way he cleared his throat, but when Megan opened her eyes and looked over her shoulder, she'd almost wished she hadn't. His brows were knit together and there was a look in his eyes she'd seen too many times before.

"I have," she whispered. When Peter sighed, something sparked inside Megan. She needed him to listen to her, to understand. "It happens to me a lot, Peter." She turned her back to the glass and leaned on it.

Peter shrugged. "Why?"

Why? He had to ask that? It didn't take a psychiatrist to understand that if a child didn't respond to her name when called, there might be an issue. There had to be some reason she didn't respond. Unless . . . this was Emma's way of holding on to a life no longer hers? Would she do that on purpose though? At five years of age? Megan wasn't too sure.

"Do you think something's wrong with her hearing?"

Megan ground her teeth before she shook her head. "No, Peter. I think her hearing is fine. I think that she doesn't want to be Emma. I think that—"

"She probably didn't hear you," Peter interrupted. His eyes were turned back down toward the flyers.

Megan seethed inside. How could he discount so quickly what she'd just said?

"She heard me when I called her Emmie."

The look on Peter's face said it all: disbelief, anger, confusion. His gaze shot from one corner of the room to another before resting back on her. She caught the way his fingers turned white as he clutched the coffee mug. Good. Maybe now he understood. Maybe now he would listen to her.

"You what?" His voice lowered about ten decibels, the anger she'd read on his face clear in his tone. No, he didn't understand.

"I wanted to see. I called her name a few times and didn't get a response. So I called her Emmie." Megan toyed with her coffee cup, turning it in circles. "That's all it took, for her to hear her old name. It scared me."

Peter's brows shot up. "Scared you? What do you think you did to her? How do you think she must have felt to realize you called her by that other name?" Peter stood, his chair scraping along the floor again as he pushed it back.

"What is wrong with you? What will it take for you to be happy?"

CHAPTER FIVE

August 5

I burned the bread again today. I never do that. It's the second time this week. Such a waste.

I laid Emmie down for her nap and fell asleep with her again. She doesn't like to take many naps; sometimes I have to read her more stories than I prefer before she'll settle down. Today I had to threaten to turn off her fairy lights if she didn't fall asleep.

Jack brought her home some balloons today. I made him use the tire pump we used to use for Mary's bike. I swear, that man is so stubborn sometimes. What does it matter if he blows up the balloons with his lips or with a pump? She has this fascination with red balloons—says they look better in the sky. For a girl who prefers pink, yellow, and white, I would never have thought she'd want only red balloons. Good thing the bag had plenty of red ones; otherwise, knowing him, he'd have gone back into town to buy more.

Jack commented that I've been more tired lately, so he made an appointment with Dr. Stewart. Meddlesome old fool, but he won't listen to me. I've always been healthier than I should be for my age. Perhaps raising a child is catching up to me. There are times I don't understand how Mary could do this to me—have a child and never tell me, her mother. Emmie is a sweet girl, so I know Mary did something right

despite her addiction, but that child of mine never thought of the con-
sequences. She never did. It was her one big fault.

I blame myself. Mary always blamed me too.

❧

Peter leaned against the doorway into the living room. He could
never get enough of the image before him: their family complete
again after so much time. He choked up and softly cleared his
throat, not wishing to disturb the scene.

A movie played while Hannah sat on a beanbag chair, her back
against the couch and her long legs stretched out in front of her.
She was going to be tall; he could see it. Alexis was sprawled on the
couch, her back against the corner of the sectional with her legs
crossed and a large bowl of popcorn in her lap. Emma sat in Peter's
favorite chair, the drawing pad he'd bought her last week against her
bent knees. Her tongue was stuck out, a sure sign of concentration.
Every so often, she'd reach down with her free hand and grab a
piece of popcorn from a bowl beside her. Not once did he catch her
watching the movie.

That didn't surprise him, though. From what he understood,
she didn't watch a lot of television at the farm. They sheltered her,
and a part of him was thankful for that. She remained a sweet little
girl, full of innocence and love.

She must have noticed him watching her. She lifted her gaze,
her soulful eyes measuring him—something he'd noticed her doing
lately. It was unnerving. What did his five-year-old see in him? Did
he measure up? Somehow, he didn't think so.

"Come sit beside me, Dad." Alexis moved her legs to make
room. Peter smiled at Emma, who watched as he crossed the room.

Hannah stuck her hand out for a high five. He went to smack her hand, but she quickly lowered it in a fit of giggles.

"Hey, no fair," he teased her before pretending to sit on Alex. They had a mini tickle fight without spilling the popcorn before Peter repositioned her legs over his. He nudged Hannah with his foot until a slight smile appeared.

"So what are we watching?"

Alexis sighed before pointing to the screen. "A movie about a dragon, duh." The sarcasm in her voice was overwhelming. Typical Alexis.

"Haven't we already seen this?"

"Only like a thousand times. But there's nothing else on," Hannah muttered.

Peter reached into the popcorn bowl and flicked a piece at Hannah's head. She ducked, but it was Emma's quiet laughter that caught his attention. He flicked one at her, but before she could duck, Daisy jumped up and caught it in her mouth.

"No way." Peter laughed. "Who's been teaching Daisy tricks?"

A light sparkled in Emma's eyes. She leaned over the arm of the chair and scratched Daisy's head. "Hannah's a good teacher," she said.

Peter nudged Hannah again with his foot. "Hannah's a great big sister." A sense of peace he hadn't felt in a long time settled in his heart as Hannah flushed with pleasure.

If he could freeze time, it would be this exact moment, with his children happy and himself at peace. The only thing missing was Megan.

"When's Mommy gonna be home?" Emma asked, almost as if she knew what he was thinking and missed her too.

"Never. She ran away," Alexis pouted. Emma's eyes widened in fear, and Peter gave Alexis a stern look.

"She didn't run away," he said soothingly to Emma. "She went out." He focused on Alexis and waited for her to look up. "Why would you say something like that?"

Alexis shook her head. "'Cause she always goes out at night without us."

Peter sighed. "That's not true. Your mother rarely goes out anymore and when she does, it's usually grocery shopping. You know that."

Alexis grunted. "She just doesn't want to spend time with us."

"What?" Was he missing something? Megan loved being home with the kids. School was out, her Safe Walks program was on break, the kids weren't in sports, and she was excited to have the summer to reconnect with Emma. So why did it bother them so much that she was gone now?

"We never spend time as a family anymore." Alexis raised her face and stared defiantly into his eyes.

Peter shook his head. That didn't make sense. "We're spending family time now."

"No, we're not. Mommy's not here."

Peter cocked his head and looked at his daughters. This had really upset them. Emma buried her head back into her drawing; she wouldn't look up. Alexis's shoulders were pushed back and her chin up high. This was his fighter. But there was nothing to challenge, nothing to fight over. The look in Hannah's eyes was sad, downcast, and defeated.

Did they honestly think that Megan didn't want to spend time with them? That she couldn't wait to go out in the evenings? He could count on one hand the times Megan had gone out alone since Emma's return. Where did this come from?

He put his hand on Hannah's shoulder and wrapped his arm around Alexis, drawing her close.

"Listen to me. Everything your mother has always wanted is right here in this room. Her family. That's you"—he nodded to Alexis—"and you"—then to Hannah—"and you, little monkey sitting in my favorite chair." Emma glanced up, her eyes wide. "The only thing that matters to your mom is her family. Nothing else."

"Are you sure about that? I heard her tell you she needed time to herself tonight." Alexis taunted him.

He had to give her that. Megan did say that before she left. He'd even agreed with her. He didn't know what was wrong with her or where her head was at but maybe some time alone, to think about how ridiculous her earlier claims were, would be good for her. He nodded.

"She did, didn't she. And that's allowed. Just like when you go up to your room for some quiet time and listen to your music. It's the same for Mom." Peter slowly removed his hand from Hannah's shoulder and laid it on his leg, inches away from Alexis's bare foot. "Right, kiddo?" He started to tickle her foot and waited for her belly-wrenching laughter.

Alexis tried to yank her foot out of his grasp, but it was pointless. He continued to tickle, and once she started to laugh, the stress in the room dissolved. Daisy started to jump and bark and Emma even laughed a little. Peter memorized the welcome sound as Hannah rose up on her knees and reached for Alexis's other foot.

Yes, to hear all three of his girls laughing together, this was heaven on earth.

⚜

As soon as she could, Megan had escaped from the house, away from her husband and her fears, and drove to the pier. She didn't blame him, though; she wasn't sure she understood it herself. Why did it bother her so much that Emma wouldn't respond to her name in the same way she responded to that *other* name? Why was she so sensitive to this?

Was Peter right? Was she just looking for a reason not to be happy? Why couldn't she just accept life as it happened and stop trying to control it?

Megan parked by the old pier and walked along the rugged path. Once she reached the end, she dangled her legs over the water and drank in the stillness. She gazed at the lake, mesmerized by the gentle swells and the way the seagulls dipped down into the water. She breathed deeply, trying to force the calm of the scene before her into her body, but it wasn't working.

She wished she were as free as the birds above her, without the stress she heaped upon herself. Emma was home. Her family was healing. Why couldn't she be happy? Because she wanted more. The hope she felt from her morning dream lingered. There had to be more for her, for them.

Earlier she had confessed to Peter that the incident with Emma had scared her. Without asking why, he turned it around and accused her of doing the same thing to their daughter. But he never asked her why she was scared, and to be honest, she wasn't sure she wanted to admit the answer.

What she needed was a fresh perspective. Someone to help her understand her doubts and worries. And she knew exactly where to go.

Megan climbed to her feet and headed back toward her vehicle. Something was wrong, but she wasn't sure if it was with her or her daughter.

Megan pushed open the door to Dr. Kathy Graham's office and glanced around the waiting area. The eight chairs were empty, as well as the coatrack. A small folded sign sat on top of the desk with "Please Be Seated" scrawled across it.

She placed a coffee from the drive-thru on the desk and sat down in one of the chairs, clasping her purse tightly between her fingers. She prayed that coming here was the right decision.

"I'll be right with you," Kathy, their family counselor, called out.

Coming here was an impulsive decision made on the pier. Peter would never know.

"Megan, come on in." Kathy stood in the doorway, wearing a light-blue summer dress with her hair in a ponytail.

"Thanks for seeing me on such short notice." Megan grabbed the coffee she'd set down on the desk and offered it to Kathy.

Buying Kathy a coffee for seeing her after hours was the least she could do. A tiny seed of doubt wormed its way through Megan. She should have taken the time to calm herself down instead of panicking over something as silly as Emma not responding to her name. It wasn't a life-or-death situation. Just groundless fears.

Megan followed Kathy into her office, and they both sat down in the leather armchairs. There was something about this office and the way it was decorated, as if it were a room in a friend's house instead of a doctor's office. This helped ease some of the tension in Megan's shoulders. Off to the side, by the large bay windows, were framed drawings that had been made for Kathy. Megan immediately picked out the picture Emma had drawn during the first few weeks she'd been home. It was a picture of a little girl and a dog, sitting in a field with trees all around them. She had drawn large blue swirls indicating a brisk wind that wrapped itself around the little girl. Megan hated that picture even though Emma had been so proud of it and asked if Kathy could put it on her wall. She hated that Emma had felt so obviously alone and unsettled.

Kathy crossed her legs and sipped her coffee while Megan sat straight in her chair.

"What's going on?" Kathy asked.

Megan bit her lip as she searched for the right words. Words that wouldn't make her sound crazy or ungrateful. Words that would convince Kathy that she wasn't a bad mother for doubting her child.

"I don't think Emma is really my daughter," Megan blurted out instead.

She waited for Kathy's reaction, for the confusion, the worry, and then the doubt that she knew she deserved. She steeled herself, knowing that she'd been foolish to come and admit her fears. Her grip tightened around her purse strap.

"Why is that?"

Megan was surprised to hear the sincerity in Kathy's voice. She glanced up and saw the concern in Kathy's gaze. She relaxed a little and set her purse on the floor.

"I know it sounds odd and might not even make sense. But it's things she says or remembers."

"What kinds of things? It's possible she's confusing early memories with those from living with Jack and Dorothy."

Megan shook her head. "Why would she respond to being called Emmie and not her real name? It's not like the two names are completely different. Plus, I thought she would have been more settled and happier by now." Megan sighed. Was it all her fault? Was she failing her daughter somehow?

Kathy leaned on the armrest. "She still needs time, Megan. This could be Emma's way of keeping the memory of that life alive."

Kathy gave a small smile. "Let's talk about how she's adjusting. Is she talking more?"

"A bit. She offers more to a conversation now if she's involved in some way. But . . ." Megan hesitated.

"Is she talking about things from the farmhouse?"

Maybe it was the way Kathy asked, or the tone of her voice when she asked it, but tears welled up in Megan's eyes. All she could do was nod.

"Remember, we talked about that. It's completely normal— healthy even. She's trying to find ways to involve herself with you. For her, sharing memories still fresh in her mind is one way of doing that. It's good, Megan." Kathy leaned forward. "Really, it's a good sign. She's engaging more."

Megan's brow rose. "So am I being oversensitive? Am I making the whole name thing more than it is?"

The way Kathy crossed her legs and took another sip of her coffee angered Megan. She wasn't sure what it was—maybe it was how relaxed she appeared or the look in her eye, like she was only appeasing Megan.

"Why would she respond to Emmie and not Emma?" she blurted out. That was the real question, the one that bothered her the most.

Kathy cocked her head and reached for the pad of paper on the small table beside her. "Maybe she was responding to the first few letters of her name, the Em part. It's possible that's all she heard."

Megan shook her head. She leaned forward and rested her elbows on her knees. She knotted her fingers together. "No. I called her name repeatedly, but she didn't hear me. The moment I called her that other name, she did."

Kathy scribbled some notes down on her sheet, and Megan couldn't help but wonder whether she was going to suggest that

Megan go on some type of drug again. Just like before. She was not crazy. She knew something was wrong.

"What was she doing before all this happened?"

"Excuse me?"

Kathy set her pad back down on the table and folded her hands together. "Was Emma in the middle of something when you called her name?"

Megan recalled the quiet conversation she'd overheard between Emma and Daisy.

"She was talking about how much she missed *them*. The others."

She didn't tell Karen about the fairy lights. She didn't need to. The way Emma's eyes lit up when Megan said she could have some in her room confirmed that had been the right thing to say.

"Kathy, she's been with us now long enough that she should remember what it was like to be part of our family. How much we loved her. I've done everything you suggested, and I'm very aware of when Emma's had enough. I don't force her to interact with us; I give her as much time as she needs while still accepting her feelings. But . . ." She hesitated, unwilling to say what she'd feared all along.

Kathy waited.

"It was as if she had been waiting all this time to be called Emmie again."

CHAPTER SIX

Peter stood at the back door and whistled. Where was that dog? He was ready to relax, maybe start a new book or watch a movie that didn't contain animated creatures, but he couldn't do that until everyone was tucked into bed, including Daisy. He had no idea what Megan was doing. How long did she need to take? He wasn't upset—but a text or phone call would be nice.

He'd already said good night to Hannah and Alexis, but Emma refused to sleep without Daisy, and that was a battle Peter wasn't willing to fight. Megan was the one who did the kids' night routine, so he wasn't sure about Megan's habits with Emma. But if having the dog by her side meant less hassle for him, he considered that a win-win situation.

His phone vibrated in his pants pocket as Daisy scampered up onto the deck and sat, waiting for Peter to let her in. He pulled out the phone and absentmindedly opened the door for the dog.

He expected it to be a text from Megan letting him know she was on her way home, so he was a bit surprised when he saw it was from Sam.

Still up?

His fingers danced over the keyboard on his phone as he followed Daisy through the house and up the stairs.

Just putting kids to bed. What's up?

He stood at the top of the stairs and waited for Sam to respond. Something must be wrong for her to text him this late.

Emma's door was directly on his left. Peter glanced in and saw her lying on the floor beside her bed, coloring. On the other side of the hall was Alex's room. She was sitting in her bed, earphones on, swaying to a song. She glanced up and waved at him. He held his hand up, fingers splayed. *Five minutes*, he mouthed to her. She nodded before blowing him a kiss. He reached out his hand, pretending to capture the kiss in his hand and holding it to his heart.

"Hey, Dad?" Alexis unplugged her earphones. "When can we go golfing?"

"Soon, hon. I promise."

"You said that last time I asked." A pout formed on her face. "You're never going to take me, are you?"

Peter shook his head. "What? Of course I am."

"When?"

He wasn't sure he liked her tone or the defiant look in her eyes.

"You promised once school was over. You even said you'd take some afternoons off and we could go out, just you and me."

She was right. He did promise that.

"Let me see what I can do to rearrange some meetings, okay?"

She must have been trying to read the honesty in his eyes, because she didn't say anything for a moment. Then she nodded and put the earphones back in before giving him the thumbs-up.

Okay, then. He returned the gesture and blew her another kiss good night before walking to Hannah's door. He knocked softly, and when she called out to him, he peeked inside.

"Hey, I love you," he said as he watched her fluff her pillows behind her head. The beaming smile on her face lit his heart.

"I love you, too, Dad. It was nice to have you home tonight."

The honesty in her gaze hit him hard. He stepped into the room and sat on the edge of her bed. He reached for her hand and raised it to his lips for a kiss. She giggled, and it brought him back to when she was only a little girl, maybe three years old, who loved pretending she was a princess.

"You'll always be my little princess, you know." She was growing up so fast.

Her head tilted to the side as she gazed at him.

"What are you thinking?" He gently squeezed her hand.

She fiddled with her blanket. "Just wondering if you're happy." She dropped her gaze.

Peter rubbed his chin as he thought about her remark. Was he happy?

"Right here, right now, I'm more than happy, love. Do you know why?"

Hannah shook her head.

Peter leaned forward. "Because I'm with you."

He wasn't prepared for her leap as she threw her arms around his neck and held on tight.

"I love you, Daddy," Hannah whispered in his ear. Peter stroked her hair and tried to speak through the lump in his throat. His phone vibrated in his pocket, but he ignored it.

"I love you more, princess. I love you more."

Closing Hannah's door behind him, Peter checked the message on his phone.

I've given a lot of thought to what's been happening. We need to talk.

Peter hesitated for a moment. *This is not the time. Can't it wait?* He waited for her response. But it was the sound of Emma's quiet voice that forced him to replace the phone in his pocket and move forward.

He knew what Samantha wanted to talk about, but it wasn't a topic for tonight.

Peter pushed any thoughts of Sam out of his mind the moment he stood at Emma's door. He still couldn't believe she was home. There had been so many sleepless nights when he'd find himself in Emma's room, trying to remember her laughter. He'd almost forgotten. He shook his head. Who was he kidding? He had forgotten. And for some reason, he had a feeling Emma knew he had.

"What are you drawing?" He sat on her bed while she still lay on the floor.

If there was one thing he was learning about his youngest daughter, it was that she loved to draw. Megan had bought a folder last week for all the pictures she'd drawn, and every night when he came home late from work, he'd find something special from Emma on his desk. He liked to consider them her letters to him. Almost like the journal he'd kept for her while she'd been missing.

"A picture for Mommy."

He leaned down to look at her picture and smiled. Megan, a woman who hated to wear dresses, was dressed in a bright-red dress with a yellow apron. Emma stood beside her holding a very large circle in her hands.

"What's that circle?"

Emma looked at him over her shoulder. "A cookie."

His brow rose. "That's one big cookie. Sure hope you saved some for me."

She reached for another crayon and started to print in the corner, *I am*, before she stopped and looked at him again. "How do you spell 'sorry'?"

Peter spelled it out for her, watching her carefully form the letters across the page.

"What are you sorry for, Emma?" He couldn't think of any reason she would need to apologize to Megan.

Emma didn't answer. Instead, she carefully took each crayon scattered around her and returned them back to the container.

"I hurt Mommy's feelings," she finally whispered.

Peter's body wilted at her words. He waited for her to finish cleaning up, but the moment she stood, he gathered her into his arms and lifted her up onto his lap. Daisy jumped up beside them.

"Want to tell me what happened?" He pulled her close until her back was against his chest and his arms were wrapped tightly around her. Tendrils of her hair tickled his chin as she shook her head.

Peter rested his chin on the top of her head. "Did you eat all the chocolate chips that were supposed to go in the cookies today?"

Emma shook her head again.

"Did you eat all the cookies and forget to leave her one?" He made sure there was a lighthearted tone to his voice.

She shook her head again, but this time she looked back at him.

Peter lifted his shoulders up high and then dropped them down. "I don't know what you would have done, then, to make her sad."

Emma's bottom lip protruded before she lowered her gaze and snuggled back close to his chest. Peter tightened his arms around her.

"I miss Grandma."

Peter's heart crumbled inside his chest. It wasn't the words that hurt, but the way she spoke them. As if he would be angry with her.

"I'm sure you do, honey. She was very special to you, wasn't she?"

Emma didn't respond. It didn't take much for Peter to realize what might have happened today.

"Did you used to make cookies with . . . her?"

Emma nodded. "And muffins, bread, cakes. She let me break the eggs too." She squirmed in his arms until he loosened his hold on her.

"Breaking those eggs can be pretty tricky. You must be really good at that."

Emma's head bobbed up and down. "But Mommy didn't let me do the eggs today."

Peter tilted his head. "Does Mommy know how awesome you are at breaking eggs?"

Emma shook her head.

"Then I guess we'd better tell her, huh? I happen to know that's her least favorite part of baking. Did you know that?"

Emma's eyes widened at the news.

"Yep." Peter nodded. "She always gets pieces of shells in the batter, and I always end up eating them. Have you ever eaten an eggshell?" Emma shook her head. "Trust me, it doesn't taste good."

"I can do it, Daddy." Emma leaned back and straightened her shoulders.

"I know you can, honey. Of that I have no doubt. Now, how about we get you and Daisy all tucked into bed before Mommy comes home, okay?" He lifted her off his lap and stood. Emma scampered under the covers and then straightened the small blanket that Daisy slept on. It was their one condition for the dog sleeping with Emma: never under the covers and always on top of the blanket.

Peter reached for her lion and stroked its fluffy mane. Emma reached out her hands. "Can I have Tiger, please, Daddy?" He loved the fact that this was still her favorite stuffed animal. He'd bought it for her the day she was born. When she'd first disappeared, Peter was able to find a little bit of comfort knowing that the lion was with her.

"You know this is really a lion, right?" He winked at her.

Emma shrugged. "I know." She tucked her lion beside her, beneath the covers.

Peter picked up Emma's clothes from the floor and dropped them into her hamper. The closet door stood open, and he couldn't help but notice the pile of clothes on the floor. The other day, Megan had mentioned that Emma's room was always so neat. She must not have seen her closet.

"Emma, why are all these clothes on the floor?" He glanced over his shoulder and saw a flash of anger on his daughter's face. Anger?

"I don't like them." She crossed her arms over her chest and pouted.

Peter knelt down and picked up a shirt from the pile. "But this is a nice top your mommy bought you. What's wrong with it?"

She gave him a look he would have expected from Alexis. "I like dresses. I feel pretty in them."

Peter dropped the shirt and picked up a skirt. "Will you wear a skirt then?"

Emma shook her head.

"Why not?" Peter reached for another top in the pile and stood. He paired the two together and held them up for Emma to see. "It's just a dress cut in half."

Emma frowned as she glanced from the outfit in his hands to the dresses hanging in her closet.

Peter reached for a hanger with two clips on the bottom. He struggled to clip the skirt onto it before adding the shirt on top, pushed some dresses aside, and hung it in the middle.

"I remember Mommy coming home with bags and bags of clothes for you. Don't you? She was so excited to buy you new clothes and couldn't wait to see them on you. How about if you try to wear one new outfit for Mommy?"

Emma's eyes widened. He knew she was about to panic. She clutched the blanket in her hands, and her nose flared as she tried to breathe.

"Not every day, Emma. How about . . ." Peter tried to think of a day when they had nothing going on. "Sundays? How about on Sundays you try to wear something Mommy bought you? The rest of the time it can be one of your dresses." He didn't like seeing Emma this way. Even now, two months later, that woman still had a hold over Emma. He felt helpless.

It wasn't until Emma released her grip on the blanket that Peter relaxed. And when she nodded her head in acceptance, he struggled to keep the smile off his face. It was a step in the right direction, at least. He sat back down on the bed and put both of his arms on either side of Emma's legs. He waited for her to lie back on the pillows before he leaned forward to kiss her forehead.

"I love you, Emma." There was so much more he wanted to say. Like how she was the glue that put him back together, and that every time she smiled at him, his heart melted. That all he wanted was for her to be happy and loved, and he would do anything, anything to make sure she was always happy. But he couldn't say it. He didn't know how to say it.

But when she reached up and touched his cheek, he knew that she already knew the words he couldn't say. He patted the dog gently before leaving the room. He switched off the light and was about to close her door when she called out.

"Daddy?"

He turned the light back on.

"I made a picture for Papa today. I think he misses me."

Peter leaned against the doorframe.

"Could you give it to him?"

He wanted to say no. But when he saw the look in Emma's eyes, he realized that was the last thing he could say to his daughter.

"Tell you what. Why don't you and I go out for breakfast tomorrow and on our way home, we can drop it off at the mailbox."

When her eyes lit up, he knew he'd just said the right thing.

"Really, Daddy? A date, just you and me?"

Peter winked. "Just you and me, kiddo." He should have done that a long time ago.

"Daddy? Thank you."

"For what?"

"For making Papa happy. I know he misses me, and my letter will cheer him up."

Peter could only nod. He didn't really want to think about Jack. He honestly didn't care about what would make the old man happy. But the light in his daughter's eyes told him it made her happy, and that was all that mattered.

Even if it meant making his wife angry.

The phone in his pocket vibrated once again.

CHAPTER SEVEN

Megan thought she'd given herself enough time to make some stops along the way and still arrive before Laurie. She always used to come to Brewster's Bakery for her morning coffee after dropping the girls off at school, until the Safe Walks program took up more of her time. As the school year ended and after Emma was found, well, she'd kind of preferred to stay close to home.

She opened the door and the bell above it jingled. She immediately looked down to see whether Shelly Belle was there. Sure enough, the old dachshund raised her head and huffed. Megan bent down and scratched the dog's big ears and then glanced up at framed photos of Jan's three dachshunds when they were all young—her babies. Two had died in the last few years, and Megan worried about what Jan would do when Shelly died too.

Megan couldn't stop the smile that grew when she thought of Jan Brewster, the owner of the shop who'd helped to raise funds when Emma first went missing.

During those first few weeks, Megan had lived in a perpetual fog. Jan had come to her rescue. First, she'd brought over treats like chocolate croissants or almond scones, coaxing Megan back into the land of the living. Then, she started leaving pamphlets about organizations for missing children in Megan's mailbox. It took one brainstorming session over coffee and cookies to come up with a plan beyond the local authorities' to ensure that Emma's photo was plastered everywhere. Jan was the driving force, and set up the fund-raising barbecue in the town square. Megan would forever be in Jan's debt.

She dropped her purse at the corner table and headed to the counter. She smiled as she heard the slight shuffling behind her. On the corner of the counter, Jan kept a basket of homemade dog treats for Shelly Belle. She put out only a few each day, but it quickly became a favorite thing for customers to do. Megan picked out a flower-shaped treat, turned on her heels, and waited for Shelly to sit before offering her the treat.

"Well, good morning, darlin'." Jan pushed open the swinging door from the kitchen, holding a tray of fresh muffins. Megan leaned over the counter to see what type Jan had made. Today was her lucky day—banana nut, her favorite.

"These look delicious." She inhaled the sweet smell.

Jan smiled as she set the tray down. "They taste good too." She poured coffee into two mugs and placed a small plate on the counter.

Megan picked a muffin and headed over to a table.

"It's been a long time since you joined me for morning coffee. I've missed you." Jan lowered herself into a chair and sighed.

Megan glanced around the bakery. The place was homey. The walls were lined with shelves of wooden birdhouses and pictures of people and events special to Jan. One of Megan's favorite photos was a shot of a cloudy sky over the lake. The way the wind had blown the clouds and the way the light shone through them made it look like angels' wings in the sky. Seeing it always calmed her.

"I've missed you too." Megan smiled and briefly touched Jan's hand.

The moment Megan had met Jan, there was a connection. It had been more than five years ago on a cold winter night in the town park. The locals had been putting on a nativity play, and Jan was passing out Styrofoam cups of hot chocolate. Seeing that she was shorthanded, Megan had offered to help. The day after the play, Jan showed up at Megan's door with a basket full of freshly baked muffins as a thank-you. They'd been friends ever since.

"Where're the girls?"

Megan leaned back in her chair. "I have the morning off. Hannah and Alexis are with friends for the day, and Peter took Emma out on a date."

Jean's brow rose. "On a workday?"

Megan nodded. "For breakfast and coffee before he heads in to work. He took her to the donut shop down the road. It'll be good for them. Peter has had a hard time figuring out how to deal with Emma. She's not the little girl we knew before everything happened."

Jan leaned forward and placed her elbows on the table. "Of course she's not. She grew up without your influence in her life."

Megan shrugged. "Right. Someone else raised her, read her stories at night, and taught her how to bake." She squeezed her eyes shut for a moment and shook her head. There was no sense dwelling on it. She couldn't change things.

Jan leaned back, her eyes full of pity. "You need to learn to forgive them, honey."

Megan shook her head. "No, I don't. What I need to do is learn to let it go and move on. I know that. It's just hard sometimes."

Jan snapped her fingers and waited as Shelly Belle trotted over and sat at her feet. "You know, when my other babies died, I was mad. Mad at God for taking my babies away from me, even though I knew they were old and ready to rest. But that didn't matter. What I knew in my head and what I felt in my heart were two very different things. I convinced myself that the only person my feelings were affecting was me. But I was wrong." A low groan came from the floor. "Poor Shelly Belle was affected as well. She'd just lost her family, and instead of being there for her to help her deal with her loss, I took it out on her." Jan shook her head as a tear welled in her eye. "Oh, I wasn't mean or anything, but I didn't show her as much love as I could have."

Megan broke off bits her muffin and cast her eyes downward, thinking about Jan's words. "I do love my children." Her voice lacked conviction, because she understood exactly what Jan was saying.

"No one doubts how much you love your girls. But, honey, you need to learn to love yourself too."

Megan sighed deeply. "And how do you do that? My girls mean the world to me. They are my everything. How exactly do I put myself first without losing that?"

The bell above the door jingled. Without glancing behind her, Jan stood up and laid her hand on Megan's shoulder. "Honey, the only babies I ever raised were my pups, so I can't tell you how to parent. But I can tell you that the first step to loving yourself is learning how to forgive yourself."

⚜

Jack and the boys were the only ones in the donut shop, the place nearly silent. Jack cleared his throat but wasn't sure what to say.

They were all tired. They'd stayed late at the races, spending a fortune at the slot machines. Doug won a measly hundred dollars on a horse no one expected to win and was convinced his luck had turned. And it had. He walked away winning another hundred at the penny slots. Jack just shook his head as he slapped his friend on the back and told him it was time to go home.

He almost didn't make it this morning. He'd considered staying home, sleeping in, and puttering around in his garden, but he showed up anyway, knowing that if he didn't, the boys would come looking for him.

They sat for at least twenty minutes in silence, watching the line of cars and drivers ordering their coffees at the drive-thru window.

Jack thought about what he'd do when he went home. Dottie's vegetable garden needed tending. Although, what he'd do with all the veggies, he had no idea. Maybe his neighbor Sherri could use some. Ever since the day he'd found Dottie on the floor, Sherri had been there for him. She became his spokeperson when the pesky media parked along the road waiting for him to venture out; she cooked him casseroles and cookies and invited him over for coffee more times than he could count. He knew she felt guilty for her part in Emmie's . . . in Emmie going back to her parents. She shouldn't. If anything, he was the guilty one.

Maybe he'd just tell her to consider the garden hers. Lord knew he couldn't do any pickling or jarring like Dottie would have. He also needed to do some cleaning. It had been a while since he cleaned the floors or the bathroom. How Dottie kept the house spotless was beyond him. Sometimes, he wondered whether the house was too large for one man.

Jack pushed himself up from the chair and groaned. His body sure was stiff today. More so than yesterday.

"Leaving already?" Kenny asked.

Jack shook his head. "Just heading to the can."

Doug stood up as well. "I could go for another coffee and fritter. They sure taste good today."

Kenny snorted. "When don't they?"

Halfway to the restroom, Jack called over his shoulder, "Might as well grab me one too. And a refill." He ignored Doug's muttering. After all his winnings last night, Jack knew the old man could afford it. He'd eat his fritter and drink another cup of coffee and then head back to the farm. He had a hard time calling it home lately. Home was supposed to be where the heart was, but with Dottie gone and Emmie out of his life, there was no heart left in that house.

Now it was only an old, empty farmhouse filled with memories of laughter and love.

CHAPTER EIGHT

September 3

I'm sitting at the kitchen table, alone. There is a single candle flickering beside me. Jack is a sensitive sleeper and would probably wake up if he noticed the kitchen light on.

There's a cup of tea in front of me, but I don't remember pouring it. Just like I don't remember putting Mary to bed or baking the Dutch apple pie sitting on the counter. I know Jack didn't bake it. He can never get the recipe right.

I also don't remember what we did today. I don't remember any of it. I think I remember being out in the garden, but it could have been yesterday or last year.

I can't rely on my memory anymore. I get glimpses of things that happen, but when I ask Jack, he just gives me a weird look and pats my hand, telling me not to worry so much. Of course I'm going to worry; I used to have a crystal-clear memory. I need to know what is happening to me. I need to remember.

What if I do something that could hurt someone? What if I take the wrong medication, or forget to take it? What if I take Mary someplace and then leave her there, forgetting that I took her in the first place? No, not Mary. Emmie. Emmie. Why do I keep confusing the two?

My father was like this. Alzheimer's is a nightmare. It's hell on earth—except the ones who live it are the family members. It was horrible to watch him lose the life he'd built for us, his family. It was hard to see him forget who we were.

Please God, I don't want that to happen to me. I don't want to forget Mary. I don't want to lose Jack. Not again. Losing him the first time almost killed me. If it weren't for Doug and Mary . . . I can't lose anyone else in my life.

Peter glanced in the rearview mirror and knew he wouldn't have been able to keep the smile off his face if he'd tried. Emma bounced in the backseat as he pulled into the local coffee shop's driveway.

When he'd asked Emma where she wanted to go on their date, her first choice would have been his last. He figured she'd want to go to the local fast-food place, or even Brewster's Bakery to see Shelly Belle and Jan. But instead, she wanted to go to the local donut shop, where Megan would often visit the drive-thru for coffee.

"I've never been inside, Daddy. Papa and I used to go through there"—she pointed to the drive-thru entrance—"and get tiny donuts."

Peter pulled into a parking space and shut off the engine. He twisted in his seat to look at her. "You used to come here?" She'd been so close, only blocks away, and they never knew it.

Emma's attention was focused on the store in front of them. She nodded. "Yep. I even saw Mommy a few times too." Her brow furrowed. "But Papa always told me my eyes were playing tricks. I would wave at her from Papa's truck window, but she would only shake her head. It made me sad." Emma's lips formed into a pout before she turned her head and stared out the side window.

Peter's body stilled. His whole world stopped for a brief second, but it felt like it was forever. "What do you mean, princess? When did you see Mommy?" It wasn't possible. After all the false sightings when Megan thought she'd seen Emma, it couldn't be true that one of those times was real. She'd been right, and he never believed her. What if he had? What if, just one time when she thought she'd seen their daughter, he'd believed her? Would they have found her sooner?

Was it all his fault?

The tiny pressure of Emma's hand on his shoulder jolted him from his realization. "I wasn't allowed to come a lot. Grandma didn't like to leave the house very much, and she needed me to be her helper. But Papa would bring me with him when Grandma was sleeping." Emma bit her lip. "Papa would always get in trouble when Grandma woke up. She didn't like me going places without her. She said that all it would take was Papa seeing a new toy he'd want to buy, and the moment he let go of my hand, someone would take me."

Peter blinked a few times, attempting to wrap his mind around what he'd heard. "Who would take you?"

Emma was concentrating on releasing the buckle from her car seat, so she didn't look up. "Anyone. It would be easy. Grandma told Papa it would be too hard for people to resist such a sweet little girl. Papa told her she worried too much, but Grandma always said"— Emma's face grew grave—"you can never trust strangers."

A load of bricks landed on Peter's shoulders. In all the counseling sessions, Emma had never talked about what happened after she'd been taken. She'd withdraw into herself and color instead of talking about the past. Megan didn't think anything of it; she'd tell him it was normal, that she would have been too young to remember. Even Kathy Graham, their counselor agreed. But they'd been wrong. All of them.

Ignoring the cramp in his side from being twisted in his seat, Peter reached his hand out and laid it on Emma's knee. "Honey, why haven't you ever told me or Mommy this? Why didn't you tell us that you saw Mommy before?"

Emma shrugged. "I didn't want to make her sad."

"How would you make her sad?" That didn't make sense.

"Grandma said Mommy was too sick to take care of me; that's why I came to stay with her. She'd be sad if I told her the truth, and then she'd die. That's why Grandma died, Papa said, 'cause she was so sad." Tears welled up in Emma's eyes. "I don't want Mommy to die."

Peter was confused. None of this made sense to him. "When did Papa tell you that . . . his wife died?" He clearly remembered the day when Detective Riley stopped by the house to let them know about Dorothy. He would never forget the look on Emma's face when Megan said, "Thank God," to the news. How would she have heard it from Jack?

"At the hospital, don't you remember?"

Emma was looking at him now in confusion. He didn't remember this, though. When at the hospital? The only time she'd been there was at the beginning, when she was getting checked out. Shortly after . . . actually, it was right after Detective Riley's visit. Those first few weeks were a blurry memory, so many appointments and meetings and interviews because of the kidnapping. He'd hated every one of them, too, and what everyone insinuated, that their daughter might have been abused. Thank God, Emma had been okay, treated like a granddaughter instead of . . . Peter clenched his fist at how his daughter could have been treated.

Surely, he would remember seeing Jack. He'd remember if his daughter saw the man who took her from him. He knew he would.

Peter shook his head. "No, honey, I don't. When did you see him?"

Emma leaned forward and rested her chin in her hands. "Daddy, you do remember. Papa was crying, and I gave him a hug."

Peter closed his eyes. He vaguely remembered the last time they had been at the hospital. A kids' section had been set up in a sitting area off to the side. Alexis had sat at a table and was doodling on some paper while Emma curled up on a couch, Hannah by her side, and watched a cartoon on a wall-mounted television. He'd sat with Megan in the doctor's office just across the hallway. The sitting area had been empty, though, and Megan positioned her chair so that she could watch the girls. From the very beginning, Megan refused to take her eyes off Emma.

"Remember, Daddy? Mommy was in the restroom, and we were in the hallway?"

At her words, the scene played out in his head. Megan went with Hannah to the restroom while he stayed with Emma and Alexis. They'd left the sitting area and were standing in the foyer of the hospital when his phone had rung. Samantha needed to clarify some contract points, and he'd briefly taken his eyes off the girls. One moment Emma had been there, and the next moment she was at the main doors standing beside an older man with a hunched back and a sluggish step. Peter remembered that walk. He also remembered the instant panic of losing Emma, and making a mental note not to let Megan know he'd lost sight of their daughter for a minute or two. But that older man couldn't have been Jack. Peter would have known right away if it had been him.

"Are you sure that was your Papa?"

Emma nodded. "Uh-huh. Papa was crying. Grandma just died, he said. Because she was sad. I told Papa not to be sad, that I didn't want him to die too." She bit her lip and blinked.

"And what did he say?"

Something like a smile played over his daughter's lips as she thought about the words. He could see the happiness build in her face, the way her eyes brightened and sparkled, the way she relaxed her fingers and kicked her legs.

"That he loved me more than Grandma's apple pie. And that is pretty tough to beat." Peace settled upon his daughter, and she jumped out of the car seat. "Come on, Daddy. Let's go." She tugged on the door handle.

The moment they stepped into the store, Emma stopped in her tracks. "Are all these for me?" Her eyes widened and her mouth hung open as she gazed at the racks of donuts behind the counter and the window display of cookies and pastries beneath it.

Peter bent down and scooped Emma up in his arms. He'd forgotten she said she'd never been inside the store before. "No, silly. But you can choose one donut to eat now and six others that we can take home and share with your sisters."

Emma entwined her hands around his neck and squeezed tight. "I love you, Daddy," she whispered into his ear.

Peter tightened his hold on her. For two years, he'd ached to hear those words, words he never thought he'd hear again from his youngest daughter. It almost killed him to know Megan might have had their baby girl in her sights and that he had refused to believe it was possible. "I love you more," he whispered back.

They waited for an older man at the counter to grab his tray and slowly shuffle his way to the side, where he waited for his coffee. He glanced behind him and nodded his head in greeting to Emma.

Emma only smiled and burrowed her head into the crook of Peter's neck.

"Good morning," the woman at the front counter greeted them when it was their turn.

Peter ordered his black coffee and asked Emma to choose a muffin for him. He normally preferred eggs in the morning and had thought they'd go to a restaurant where he could order a real breakfast, but since this was Emma's date, he agreed. Emma glanced at the rows of muffins and donuts behind the counter, and Peter could see the anxiety well up inside of her as her body stiffened. The woman behind the counter must have noticed as well, as she began to rattle off the different varieties to Emma, who visibly relaxed. He should have given her some options to choose from instead of assuming she would know what he'd want.

"Do you like apple cinnamon, Daddy? Or would you like blueberry bran?" Emma gazed up at him, her brows knit together as if it were the most important decision in the entire world.

Peter smiled at her. "I think I'm in the mood for . . ."

"Apples!" Emma finished his sentence with a nod. "Apple cinnamon, please," she asked the woman behind the counter, who grinned as she chose the largest muffin and placed it on a plate.

"Now, what about you? Would you like a donut or a muffin?" If Emma was anything like her sisters, she would go for the donut. Didn't most little kids?

Emma's forehead bunched up as she shook her head. "Muffins are healthy, right?"

Peter shrugged. Really, there was little difference between muffins and donuts. Both were full of sugar. "Today's a special date, so you can get whatever you like."

Emma tapped her lips with her finger as she thought about her choices.

"I have some yogurt fruit cups if you'd like to try one of those too?" The woman at the counter pointed to the display case directly in front of them. There was a row of cups half-filled with yogurt and topped with fresh fruit. Emma's eyes lit up. Peter remembered Megan complaining about the large amounts of yogurt she went through during the week, thanks to Emma. Peter nodded and held up two fingers, indicating he'd have one as well.

"Do you want a chocolate-dipped donut or strawberry-filled?" Peter whispered in Emma's ear.

Emma glanced at the two choices and then whispered back, "You choose."

Peter smiled. "Close your eyes. It'll be a surprise."

He waited for her not only to close her eyes but also to cover them as well with her hands. He then pointed to a chocolate-dipped donut with pink sprinkles on top. The woman set the donut on a plate and placed a container of chocolate milk next to it on a tray. Peter tapped Emma on the shoulder.

"You can look now."

Her tiny squeal of delight was proof enough that he'd made the right choice.

He set Emma down on the ground and reached in his back pocket for his wallet. Emma grabbed the plate holding her donut. "Why don't you go choose a table for us?" he suggested. He quickly glanced around the nearly empty store. In the far corner sat two older men.

He expected Emma to choose the farthest table from the men, and was surprised when she chose the table next to them. He instead placed the tray on a table a few feet away, to give both the men and themselves some privacy, and called Emma over.

Except she stood there in the middle of the store and didn't hear him. Her back was to him as she faced a man who'd just walked out of the washroom. An older man who looked oddly familiar.

The plate Emma held in her hands dropped to the floor as she screamed.

CHAPTER NINE

October 1
Sometimes it's hard to understand why things happen the way they do.

Why did Jack have to disappear and leave me to raise Mary by myself? Why did Doug have to take his promise to the extreme and make me . . . why did Doug have to be Doug? Why did Mary have to grow up and decide I was the devil incarnate, when all I tried to do was love her the best way I knew how?

There are images in my head that I don't understand. A street lined with trees and the laughter of children, of balloons covering a clear blue sky, and a crying child. It's a street I don't recognize, and when would I have seen balloons in the air like that?

I know the dementia is getting worse and that I'll have more days when I don't remember than days when I do. Right now, that is a blessing. For Emmie. For Jack. For myself. There is nothing I can do to stop my mind from working against itself. I know that. No matter the medication I take or the specialists I see, I'll eventually forget who I am and who I love.

I hope I die before that happens. God forgive me, but I hope I do. I'm sorry, Jack. I know we made a promise, but the thought of living a life lost within myself scares me.

I hope Jack will read these journals one day when I'm completely lost to him and understand, even when I don't.

❧

Jack pushed open the restroom door with his elbow and wiped his hands on his pants. He grimaced in disgust at the wet marks along the sides of his legs.

"Papa!"

Jack's head shot up. Emmie's voice filled the store as she shouted his name again.

"Papa!"

He had to be hallucinating. There was no way Emmie would be here. Maybe he was having a heart attack and this was his punishment in purgatory—hearing his girl call out to him.

Except why would he feel her tiny arms wrapped around his leg, squeezing tighter than the fist in his heart?

When he glanced down, he saw a little piece of heaven in her crystal-clear blue eyes. Her hair was longer and curled only at the ends, and she seemed a bit more grown-up than the last time he saw her. A little wiser around the eyes. But she was still his baby girl. His Emmie.

Jack's arms reached down, and he gathered his angel close. He rubbed his cheek against her hair and inhaled a soft vanilla scent. If he died right now, he'd die a happy man, ready to see his Dottie and let her know their girl was all right.

"Papa! I missed you so much!" Emmie's face lifted, and the smile that beamed from cheek to cheek warmed his cold heart. Just her smile seemed to wake him up inside, filling him with hope. With love.

Jack knelt down but didn't release his hold on his baby girl. In-stead, he gathered her closer and lifted her up, not caring about the stress on his back. She felt lighter in his arms than he remembered, and that worried him.

"Emmie-mine, what are you doing here? Where are your parents?" He lifted his eyes from her piercing gaze to scan the room. Surely, her parents had to be here somewhere, and no doubt they would not be pleased to see her in his arms. He knew he wouldn't be if the situation were reversed.

Emmie twisted in his arms and pointed to the lone man standing across the room with a shocked look on his face. "I'm on a date with my daddy. He bought me a chocolate donut with sprinkles. Come see, Papa." Her eyes suddenly widened, and she pointed down to the floor. "Oh, no, I dropped my donut," she whispered.

Jack gave the woman at the counter a slight nod. "It's okay, sweetie. We'll get you another one. Don't worry." He stroked her back in tiny circles and reminded himself to remember this, having her in his arms once again. He had a feeling the moment he let go, he'd lose her all over again.

Knowing it was the right thing to do, Jack walked toward Emmie's father. The hesitation in his steps must have been evident, but there was nothing he could do about that. Watching her walk away the last time had been the hardest thing he'd ever had to do, and having to do it again wouldn't make it any easier.

"Daddy"—Emmie twisted in his arms—"now Papa can be on our date too!" Her voice sang with happiness.

Jack saw the look in her father's eyes and knew the feeling was not mutual. He didn't blame him. Jack cleared his throat but the words wouldn't come.

Someone else cleared his throat as well.

"Jack?"

He turned to find Doug standing beside him.

"Is this . . . ?"

Jack nodded. "This is my Emmie girl," he managed to whisper past the large rock lodged in his throat. He was not going to cry. Not here. Not now. Not with his girl in his arms and her father looking on.

Doug nodded and smiled. "Well, sweetheart, it's a pleasure to finally meet you. Your grandpa sure has missed you."

"Excuse me?"

Jack turned toward Emmie's father and sighed. He hated to let her go, but he knew he had to. He wasn't sure how, though. His arms refused to unlock from around her small frame.

"Come sit down, Papa." Emmie wiggled against him. She held tight to his hand, not letting him go as she dragged him over to the table where her father stood.

"This is the best date ever, Daddy! I can't believe that Papa is here, in our donut shop! I'm so excited!" She chattered away as the two men stood still, eyeing each other before they both sat down in unison.

Both men remained silent while Emmie babbled, picking at the sprinkles on the new donut that the waitress brought to her. She didn't seem to notice their silence. Jack listened to his girl talk, drinking in the sound of her voice as she described how Daisy had grown. He expected the little pup he'd picked up for Emmie to be almost full-sized now, although, seeing how it had been the runt of the litter, he didn't expect the dog to be too big.

Jack didn't fail to notice the way her father suddenly reached his hand across the table and waited for him to shake it; nor did he miss the way Emmie's eyes darted back and forth between the two men as if she were waiting to see what would happen.

"We were never introduced. I'm Peter." A look filtered across his eyes that Jack understood all too well. "Emma's father."

Jack gripped the man's hand and was assured of the strength in the grip.

"Jack."

Emmie shook her head. "No, he's Papa."

Jack smiled at her, his features softening as he was mesmerized by the bright sheen to her eyes. "To you, I'm Papa. But to everyone else, I'm Jack."

Emmie cocked her head. "Like how I'm Emmie to you, but everyone else calls me Emma?"

"That's because your name is Emma," Peter confirmed.

Jack nodded as the truth of what Dottie and he had done hit him square in the face again. "Do you remember when I first met you?" He wasn't sure if she'd remember that far back, or if her mind had blocked those first few months, like he'd been told might happen.

Emmie's face scrunched up. She closed her eyes, and her lips moved as if she were talking to herself. "I remember you gave me a balloon."

Jack's eyes misted at that memory. He'd found a bag of balloons in one of their junk drawers while Dottie had been out that day. Emmie looked so scared and alone, and all he could remember was how much Mary had liked balloons as a little girl.

Out of the corner of his eye, Jack noticed Peter's back straightening and the tightening grip on his coffee cup. Jack nodded, as if to assure him that he wasn't going to do anything to hurt their little girl. He could only pray that Peter believed him.

Jack lowered his voice. "Do you remember what happened before I gave you the balloon?"

Emmie shook her head.

Jack made sure he added a smile to his voice. This was just like when he'd read her a story at night. Sometimes he'd tell her stories of his daughter Mary, and sometimes he'd tell her stories of when she first came to stay with them. "Well, you were holding on to Grandma's hand real tight. You were such a brave little girl, though." He quickly glanced at Peter to gauge his reaction. Peter's lips thinned at the word "Grandma," but when he saw Jack's penetrating look, he gave a slight dip of his head. Jack took that as acceptance and continued.

"You were so quiet, and you were holding on to your stuffed animal so tight. I asked you what your name was, and you whispered it so quietly that I could barely hear. But I think Tiger knew I couldn't hear, because you whispered your name again into its ear and then held it up high to whisper in mine. Do you remember that?" Jack waited as Emmie bit her lip.

"I think so," she said. She glanced up at Peter. "Papa knows that Tiger is really a lion, so it's okay, Daddy."

Jack smiled. Apparently, they'd had the same discussion. Dottie tried to get Emmie to change the lion's name to something other than Tiger, but Emmie wouldn't have it. The girl could be so stubborn at times, just like . . .

He pushed the thought out of his mind. He'd never stop grieving the death of his child, but there was no sense bringing her into today's conversation.

"Well," he continued, "Tiger whispered your name to me and all I heard was, 'I'm me.'"

Emmie shook her head. "That's not what Tiger said." She giggled as she sipped on the container of chocolate milk in front of her.

Jack's brow rose. "It's not?"

"Daddy, I wouldn't say 'I'm me,' would I?" Emmie rested her elbow on the table and leaned her chin into the palm of her hand.

Jack caught the way Peter cleared his throat. "Well, now, I'm not sure. Maybe Tiger heard you wrong?"

Emmie glanced back at Jack. "Is that really what Tiger said?"

Jack kept the smile off his face and nodded. "Scout's honor." He held up three fingers. "That's where we got the name Emmie. Sure is close to Emma, though, isn't it? Must be my bad hearing." Jack winked.

"That's okay. Right, Daddy?"

There was a hint of hesitation in her voice, and Jack winced. She was too young to be worried about things like that. And it wasn't fair of him to put her in that position. Her real name was Emma. Not Emmie. He caught the look on Peter's face, as if he were trying to figure out how to respond without hurting her feelings. It wasn't right to put Peter in that position either.

"Emma is a beautiful name. I think it's the perfect name for a princess." Jack reached for Emma's hand and brought it to his lips. He laid a gentle kiss upon her palm, and she giggled.

No matter what, she would always be his princess.

Time stood still, and Peter had no idea what to say or how to react. A first for him. An image flashed in his mind of the first time he'd seen Jack.

Peter had stood beside Megan, his arms encircling her waist in an attempt to keep her by his side. The screen door edged open, and Jack stepped through it. He was old and worn. Tears streaked down his face, and Peter could see the anguish in his eyes. He stared at them as if trying to tell them something, but whatever Jack had to say disappeared the moment Emma stepped out of the house.

As soon as he saw her, he knew he'd recognize her anywhere. Her blonde hair, held in pigtails, framed a face that looked so much like Megan's. His heart lurched. He didn't expect this. He'd convinced himself that that day would be about accepting that Emma was really gone. After the way Detective Riley spoke to him on the phone, he'd been persuaded that this was the end to the small dream he'd held alive in his heart.

When Detective Riley stopped them from running to Emma, it took everything inside Peter to stand still and allow the older man to say his good-byes. Peter would never forget his voice, the gruffness and loss the man struggled to mask. It hurt his heart to have the other man's arms around his daughter, to see him place a kiss upon her forehead. He wanted to lash out, to protect his daughter the way he should have two years ago. But the look in Emma's eyes stopped him. She loved the older man.

Peter turned his gaze to Emma and Jack. He knew if Megan was here she'd have picked Emma up and taken her out of the store and back home within a heartbeat. And that had been his first reaction when Emma screamed.

But it was the way she locked onto the older man and the smile on her face that had stopped him from reacting and set him instead to observing. She had actually laughed. It was a sound he wasn't about to forget. For the first time since they'd brought her home, his daughter was happy, content. At peace.

Maybe Jack wasn't the monster they had made him out to be. Emma certainly didn't think so, and he trusted her judgment, even if she was only five years old. He knew all about Stockholm syndrome, had read books on it late at night while the kids were in bed, but he didn't think this was the case with Emma. They had never harmed or tortured her. And as far as he knew, Jack honestly had thought this was his granddaughter. The monster was Dorothy, his wife—but then, she was also a victim.

It was hard to stay angry with someone who loved your child almost as much as you did. His gut wrenched. He never thought of Jack and Dottie in that way. It was easier to paint them into evil villains who stole his child. He didn't want to think of them as real people who were important to his daughter.

But the way Emma glowed told Peter he needed to start.

"What if you had a special nickname?"

Peter wasn't sure where that came from or why he even suggested it, but it seemed like a good compromise. Emma cocked her head and smiled. Her fingers tapped against her lips for a moment or two. He could see the wheels turn in her mind. She wanted to please both of them but knew, even at her young age, that it was a precarious position.

She leaned over, cupped her hands over her mouth, and whispered into his ear, "Can it be Em?"

Peter stared into Emma's eyes and thought about it. Em would be acceptable and easy to remember. Em was even what Kathy, Emma's counselor, had suggested when they discussed Emma's trying to combine both of her lives into one. Em would be a sign that she didn't have to choose after all.

Peter winked and gave her the thumbs-up. She giggled and then leaned over to Jack and whispered into his ear.

"Well, now"—Jack cleared his throat—"I think that is a good nickname. And easy for my old brain to remember." He patted her hand as he visibly struggled to swallow.

This wasn't easy on him. Peter tried to put himself in Jack's shoes, to understand the man a little more. He'd lost his wife and the child he thought was his granddaughter all at the same time, while also having to deal with the consequences of his wife's actions.

The publicity surrounding Emma's return and Dorothy's death had to have taken a toll on the man.

Peter glanced at the table where the other two men sat hunched over their coffees, neither one saying a word. The man who spoke to Emma earlier watched them.

"Those men . . ." Peter nodded toward the table.

Jack grunted. "Don't mind them. They're harmless. Doug is the one watching us, and then there's Kenny."

"Are those your boys?" Emma piped up. She waved at the men before taking another bite of her donut. "Grandma says Papa only comes to town to be with his boys, and when he's with them, all he thinks about is—"

"Hush now, child," Jack quickly interrupted. "Your grandma's words don't bear repeating."

Peter had to smile when Jack's lips quirked, and he shrugged his shoulders. He took another sip of his coffee and realized it was gone. He knew what he was about to do was going to be difficult, but he needed to head into work, and Megan would be waiting for them by now. They'd stayed longer than he'd thought they would.

He reached across and placed his hand on Emma's shoulder. "Em, honey, it's time to leave."

Her whole body stilled before she lifted her tear-filled eyes to him. "Do we have to?" she whispered.

Those four words hurt him more than a jab to the heart would have. He didn't miss the way Jack straightened in the chair across from him; nor did he miss the way Emma leaned into Jack until she rested against his arm.

"I'm sorry, honey." Peter tried to smile, but he doubted it worked. "Your mom is probably waiting for us at home, and I need to get to the office."

Her head dropped, and she fiddled with her hands, which had fallen into her lap. Peter glanced over at Jack's friends and then back at the older man. He had an idea, but he wasn't sure whether it was the right thing for him to do.

Having Emma return to them was a dream come true, an answer to a prayer—except the little girl who returned was more like Emmie than Emma, and it was something neither he nor Megan wanted to accept. In the beginning, he'd agreed with Megan that immersing Emma back into their family dynamic was the right decision and that removing Jack from her life was for the best.

But what if that time had changed? What if it really was in Emma's best interest to have Jack back in her life? Who were they to tear apart their daughter's heart like that? He knew Megan would disagree. But maybe it was time for them to put their daughter's happiness first.

Emma sat quietly by Jack's side. Peter knew this was breaking her heart, having to leave Jack again, just like he knew it was tearing Jack apart to let it happen.

"Do you come here for coffee often?" Peter struggled to keep his tone neutral.

When Jack managed to tear his gaze from Emma, Peter's breath caught at the dimmed look in the older man's eyes.

"Every day. It's the only way I can keep an eye on the boys without them ransacking my house." His voice strengthened as he stared at Peter. "Every morning at this time."

Emma raised her head but kept her gaze downward. She reached up and grabbed hold of her drink container.

Peter cleared this throat. "I normally drop by for a cup a few days a week."

The light in Jack's eyes brightened. "Maybe I'll see you then," Jack said.

Peter gave a slight nod. It was the best he could do for now. He was going to have to figure out a way to bring Emma with him now and then without raising Megan's suspicions or making Hannah or Alexis jealous. He also knew that a phone call to Detective Riley would be required to see if Emma seeing Jack was even something that could legally happen given the restrictions that had been put on the older man once Emma had been found.

"Papa?" Emma's voice held a tentative note to it.

Jack leaned over and placed his arms around her. "Yes, princess?"

"I have pictures for you. Lots and lots. Daddy has one in his briefcase that we were going to mail."

Peter had completely forgotten about that picture. He lifted his bag onto the table, opened it, pulled out the envelope, and handed it to his daughter.

"I didn't want you to think I forgot about you, Papa, not like . . . not like your own little girl. I'll always draw you pictures and write you letters, I promise." Emma reached her little arms up and wrapped them around Jack's neck.

Peter glanced away briefly; the feeling that he'd intruded upon a moment he wasn't part of hit him hard. His youngest daughter, despite everything she'd gone through, had grown up a lot in the two years she'd been away from them. She accepted life more easily than he could have.

"Oh, sweetheart, I know you'll never forget. My Mary never did either. Sometimes life gets in the way and makes it hard to keep our promises. But I'll always love you. Always. That's one promise I'll never break." Jack kissed the top of her head before he unhooked Emma's arms and pulled back. "Now, scoot. Your mama is waiting for you, and I need to head back to the farmhouse. I've got some rosebushes that need pruning." Jack held the envelope in his hands. "I'll open this tonight before bed, okay?"

Emma held up her hand, and then curled her fingers into her palm while keeping her pinkie up high. "Pinkie promise, Papa?"

Peter's lips curled into a small grin as Jack struggled to keep the smile off his face. Emma had a way of wrapping people around her little finger.

"Pinkie promise."

Peter stood up from the table and waited for both Jack and Emma to do the same. Before he had a chance to take Emma's hand, she'd launched herself at Jack again and whispered into his ear. A small pang of jealousy took root in Peter's heart at the carefree way Emma responded to Jack. He wanted that with her. One day he would have it. He reached across and held out his hand. Once the older man gripped it, Peter squeezed tight.

"Thank you." His voice lowered. "I never said it that day. Thank you for loving Em and keeping her safe." Peter swallowed past the golf ball lodged in his throat. He sniffed and blinked his eyes. "And I'm sorry for your loss."

No other words were spoken, just a tight nod of the head as Jack released Emma into Peter's arms.

Peter held his daughter close as he walked out of the donut shop. Emma's arm waved relentlessly as they walked away. A huge smile filled her face. Once they were settled and Peter was driving out of the parking lot, Emma asked the question Peter wasn't sure he wanted to answer.

"Can we go back tomorrow?"

CHAPTER TEN

J ack stood at the top of his porch steps and looked out over his front yard. Weeds peeked from crevices along the stone path, flowers wilted in the hot afternoon sun, and the grass was in dire need of a cut.

He'd let things go. If Dottie were here, she'd have a thing or two to say.

Jack pulled the kerchief out from his back pocket and mopped the sweat off his forehead and neck. The cloudless sky showed no mercy of rain or shelter from the sun's rays. Last year during days like this, he was out in back beneath the trees, playing with his sweet Emmie.

He missed those days. Guilt ate at him, tearing him up from the inside out. He wished time would reverse, even if just for a moment. He wanted to go back to that day when he sat with his girls, drinking ice-cold lemonade and drawing silly pictures with Emmie while listening to the clicking of Dottie's knitting needles as she made another hat or booties for the church donation box. He wished to relive his ignorance and believe that Emmie was really his.

He'd known Dottie had been in a bad place, but he hadn't realized just how bad. When did her memory first go? How could she honestly have thought that Emmie was theirs? Why hadn't he seen it sooner? He'd never forgive himself for not seeing what was in front of his eyes.

Gripping the porch railing, Jack walked down the steps and made his way across his front lawn. In the middle of his yard, he'd stuck a bench and planted a small tree. That was the first plant he watered in the morning.

When Dottie passed away, Jack had to make a choice. He could bury her either in Hanton, where so many of their friends were buried, or in Kinrich, close to Emmie. But with the huge media outcry when Emmie was found, Jack knew the last thing Dottie would want was to be buried where anyone could find her. She was a private woman. Always had been. Always would be.

There were trees in their backyard dedicated to the memory of Dottie's family. Their ashes were buried beneath the tree roots, encased in cedar boxes that Jack had made over the years. Planting a tree was one of Dottie's family traditions, and he knew she would expect nothing less for her own remains.

He'd planted this tree in the front yard so that he'd always see it. He loved to sit on the front porch; it was his resting place, where he could look out over his flowers and feel a sense of pride. The backyard reminded him too much of Dottie, with her flower garden now overgrown, the chairs beneath the tree branches, and the tire swing he'd hung for Emmie.

He wasn't ready to sit among those memories yet.

Besides, Dottie needed a place of honor. She deserved it.

He lowered himself onto the wood bench next to the tree and pulled out some leaves that had fallen into the wooden bucket planters beside it. Otherwise, the flowers bloomed healthy and hale. But then he made sure to water them at the same time he watered Dottie's tree.

"Well, Dottie-mine. I saw her. I saw our girl." His voice choked on the words. "She looks good. Growing like a weed. And she's happy. Our girl is happy." Jack swiped away at his wet cheeks.

"I wish you could have seen her, honey, one last time before you left. She misses you. She was telling me how she likes to bake with her mom, and how she's a good little helper because you used to let her help you. She'll never forget you, Dottie. You'll always be her grandma."

Jack leaned back on the bench and crossed his legs in front of him. He should have worn his hat. Sweat dripped down his neck, and he was feeling drowsy from the heat.

The gentle buzz of a bee filled the air amid the chirping from a nest at the side of the house. He closed his eyes and let the peace wash over him. He wasn't much for getting emotional, but he couldn't hide it from Dottie. He never could. She could always see right through him.

"If you had asked me yesterday, I would have told you I'd be coming to see you real soon. I was ready, baby. To see your face again, to hold you in my arms, to listen to you rail at me for letting my flowers go . . . I miss you, Dottie-mine. But I can't now. Not after seeing our girl. I can't leave her." Jack leaned forward, resting his elbows on his knees as he stared at the tree. "I want to show her this tree, explain to her what it means. I'm not sure if that will ever happen, but I want the chance in case it does."

He reached into his pocket and pulled out a folded piece of paper.

"Her father is a good man. I knew it was hard for him when Em saw me. If I were him, I'd have taken her out of the store and called the police." Jack lifted his gaze to the sky and shook his head. "He's a stronger man than I could ever be, Dottie-mine. He's going to bring her back to the donut shop. Can you believe it? Not every day, but maybe, if I'm lucky, I'll get to see her once every few weeks. I can't let her down. What if she comes and I'm not there?" He tried to clear his dry throat, but it hurt. "I know I'm just a foolish old man, but I can't give up hope."

Jack unfolded the picture in his hands. "She drew us something. Our Emmie. She's quite the artist. I thought she'd have forgotten us by now, but she hasn't." Jack traced the images on the paper. "We're all holding hands, Dottie-mine. Our girl . . ." The image blurred in front of him. Jack berated himself for allowing his emotions to get the better of him. He didn't want to lose this picture.

"She drew us. You, me, and her. Holding hands, with Daisy. I'm going to frame it and put it in the living room, right next to the other ones she made for us."

Jack cleared his throat. "Be happy, Dottie-mine. Be happy and at peace. All is well, and I'll see you soon."

CHAPTER ELEVEN

December 9

My heart is so heavy, and I'm so angry lately.

I know Jack is concerned. He has an anxious look in his eyes when I lash out at him, but the old man, he doesn't say anything.

I'm afraid that I'll lose everyone I love, and I'm afraid of what that means—being alone. I'm scared.

I have nightmares most nights. Even my dreams are filled with empty coffins.

Yesterday passed so quickly. There are moments I can't recall anything that went on.

I almost broke down last night with Jack during our tea, but then I heard Emmie's cries throughout the house and I went to comfort her. She still cries in her sleep, wanting her mommy. When I came back down to the kitchen, I noticed Jack holding his pill bottle. Just a little chest pain is all, he said. But I know that man better than he thinks. He would only take those pills if he was in a lot of pain. The radio was on low, and the story of a woman trying to find her daughter came on. It's been on the radio all day. The sound of that woman's pleas haunt me. I know what she is going through. I understand her fears. I wish I could write her a letter and tell her to never give up, not like I did. But I won't. Sometimes the lessons we learn in life aren't meant to be shared.

I often wonder if Jack ever thinks about when Mary went missing all those years ago. How worried we were. How we searched all over only to realize that our child wasn't missing—she'd run away from the ones who loved her most.

A woman can handle only so much weight on her shoulders before her knees give out and she can't get back up again. I'm not sure how much more I can take.

Emmie is a beautiful child. I see so much of Mary in her. She has Jack's eyes, pale blue that darken when she cries or gets sad. The poor child is so scared and sad. I just want to wrap my arms around her and never let her go. I made so many mistakes with Mary, but I can only believe that this is God's way of giving me another chance. Those rare moments when she smiles are priceless. Why didn't I treasure Mary's smiles when she was this age? I can't stop thanking God that I found her when I did. Otherwise, my granddaughter might have forever been lost to me.

Please, Mary, if you are looking down, know that I never stopped loving you. I promise to be a better grandmother to your child than I was a mother to you. I promise.

⚜

Megan rocked herself in the back-porch swing, enjoying the gentle summer breeze kissing her shoulders and arms as she drank in the silence.

She loved this time of day best, when the birds' sweet songs filled the summer air and the sun dropped slowly into the horizon. Sometimes Peter would sit out here with her on the swing, coffee in hand, as they struggled to reconnect with each other. It had been Kathy's suggestion that they do this, a means of rebuilding the tenuous bonds of their marriage. So far it wasn't working. Most of the time she was out here alone while Peter was stuck at the office.

Although she wasn't sure "stuck" was the right word. It was his choice to work late nights. She wasn't sure why he needed to—Samantha was supposed to help lighten his load. Unless . . .

In the beginning, it was almost as if he were trying to avoid Emma, which made no sense. But lately, all the two seemed to do was spend time together. Their bond was growing stronger, and while Megan loved to see it develop, she also felt left out. The thought made her sigh deeply.

Emma was smart for her age. She'd have no problems going to kindergarten in the fall. At night, when Megan tucked the girls into bed, Emma was always waiting with a book she'd picked out. She'd snuggle tight beside Megan, pointing out the smallest details in the pictures.

Megan lifted the phone and stared at the text message she'd received earlier. She'd asked Peter whether he would be home for dinner. The only reply was that he was working late. Again. Seems like that was all he did—even on the weekend. She'd canceled going to the movies with Laurie too many times to count. Just to make amends, she'd been spending the hot days in Laurie's pool. The kids loved it, and to be honest, so did she. But she was finally ready for a girls' night out without kids. She needed it, and she'd asked Peter to be home tonight by seven thirty at the latest. He still hadn't responded. She was desperate enough that if he didn't call soon, she would pack the kids up and take them to her mom's house—something she rarely did.

She stared out at her yard and noticed the sprinkling of toys layered along the grass. Peter had built Daisy a little run alongside the house; thank God, the dog was learning to go to the bathroom there.

The sound of light squabbling filtered through the open sliding doors. The girls were watching a kids' special on the television. Megan had popped some popcorn and was letting them have a pajama party in the living room.

The phone buzzed in her hand. *Be home soon.* Her brow rose in surprise. Nothing like leaving it to the last minute; Laurie was due to arrive within half an hour.

"Mom! Emma won't share the popcorn." Alexis stood at the sliding doors with her hands on her hips.

Megan planted her feet on the ground to stop the rocking motion of the swing and stood. "Really, Alexis? It's a bowl of popcorn. Not really something worth fighting over. We can always make more if you want more."

The frown on her middle daughter's face was priceless. Megan struggled not to laugh. It was only popcorn. Did she really expect to get Emma in trouble over this?

"It's not fair. You said we all had to share." She took a few steps back to allow Megan room to enter the kitchen, but now her arms were crossed over her chest.

"And did you get any?"

The scowl deepened. "That's not the point."

Megan shrugged. A third child added an extra element to their family's dynamic. Hannah and Alexis were still in the adjustment stage of accepting their sister into the house, even though the fact that Emma had been taken wasn't anyone's fault.

"So we'll make more. Why don't you go bring in the bowl, and you can help me."

"Can't we just get a new bowl? Emma's hogging the other one."

Megan rolled her eyes and then pointed to the cabinet where they kept the Tupperware bowls. "Go ahead." With Alexis, she'd learned a long time ago to pick her battles. This wasn't one of them.

Megan pulled a white canister over to the popcorn machine and opened the lid. She let Alexis pour two spoonsful of kernels into it before she plugged it in. Alexis stood there, watching the swirling kernels, and jumped at the first pop. Megan couldn't help but smile. She always jumped too. They waited for the bowl to fill with the fluffy white popcorn and then unplugged the machine.

"Make sure you don't touch this, okay? It's pretty hot. And please share with your sisters. This bowl isn't all yours." Judging by the scowl on her daughter's face, being told to share wasn't quite what she wanted to hear.

Megan turned to glance at the clock and frowned. Laurie sat at the kitchen table.

"How did you get in?" The door should have been locked with the alarm set.

"With my key." Laurie held up her key ring.

"Was the alarm on?" Megan's heart beat a little faster at the thought that Emma could have left again and no one would have known.

"It beeped. I figured you didn't hear it over the popcorn machine. Don't worry; I reset it and locked the door."

Megan unclenched her hand and took in a deep breath.

"Hey, Lexi, how ya' doin', girl?" Laurie snaked a hand out and grabbed a handful of popcorn before Alexis could pass her.

Megan was jealous of the special bond between the two of them. Laurie was the only one who could call her daughter Lexi. The last time Megan tried, Alexis had bitten her head off. Peter could get away with calling her Lex, but everyone else had to use Alex or Alexis. "Mom says I have to share. But Emma ate the other bowl. It's not fair." Alexis pouted. Megan frowned before shaking her head at Laurie. Alex had been complaining about Emma all week. It was tiring.

Laurie leaned forward in the chair. "I bet Emma is so full from eating all the other popcorn that she won't even want any."

Alexis groaned. "She will. I know it."

"Then let her have a few handfuls. I bet she won't want more than that." Laurie shrugged her shoulders before leaning back.

Alexis glanced over her shoulder and stared at Megan before looking down at the bowl in her hands. "Yeah, probably. Have fun tonight."

Megan crossed the kitchen, sat across from Laurie, and sighed as they both watched Alexis walk away.

"Any plans yet for her birthday?" Laurie tapped her fingernails on the table.

Megan's eyes widened. She looked at the calendar on the wall and winced. Alexis's birthday was in five days. Five days. How could she have forgotten that?

"You forgot, didn't you?" The gentle accusation in Laurie's voice rang loud and clear.

Megan frowned. She struggled to recall anytime Alexis had mentioned her birthday, but she couldn't think of a single time. Normally, Alexis would be brimming with excitement and plans. With her birthday in August, she normally wanted to do something outside, a pool party or picnic. Last year, they held a mock summer Olympics in their backyard, complete with an egg toss, a waterslide, and horseshoes.

"I'm sure she's talked about it with Peter, and he's told her he'd talk to me." At least, she prayed that was true.

There was a slight rise in Laurie's eyebrow. "I'm sure. And where is your husband anyway? If you cancel on me again, I'll scream."

Before Megan could respond, the sound of the front door opening and then closing caught their attention. She cocked her head before looking past Laurie's shoulder, and waited for Peter.

There was a small thud of what she imagined to be Peter's brief-case as it hit the floor, and they heard the jingle of keys dropped into the bowl on the front table. Within moments, her husband walked down the hallway and stood at the kitchen doorway.

There were visible creases along his face, and a strain to his smile as he nodded to Laurie and then leaned down to brush his lips against Megan's cheek. She smiled up at him before reaching for his hand. She needed to touch him, to feel a connection between them, but he only grazed her fingers before turning away. She could see the look on Laurie's face out of the corner of her eye but refused to meet her gaze. Megan wasn't in the mood for sympathy.

"So you're going on a girls' date? What movie are you going to see?" Peter reached into the fridge and grabbed the water jug.

"Some chick flick Laurie's been wanting to see." Megan smiled before narrowing her gaze. "Has Alex mentioned anything about her birthday to you?" She kept her voice down, just in case her daughter was eavesdropping.

Peter only shook his head as he gulped down the glass of water. "No. I figured you were on top of that." He reopened the fridge door and peered inside. "Did you leave me anything for supper?" He pulled open the oven door before reaching for the microwave and finding the plate of food in there for him.

Megan's heart sank. She had five days.

"You forgot, didn't you?"

The look in his eyes said it all. Megan sighed.

Peter shrugged it off. "I'll talk to her tonight about it. Explain that we just lost track of time." She noticed the thin crease around his mouth.

"Or," Laurie interrupted, "we could plan a surprise party. There's that new go-kart track that opened just out of town. They have miniature golf too. You could call and see if there is an opening. Invite some friends . . ."

Megan smiled. "I like that idea." She could ask her parents and some of Alexis's friends to join them. A surprise party would be perfect. Then Alexis would never know Megan had completely forgotten her birthday.

"That will work." Peter nodded. The look he gave Megan told her he thought she should have come up with that idea rather than Laurie. Waves of his disappointment and disapproval washed over her as a glower settled on his face. Now that Emma was home, he thought she should be there 100 percent for Hannah and Alexis. And he was right. She should.

"Did you at least remember to order that gift I wanted for her?" His brow rose as if he didn't expect her to say yes.

Megan stared at him blankly, trying to remember what gift he had wanted ordered. It sounded vaguely familiar.

"The golf bag, Megan. I wanted to get her a new golf bag with her name on it to go with the golf clubs I ordered. Remember? You told me you'd take care of it." Peter sighed as he laid his plate down on the kitchen counter.

Right. She bit her lip while remembering the phone call she'd made. "They were out of the bag you wanted with the purple camouflage fabric, so they were going to see if they could locate one in their other store." She caught the skepticism in his gaze. "I'll give them a call tomorrow." She made a mental note not to forget.

Peter thought her lack of memory was due to laziness. Her counselor said it was because she didn't view the small issues as important enough to remember. But Megan feared something different. For two years, she'd been so focused on finding Emma that she'd gotten in the habit of putting off everything else until the last minute. She wasn't lazy or forgetful. She had simply forgotten how to prioritize.

The problem was that she needed to make her entire family a priority now. Not just Emma.

The guilt she'd felt earlier intensified. She could tell Alexis until she was blue in the face that her birthday was more important to her than anything else, but they both knew Megan would be lying.

There was nothing Jack loved more than being in his woodshed. Sure, the sawdust made his eyes water and he'd sneeze for the next day or two, but there was something about the smell. Dottie used to say it offered promises of what was to come; he personally believed it offered the promise of the unknown.

Being out here kept him busy and kept his mind off what he'd found earlier.

Jack set the piece of quarter-inch-thick plywood he'd just cut on the side table and picked up another piece. Only three more to cut. He knew it was early, but before Emmie had been returned to her parents, he'd been planning to build her a Victorian dollhouse for Christmas. Now that his girl was back in his life, he wanted her to have it.

He took a quick look at the drawings he'd made to confirm that the markings on the wood were correct, and then powered up his table saw and gently pushed the wood along until it was cut in half.

He'd spent a long time on this drawing. There were a few designs in one of his books Dottie had bought him a few years ago that he liked, but instead of choosing just one, he decided to incorporate what he liked from several. The only problem was that the house looked like a mishmash now.

He grabbed the design from the corkboard across from him and gazed at it. Maybe if he added some lattice around the roof, a wrap-around porch, and extra doors . . . he grabbed the pencil behind his ear and was sketching the layout of the porch when a car horn interrupted him.

Jack stepped out of his woodshed and hesitated before waving to Doug. Not sure whether he'd kept the surprise off his face, he stepped back into his shed and kicked open the old fridge in the corner. By the time Doug walked in, Jack had two cans of root beer opened and had already chugged half his can. It felt good to taste something other than sawdust in his mouth.

"Thanks." Doug took the offered can and sipped. There was a gleam in his eye as he looked around.

Jack puffed out his chest before taking another long drink. He was proud of his shed. He'd added on to it last year, enlarging it so that he had more room to store his projects and keep them out of Dottie's way. Off to the side was a table he'd lowered for Emmie. On days when he wasn't cutting wood, she'd sometimes sit out here with him and color while he tinkered. He missed those days.

"It's been a long time," Jack muttered. Ever since Dottie banned Doug from her life, he'd never stopped by. Not until now.

"Need some help?" Doug's gaze shifted to the corner where Jack's half-finished projects collected dust. Most needed to be stained or painted.

"I'll get to them eventually." Jack shrugged before emptying his can and throwing it in the recycle box beneath his table. A metallic sound filled the silence.

Doug's lips tightened, but Jack was glad he didn't say anything. Having Doug here was uncomfortable, and he wasn't sure how to handle it. The coffee shop, the races—those were neutral grounds. But here, where Doug's presence hadn't been allowed since Jack had come home from the war . . . well, Dottie was probably glaring at them right now, angry beyond words that Doug would have the audacity to go behind her back.

"Think Dottie's turning in her grave?" Doug's voice was gruff.

"Why not go find out for yourself. She's out front, beneath the new sapling." Jack nodded toward the door and waited to see whether Doug would leave.

"Thought for sure you would have put her in the back with her brother." The surprise in Doug's voice caught Jack off guard. A tremor worked its way through his body, but Jack fisted his hands and ignored it.

"Sometimes Dottie didn't know what's good for her. She was too focused on the past. I can't go back there anymore," he mumbled.

"So don't." Jack jumped at Doug's brief touch on his shoulder. Jack cleared his throat. "Why'd you come anyway?"

Doug's shoulders relaxed as he let out a sigh and pulled out a stool from beneath the table.

"I'm tired, old, and lonely as hell. And I know you are too. You heard Kenny; he knows he's dying. We know he's dying. And you . . ." Doug gave him a pointed look. "Something's up with you, but you're too pigheaded to ask for help."

Jack buried his hands in his coverall pockets. He had half a mind to stop his old buddy from going any further, and yet he didn't.

"You've got this big old house that's falling apart around your ears, and you're too stubborn to sell it, but you can't fix it up either. Let us move out here with you. Kenny has a day nurse; she'll even cook up dinner if we ask nice enough. The three of us, we've been through hell and back together. Why not die together too?"

Jack shook his head. "Who said anything about dying?"

He'd already had that conversation with Dottie earlier. He wasn't going anywhere. He had his little girl to take care of.

"Then let us help you make sure you live long enough for her."

Jack hadn't realized he'd spoken aloud.

"Just think about it."

Jack grunted. He'd already made his decision.

He pointed to a small rocking horse on the floor.

"Stain is on the top shelf. Go with the dark stuff. If you're sticking around, you might as well make yourself useful."

CHAPTER TWELVE

Christmas Eve

We're snowed in. The tractor is broken, and Jack hasn't been able to keep the lane clear during the heavy snowfall today. Thank goodness we don't go anywhere for Christmas anymore.

Our front yard is decorated with lumpy snowmen and tiny snow angels. Jack convinced me to put my knitting aside—I had just finished a dress for Emmie—and dragged me outside. We taught Emmie how to make snow angels and then Jack insisted on rolling mounds of snow together to make a snowman family. I swear my bones refuse to get warm now despite the blazing fire in front of me.

In the months that Emmie has been with us, I've seen a change that warms my heart. She's accepted us completely as her new family and rarely cries out at night for her mommy anymore. I still catch the moments when I know she's thinking of the life she used to have, and I wonder what I could have done differently, but there's no going back. No changing the past. What's done is done, and I can't let it eat me up.

She is Mary's daughter. I know she is. I have moments of doubt—that is common, I think. I never knew about Emmie until the day I saw her. So much from that day is a blur. There are so many things I question and wish I could remember, but one thing I know for sure is that I love this little girl more than anything.

This is her first Christmas with us, and I think it will be wonderful.

Jack loves all the cookies and squares that have filled the kitchen. Emmie is a natural baker and a good helper. I think she'll like the matching aprons I made for her and me to wear while we are baking. Our freezer is full of containers of baked items for Jack to donate to the local churches. He was supposed to have done that today, but with the snowfall warning for the county, I'm glad he didn't. The cookies can wait.

This is the first Christmas in a long time when I'm actually looking forward to the day. Our tree is up and decorated, the lights are strung, and the giggles of a young child remind me of the days when Mary was a little girl.

The only thing more perfect would be for Mary to be here as well. But there's a snowman outside with her name on it, so that will have to do, as Jack says.

⚜

Brewster's Bakery was packed. All the tables and chairs were full of people sipping cappuccinos and eating the shop's famous home-made pastries. Laurie spotted two seats left at the far counter and sidestepped through the packed house. Megan followed after her, but not before stopping to look at the plated desserts in the cooling case. There were two pieces of Jan's homemade coconut cream pie left.

Luckily, Jan was behind the counter and saw her looking at the pies. She pulled the pie plate out of the case and held it up. Jan's petite frame made it seem like she never touched a single dessert in the store, but Megan knew otherwise and often wished for her metabolism. Regardless, it was Jan's sweet tooth that made this shop what it was.

"Two pieces, please. I'd be in the doghouse if Peter knew I had a piece of your pie and didn't bring him one." She smiled, knowing Peter often teased that he should have married Jan when he had the chance back in third grade when she'd kissed him on a dare. Jan's husband, Charlie, would blush and stutter in mock protest, while Jan herself would laugh and punch Peter in the arm, claiming he never had a chance compared to Charlie.

Jan shook her head. "Sorry, sugar, but someone already claimed these." She set the pie plate on the counter and slid the slices onto individual plates. She then reached below her and pulled out a shaker, with which she dusted a fine coating of chocolate powder on top of the pies.

Megan groaned. She'd been looking forward to having a piece of pie all night. She studied the other desserts in the case, but nothing else called out to her.

"However, your handsome husband did call me earlier and warned me you'd be in, so I set aside a full pie for you to take home. He wanted me to remind you to share." She winked at Megan before handing the two plates to the customer, who waited patiently.

Megan smiled. It figured that Peter would guess they'd come here after the movie. She glanced around the crowded shop and waved at several people she recognized. When it was Megan's turn to order her cappuccino, she tried to get Laurie's attention to find out what she wanted, but she seemed to be too engrossed in whatever she was looking at on her phone.

"Two mocha lattes, please. One with soy milk and no whip. Jan has a pie set aside for me, but"—she leaned over to peruse the treats again—"two almond biscotti. Please," she added to the teenager at the till.

After paying, Megan made her way over to sit beside Laurie. She must have surprised her because it took a bit for Laurie to realize she'd sat down, and when she did, she quickly turned off her phone and threw it in her purse.

"Something you want to tell me?" she teased at her friend's furtive demeanor.

A red flush crept its way up Laurie's face as she looked away. Megan gasped in surprise.

"No way. You're not holding out on me, not now. How long did you think you could keep it a secret?" The way Laurie's eyes widened, Megan knew she'd hit it dead on. Laurie was finally involved with someone.

"What's his name?" Megan turned her chair slightly so that she could face her best friend.

Laurie shrugged, trying to hide her embarrassment. "It's probably nothing, which is why I haven't said anything yet."

Megan narrowed her eyes. "Not buying it." She reached out and gently touched Laurie's hand. It shocked her to feel her friend's body tremble. "Laurie, are you okay?"

She witnessed the struggle on Laurie's face, and realized that this must be harder on her than she thought.

"It's been over four years; it's okay, you know. He would want you to move on and be happy," she whispered.

Laurie shook her head. "I know. I tell myself that all the time. But it's hard. Kris was the love of my life. But . . ."

Megan leaned back as Jan set their coffees on the counter. Megan smiled at her in thanks. She wished Jan would walk away, but she didn't know how to say it without hurting her feelings.

"It's good to see you finally in the land of the living, honey." Jan leaned her hip against the counter. "You have no idea how much people have missed you."

Megan snorted. "I've always been living. I just prefer to do it quietly right now. The last thing Emma needs is to be in the spotlight. She didn't handle it well when she first came home."

"This town just needs to learn to mind its own business," Jan grumbled.

"That's the pot calling the kettle black, isn't it?" Laurie muttered as she dropped her gaze to her coffee mug.

"Really? You're going to go there?" Jan's eyebrow rose.

When Laurie's face burned bright red, Megan crossed her arms and leaned back in her chair. "Someone want to tell me what's going on?"

"Nothing," Laurie mumbled.

Jan snickered. "I can't believe you haven't told her yet." She crossed her arms over her chest.

Megan kept silent. Something was going on, and she had a feeling it had to do with whatever Laurie had been doing on her phone earlier. The question was why was she the last to know? With Laurie's gaze burning holes into the counter, Megan reached for her latte and took a sip, waiting for the delicious warmth to flow into her. Jan made the best mocha latte around.

"Hey." Laurie glanced around the shop. "Where's Shelly Belle?"

"It's too busy in here, so she's sleeping in the back office. Now stop trying to change the subject."

The flow of voices surrounded them as they waited for Laurie to respond. Laurie bowed her head before finally raising her tear-filled eyes. The look on her face, the uncertainty and doubt, had Megan reaching across and enfolding her best friend in a hug.

"Oh, for Pete's sake," said Jan. Megan pulled away. "It's not the end of the world, and no one is dying. Our girlfriend here"—Jan cocked her head toward Laurie before lowering her voice—"was caught in a heated embrace last night with—"

"Just a man," Laurie interjected.

Jan's brow rose.

"What man?" Megan asked. Something was up. "Who is he? Where did you meet him? Why don't you want me to know about this? Why didn't you say something when you showed up this morning?"

Laurie shook her head. "I was going to tell you, but there was the picture, and then the . . ." Her voice drifted off.

"Oh, no, you don't. This isn't about me." Megan turned to Jan, who shook her head and clamped her lips together. "Who is it? It's not like I'm going to be upset. As long as it's not Peter," Megan joked.

Laurie drew herself up tall and reached for her own cup. She slowly brought it to her lips and took her time taking a sip before lowering it.

"It's no one, Meg. I only met the guy at the new shooting range that just opened up over on County Road 14. We chatted for a bit and then went for drinks afterward." Laurie shrugged her shoulder, yet she didn't look at her.

"So you shot a gun, had some drinks, and then"—Megan glanced at Jan—"were caught in a heated embrace, but it's nothing?" Why was Laurie hedging so much?

Her friend's cheeks bloomed a nice shade of red. "I had too many drinks, my bad."

"You're really going to use that excuse?" The challenge in Jan's voice was clear.

A sad smile flittered across Laurie's face. "It's not an excuse; it just is what it is. I won't be seeing him again, so really it doesn't matter."

Megan groaned. "I still can't believe I'm only just hearing about this. I must be the worst friend in the . . ." A blank look crossed both Laurie's and Jan's faces moments before terse smiles and narrowed eyes focused beyond her shoulder. She swiveled in her chair.

"Martha, Evelyn, how nice to see you," Megan cooed, knowing she couldn't hide the fakeness in her tone. Why, tonight of all nights, did she have to run into the two people she detested the most?

Martha Greer and Evelyn McNish could have been twins for the way they walked, talked, and dressed. Best friends for years, they were inseparable and always seemed to meddle in anything that was happening around town. Neither woman would ever be seen in Jan's bakery in sneakers; only dress pants and heels would do. Martha always wore a string of pearls around her slender neck, while Evelyn never wore less than the opulent diamond necklace her husband bought her for their twentieth anniversary. They were both slightly older than Megan, slightly skinnier, and slightly more beautiful. They were also terrible gossips and had made Megan's life miserable with all their backhanded whispers about how she was losing her mind in that first year of Emma's disappearance.

"Megan," Evelyn purred, "it's been forever since we've seen you. How are you?" The slightest smile was plastered on her face.

Megan squared her shoulders and reached for the cup she'd placed on the counter. She needed something in her hands to keep her occupied. "I'm fine, thank you."

Martha placed her hand over her heart and sighed. "We're so glad to hear that. We pray for you daily; we want you to know that. You must be feeling so relieved to finally have your daughter back home where she belongs, despite the horrible nightmare she must have experienced. I hope you've taken her in to see Dr. Brown. You never know what this type of trauma could do to such a young child." She sighed dramatically while shaking her head.

Megan didn't miss how Evelyn's lips quirked during Martha's speech.

Jan frowned at the two ladies. "Oh, for Pete's sake, Martha. Don't you read the paper? Our angel is fine; no need to be so dramatic."

Megan turned her head and smiled at Jan before looking at the two women again. "She's right. Emma is fine and adjusting well. I appreciate your concern."

Evelyn placed her hand on Megan's shoulder. "Of course she's not fine. You don't have to pretend to us. To be ripped out of her mother's arms and forced to live secluded . . ."

"She wasn't ripped out of my arms."

"And who knows what could have happened to her during the last two years."

"Nothing happened to her."

"Of course she's not okay. But don't you worry. We're all here to support you." Evelyn squeezed Megan's shoulder with her thin hands, her grip stronger than expected.

"I assume that program you forced parents to participate in will cease now?" Martha tsked.

"Excuse me?" Megan didn't believe she'd heard the woman correctly.

"Well, we all assumed you only started that program out of guilt."

"There's nothing for Megan to feel guilty for." Laurie stood up beside Megan and placed her arm around her. "You should be the one to feel ashamed for even suggesting that. And no, the program continues. Parents aren't forced to do anything, Martha Greer. Maybe if you and Evelyn had offered to help out, since you live on the routes, you would know that."

Martha's carefully sculpted brows rose straight to her hairline. "Why would we do such a thing? Back in our day, we took care of our own children's safety and didn't rely on others, not like the mothers of today's society." She harrumphed in disgust.

That was it. Megan had had enough. She stood, causing the women to take two steps back.

"Since you ladies are both prime examples of how to raise children, I would love for you both to help me in my program. I do need volunteer walkers, and since I know you enjoy your daily walks around the neighborhood, this would be perfect for you. I'll add you to my list." She tightened her hold on her purse, grabbed the boxed pie Jan held in her hands, and then glanced over her shoulder at Laurie.

Without any further words, Megan pushed past the two women, their exclamations of surprise and outrage ignored as she blew a kiss to Jan and waited for Laurie to join her at the front door. Inside she fumed, her entire body tense as she struggled to remain calm. She couldn't believe the nerve of those two women.

"Are the claws back in yet?" Laurie threaded her arm through Megan's as they walked toward the car.

Megan snorted. "Not yet." She needed to calm down, breathe deep, and just forget about the two busybodies inside.

"You know not to listen to them, right?"

They'd stopped beside Laurie's car. Megan gave her a reassuring smile before opening her door. "I know."

The ride back to Megan's house was quiet. Their words echoed in Megan's head until a headache formed. A tiny seed of guilt had always lingered deep inside of her. And always would.

As Megan opened her front door, she waved at Laurie, who backed out of the driveway. She thought about the tense atmosphere in the car and shook her head. She'd tried to lighten the mood by asking about Laurie's mysterious man, but Laurie clammed up and refused to say anything more on the topic. Laurie also begged off their morning run, claiming her parents were coming over for the day, so she needed to clean.

Megan heard the lie in Laurie's voice but kept quiet. Laurie's house was spotless.

Laurie rarely dated, but when she did, she was like a kid in a candy shop, so for her to clam up and not tell Megan who the man on the shooting range was seemed odd.

Unless she thought Megan wouldn't approve?

After keying her security code into the house alarm, Megan placed her keys in the dish on the side table. Peter's office light was on, so she took the pie into the kitchen to cut two pieces. She ignored the cluttered countertop with a half-filled popcorn bowl and dirty water glasses. Her attention was drawn to the lit screen of Peter's cell phone on the counter. She didn't see much before it went dark, but she did see the name. It was *her*. Samantha Grayson.

She should ignore it or possibly turn the phone off, but she couldn't. It was late—really late—and there would be no reason for Samantha to be texting her husband this late at night unless it was an emergency, or . . . she didn't even want to finish that last thought. She turned her gaze away from the screen and focused on opening the box of mouthwatering pie. Part of her wished Peter would walk into the kitchen and see his phone on the counter; another part of her wanted the screen to light up again so that she could see what the text said. They were struggling to rebuild their trust in each other, and searching through his messages was definitely not a sign of trust. No matter how tempted she was.

After sliding the pieces of coconut cream pie onto their plates, Megan stood there, listening to the stillness in her house. From Peter's study came the distant sound of paper rustling, but other than that there was blissful silence. She loved it. Loved knowing that her family was all under one roof. She felt whole, complete. She cherished the feeling for the few seconds it lasted—until the screen of Peter's phone lit up again.

This time she didn't stop herself. She grabbed the phone and read the message.

She needs to know.

The phone fell out of her hand, hit the corner of the counter, and dropped to the floor. A sick tumult of emotions swirled inside of her as she repeated the words over in her mind. Her chest ached, and her heartbeat quickened until she felt like she was running a marathon. She shouldn't have looked. Prying never turned out well. She knew that. Oh God, why did she look?

A creak on the floorboards from the hallway shot through the house like a gunshot. Megan jumped and quickly bent to pick up the phone. Halfway down, she realized her hands shook. She grabbed the phone and slid it across the counter back to where the half-filled popcorn bowl sat and whirled around to greet Peter with a smile.

"I was just about to bring you a piece of Jan's pie." She plastered a smile on her face and hid her trembling hands behind her back as she watched Peter approach.

"I've been waiting for this all night. What took you so long?" He bent down and inhaled the coconut cream aroma before dipping his finger in the whipped cream on his piece and scooping up a large portion. "Want a taste?" he asked, his voice husky with emotion Megan didn't understand, especially after the text message she'd read.

Instead of responding, she reached across to grab his phone and handed it to him. "You have a text." She busied herself by grabbing the dirty water glasses and placing them inside the dishwasher. She waited to see whether Peter would say anything to her, but he'd just set the phone back down on the counter and was eating his pie instead.

"Who texted you?" The question rushed out before she had a chance to bite her lip. She reached for her pie and sank her fork into the creamy center.

His brow furled as he looked up from his pie. "Just Sam. Why?"

Megan shrugged. "Just wondering why she would text you so late at night." She feigned indifference. Or at least she tried to. Peter must have caught a tone to her voice.

"Did you read it?"

Megan raised the fork to her mouth. "Do I need to?" What she should have said was yes. So why didn't she? Why not just admit she read it and have him explain her fears away?

Maybe because she wanted him to be truthful without forcing it out of him.

Peter shook his head. "No. It's just about a deal we're working on. I was going over the numbers after the girls were in bed and had some questions for her."

Although the slight hesitation in his voice was barely discernible, she caught it. There was something he wasn't telling her. Something he didn't want her to know. A flash of uncertainty crossed his face, so she swallowed her words and took another bite of the pie that crumbled like dust in her mouth.

She set her pie down. She'd leave it for the morning. "How was your night with the girls? Any problems getting Emma to bed?" Peter didn't seem to notice the change in her voice, or that she'd discarded the pie, something she rarely ever did.

Peter finished his pie and then leaned against the island. "Everything was good. They were up late, so hopefully they'll sleep in."

Megan chuckled. "You're kidding, right? Emma is always up at the crack of dawn." She yawned at the thought. Sleeping in would be nice, though.

Peter stepped toward her and placed his hands on her waist. "Is Sleeping Beauty tired?"

Megan let out the breath she didn't realize she had been holding as his hands touched her. She forced herself to relax. She shrugged her shoulders and yawned again. "It's a little past my bedtime," she admitted.

He leaned forward and placed a light kiss on her lips. "Why don't you go on up to bed, and I'll put the pie away."

Megan glanced down at the pie and then back up into Peter's eyes. Were there ulterior motives to his offer? Was he going to text Sam back?

"Will you be long?"

He must have caught her glancing down at his phone. He picked it up and held it out face-first so that she could see him hold the power button until it turned off. He then replaced the pie in the box and found a place inside their overstuffed fridge. Megan continued to stand there, just watching her husband. It wasn't that she didn't trust him, but knowing he kept a secret from her bothered her. More than it should. What if he was telling her the truth? What if she was reading into it more than there was?

Peter reached for her hand and smiled. He gently tugged her into his arms and started to walk backward, out of the kitchen and up to the stairs. Megan couldn't help but notice that he'd left the phone on the counter. This time, the smile that bloomed across her face was real.

❧

Peter's fingers trailed up and down Megan's arm as they lay snuggled close together.

"Did you know Emma thinks she saw you?" His movements stilled for a brief second before continuing, but the gentle caress she had just been enjoying now tickled and annoyed. She lifted her arm to move his hand.

"I don't understand." She turned to face him and saw the hesitation in his eyes.

"When I took her out for breakfast, she told me she thought she'd seen you in the drive-thru." Peter's lips tightened.

Megan shook her head. "When did she see me?"

Peter twisted so that he was on his back and anchored his arms behind his head. Megan had to dodge his elbow before he hit her in the head. His Adam's apple bobbed before he looked at her out of the corner of his eye.

"Apparently, Jack would bring her into town and go through the drive-thru for donuts."

Megan's breath caught. "She was here? Just down the road?" She shook her head. No, that wasn't possible. She couldn't have been. For two years, Megan had searched for her daughter. There was no way she had been just down the street.

Peter's chin jutted out. "She said you were behind her. Several times. She waved but said you didn't see her."

Megan tried to recall ever seeing Emma in the drive-thru line.

She couldn't. She recalled the time at the playground when she thought Emma was skipping down the sidewalk, or when they were at the pool and Megan thought for sure she'd seen Emma disappear behind a curtain in the changing room. There was the time when the kids were in line at the local ice cream shop and Megan thought Emma was standing outside with another family. And then the little girl at the donut shop. But that girl had been inside the store, and Megan knew for sure it wasn't her daughter.

"How did I not see her? How could I not know it was her?" Her chest tightened. "I wasn't crazy then. All those times you . . . it was real, not a figment of my imagination." Resignation swept over her. She let out a large sigh, threw the covers back, and grabbed her bathrobe. "We could have found her sooner, Peter." Her voice rose as she tied a knot around her waist. "Damn it, I could have found her sooner!"

Peter propped himself up in bed. "Don't you think I know that?" He rubbed his face with his hands.

"You could have believed me." Megan's hands trembled as she opened the drawer to the bedside table and pulled out a green leather-bound book with a cord wrapped around it. "Read my journal, Peter. I wrote down every time I thought I saw her. Every time." Her voice shook. "How many of those times do you think I actually saw her?" She tossed the journal onto the bed, regretting it the moment she did so. She'd poured her heart into that journal, and she wasn't sure she wanted him to see her that way.

He picked up the book and held it in his hands before offering it back to her. "How many times did you think you saw her?"

Megan breathed slowly through her nose, consciously letting the anger that welled up inside go, before taking the journal and placing it back in the drawer. "Too many times. I didn't tell you half the time." She sat back down on the bed and lowered her head to her chest.

The room was quiet. The gentle music of the wind chimes in their backyard sang out against the warm night breeze.

"Oh my God, Peter. Why didn't I trust myself enough?" Tears welled up as the realization that she'd actually seen her daughter hit her.

"Because I didn't trust you." Peter's voice lowered as he admitted something Megan had been waiting for a long time to hear.

She ran her hands through her hair before shaking her head. "You should have." Her throat hurt as she pushed down the urge to cry. All of this could have been avoided. They could have had their daughter back sooner if only . . .

Peter bit his lip. "I should have."

Megan pinched the top of her nose. "She waved to me?" Her voice broke. She waved to her. Emma had been right in front of her, and she'd missed her. "How could I not have seen her? How? I was always looking for her." She rubbed her eyes. "How did I not see her?" Anguish filled her voice as she looked to Peter for answers.

He reached for her hand and pulled her back down. "Maybe she didn't see you, Meg. Maybe she saw someone else." He laid a kiss on her forehead and wrapped his arms around her.

Megan tried to stop the tears. She curled her arms up across her chest and let herself believe him. Maybe it was true. Emma must have seen someone else. There was no way Megan would have not noticed her. No way. If there was one thing her counselor had mentioned, it was that Megan had been hypervigilant about catching a glimpse of Emma. She didn't trust anyone else to know her daughter the way she did.

"It had to have been someone else. I would have known it was her." She breathed in the musky scent of her husband and was soothed by the gentle strokes on her back.

"Of course you would have." He tightened his grip, and Megan cuddled in closer. "You found her when no one else was looking."

CHAPTER THIRTEEN

February 7

Jack handed me a box today and asked me to mail it while in town getting groceries. It was only a small box, not heavy, and I could hold it in one hand. I knew before I asked what it was for; why didn't I just keep quiet? Every year, every holiday, Jack sends boxes like this. A shadow passed over his eyes as he whispered that it was for Valentine's Day.

What he didn't say was that it was for Mary.

I hid myself away in our bedroom. Luckily, Jack understood. I used to do this when Mary was a young child. I needed time to myself. Quiet time, when I could get lost in my own thoughts and not worry about anything else. I'm too old to raise a child. We're too old.

Jack wants to reach out to Mary, to convince her to come home and raise Emmie. I think it's a bad idea. I'm not sure why, but something inside me tells me it wouldn't work. I told Jack I would try to contact her. But I won't. I can't.

Her last words to me were, "I hate you." I'll never forget her tone. Children eventually say that to their parents, but they never believe it, deep down. But Mary did. I heard it in her voice. I don't know what I did that was so evil, so horrific, to earn her hatred, but it's there.

Every day I remind myself that I can do it differently. That I can raise Emmie to be a loving young woman. But every day I'm also reminded of my age and how tired I am, and I get worried. What happens if I die too soon? What if Jack is the one who dies first? What if we die together, like we had talked about, knowing that without each other there is no reason to live? What would happen to Emmie then?

❧

Megan's running shirt was soaked. Despite the early hour she'd left the house for her morning run, the humidity had made it a struggle to breathe. Peter had warned her to use the treadmill today, but she thought she'd be able to beat the weatherman at his prediction. She should have listened.

Hannah opened the door as Megan stumbled up the walkway.

"Thanks, kiddo," Megan huffed. Throughout the last half hour, all she could think about was walking into her air-conditioned home. Not even jumping off the pier and into the lake had cooled her off.

"Dad asked me to keep an eye out for you." Hannah skipped ahead into the kitchen.

"Thanks, hon," Megan called out. She plopped herself down on the stairs and eased off her running shoes. Her entire body was drained. More than likely, she was dehydrated. Her head dropped down to her chest as she reclined against the steps, not caring how uncomfortable it was for her back. She wouldn't have been able to move if she'd tried.

"Here." She opened her eyes to see Peter squatting down in front of her, holding a glass of water with a straw. Megan smiled at him, thankful for his foresight. With her hands heavy at her sides, she let Peter guide the straw to her lips, and she sucked at the water.

"Do you need me to carry you up to the shower?" His eyes twinkled. "I could always wash your back."

Megan rolled her head back and didn't respond. She wasn't in the mood to say yes, but she was too tired to say no. Instead, she grunted as he lifted her in his arms and carried her up the stairs. She felt the strain of his muscles against her back as they flexed holding her.

He sat her on the bed, where she flopped down. Minutes later, the sound of the shower filled their bathroom. She should move, make it look like she was putting an effort into undressing, but her body was drained.

Peter grabbed the waist of her shorts. "I wish you'd listened to me when I told you not to go out this morning," Peter admonished her. He peeled the shorts off her body.

"I hate the treadmill."

The bed dipped as Peter knelt beside her. His arm snaked beneath her, and he lifted her up. She raised her arms as he pulled her shirt up over her head.

"What did you do? Jump in the lake?" Peter chuckled at her as he worked her sports bra over her chest before throwing it across the room to their clothes hamper.

"I thought it would help cool me down." She opened her eyes and stared at her husband's naked and chiseled chest. There wasn't an ounce of fat on his body, unlike the pudginess that covered her midsection.

"Wasn't the Sunset Cafe open to at least fill your water bottle?"

Megan shook her head. "It was too early."

Peter stepped off the bed and reached for her hands. He pulled her up and into his arms. "It's going to be like this all week. Use the treadmill next time, okay?"

Megan rested her head against his chest and nodded. She'd probably skip her runs for the next few days. Maybe she'd take the kids to the beach and just relax. She'd only been down to the beach once this summer, and it had turned out to be a mistake. Despite finding a quiet spot in the sand where they could build a sand castle, they'd quickly been swarmed by well-wishers wanting to welcome Emma home, and what should have been a calm afternoon turned into an overwhelming experience. Yesterday, Alexis had asked while they were making cookies if they could go back to the beach, and Megan said she'd think about it.

Maybe she'd ask Laurie to join them to help keep an eye on the girls. On a day like today, the beach would be swarming with people. The lake breeze was refreshing in the humidity.

"Do you think Emma is ready to try the beach again?" she muttered against Peter's chest.

He gently pushed her away and stared down at her. She tried to read the emotions in his gaze, but he quickly shut his eyes before leaning forward and placing a kiss on her forehead.

"I think it wouldn't hurt to try. And you know Hannah and Alexis would love it."

After their shower, Megan sat down on the bed and towel-dried her hair. She didn't catch Peter's words.

"What did you say?" She lowered the towel into her lap and pushed her hair off her face.

"I said Emma has a surprise for you downstairs."

Megan nodded. It was probably another picture. She was going to need to buy a new scrapbook soon, the way Emma was drawing her pictures. She picked up the towel again and squeezed the water from the ends of her hair.

"We had a good talk the other night," he said.

She stopped and looked over at him. Peter had his towel wrapped around his waist as he stood in front of his closet looking for a shirt to wear.

"And?"

Peter shrugged. "That's quite the little girl we have. I always wondered what type of child she would grow up to be, but I'm beginning to realize there is a layer of stubbornness beneath the layer of sweetness."

Megan smiled. He was only now realizing that?

"I was able to make a deal with her, but only after some careful negotiating."

She nodded. "So you used your power of persuasion against your own daughter?" She wanted to laugh, but the look on his face told her he was serious.

"She's going to start wearing the clothes you bought her."

Megan's grip on her hair tightened. "Seriously?" If she actually started to wear different clothes, that meant she was starting to accept the changes in her life.

Peter nodded. "Just on Sundays, though. At least, that was the agreement. I figured if we started with one day a week, then it might progress into more. But she put on that skirt and tank top you bought her last week."

Megan's eyebrow raised. "I'm shocked." She'd seen the pink-and-yellow polka-dot skirt and a sunflower-yellow shirt in the local children's store downtown and couldn't resist. It screamed Emma.

Peter sat down beside her on the bed. "It's a good thing, right?" He stared down at his clenched hands in his lap. Megan reached over and laid her hand over his.

"Yes, it's a very good thing. This was one of the breakthroughs the counselor said might occur." She took a deep breath and slowly let it out. Might. Kathy had warned her it would be a slow process and not to expect major changes overnight.

Emma's sleeping through the night had been the first step, and that had taken a few weeks. Megan and Peter took turns trying to soothe Emma during those long nights. Her wanting to venture outside their home to play would be another. That one hadn't happened yet, but Megan thought it was due to her own hesitation in taking Emma out in public.

Emma's willingness to wear clothes other than what she'd brought home with her was a huge step forward. Megan had feared that she'd have to outgrow the old clothes first for that to happen. Kathy suggested that Megan use the clothes Emma did outgrow and make them into a quilt or miniature clothing for her dolls. Megan did not like that suggestion. She couldn't wait to create a bonfire out in the backyard and personally toss each dress into the flames.

⚜

As Megan walked down the stairs, she reminded herself to act casual when she noticed Emma's outfit. She wanted to show her happiness without making it too obvious. There were days Emma seemed as skittish as a newborn colt, and it was all Megan could do to not say or do anything that might force her back into her quiet shell.

Her hand gripped the handrail as she stood on the bottom step. Today was a new day. One full of new beginnings. New adventures. Did Dorothy and Jack take her to the beach while she lived with them?

"Mom, can I have the last waffle?" Hannah stood in the kitchen doorway wearing pink track shorts and a black tank top.

Megan placed her arm around Hannah's shoulder and gave her a slight squeeze. "Morning, sunshine," she laid a gentle kiss on the top of Hannah's head. "You're kidding me, right? I just bought those yesterday. There's only one left?" She knew the waffles were a favorite with the girls, but she didn't expect them to disappear so soon.

"So who ate all the waffles?" Megan glanced around the kitchen. Peter stood at the counter pouring a cup of coffee. Alexis sat at the table scarfing the last bite of waffle, while Emma's head hung low as her hand rested on top of Daisy's head.

"Let me guess: Daisy had breakfast too." Megan crossed her arms and frowned. "Emma, honey, we talked about this. It's not healthy for Daisy to eat people food. Remember?"

As Emma slowly nodded her head, still not looking up, Megan glanced over at the empty dog bowls.

"Daisy has no food or water, honey." Megan lowered her voice as she leaned over the table. It was hard to keep the smile both out of her voice and off her face as Emma slid off her chair and headed over to the cupboard where the dog food was kept.

While Emma filled Daisy's bowls, Megan reached for an envelope she kept tacked to the bulletin board by the phone. When Emma was finished, Megan held out the envelope and let her youngest daughter go through and pick out a sticker. Megan winked at her when she pulled out a bright-yellow daisy and placed it on the chore chart they'd made up.

Integrating Emma into their family routine also meant allowing her to take ownership of certain chores. Feeding Daisy was one of them. For every chore completed, the girls would place a sticker on top of that specific chore, and if they were all covered by the end of the week, they received a special reward. Normally, it was ice cream or a small item the girls had requested.

"Coffee?" Peter held out a mug. Megan reached for it and took a sip. Peter made the best coffee. Years ago, they'd both decided Peter's strong brew was preferable, especially since Megan always seemed to make a weak pot.

"Hey, Mom?" Alexis raised her head from the plate she was licking clean. Smears of maple syrup covered her mouth and the tip of her nose. "Do you think we could go over to Laurie's pool today? It's gonna be a scorcher." Alexis pointed to the small kitchen television that sat on a shelf above the built-in desk.

"Scorcher, huh?" Megan winked at Peter before taking another sip. At Alexis's nod, Megan smiled. "Actually, I thought maybe we could have a picnic lunch down by the beach today."

A wide smile crossed Alexis's face before she launched herself at Megan and threw her arms around her. Megan held up her coffee just in time and laughed.

"Really?" A look of disbelief covered Hannah's face.

Megan nodded. "Really. Your dad might even join us for lunch," she said.

"Awesome!" Alexis untangled herself from Megan and ran over to Peter, who was waiting. He gripped her in a bear hug and lifted her off the ground.

Megan bent down and stared into Emma's eyes. They were as round as saucers. "Do you like the beach?"

Emma nodded her head, the little curls bouncing at the movement.

"Do you want to go today? We could build a sand castle together."

Emma continued to nod. A tiny tear ran down her cheek, and Megan wiped it away.

"What's wrong, honey?" Her heart ached. The only time Emma cried was when she was thinking of Dorothy and Jack.

"Papa said he was going to take me to the beach this summer," Emma whispered.

"Well." Peter squatted down beside them and reached for both Megan's hand and Emma's. "You can always draw him a picture. We'll make sure he gets it, right?"

Megan dug her fingernails into Peter's hand at the suggestion. She hoped he caught the daggers in her eyes as she glared at him. He shook his head at her in reply.

Emma's eyes grew wide and a tiny smile teased the edges of her lips. "Today?" Emma's fingers splayed across Peter's cheeks as she stared into his eyes. When he shook his head, she burrowed her face into his chest. Peter held Emma as he stood up and patted her back.

Conflicting emotions raged through Megan. Part of her loved to see Emma in Peter's arms like this, going to him for comfort. That was how it should be between father and daughter. But the other part of her wanted to scream at Peter for knowingly giving Emma false hope.

Megan realized that wanting to keep Jack out of Emma's life was wrong. She knew that a gradual withdrawal would have been more beneficial to Emma than the sudden split that she had insisted on, but she also knew that until she let go of her anger toward the man and woman who took Emma, she'd never be okay with allowing Jack to be a part of Emma's life. Never.

Megan jumped when Peter's hand touched her arm. He'd set Emma on the ground, and she was looking through the papers piled up on the counter.

"I can't find the picture I drew for Papa," she said.

Megan tried to remember what picture Emma was talking about. There'd been so many.

"It has to be around here somewhere." Megan placed her coffee down on the counter and began to go through the stack of papers.

There were bills she needed to pay, letters she needed to read, and an assortment of to-do lists, but no drawing from Emma.

"We can look for it after breakfast, okay, honey? We'll find it." But then what? she asked herself.

Emma shook her head. "No, I need it."

"It's okay, honey," Peter said. "We can do it tomorrow, okay?"

Megan jerked her gaze toward Peter. "Do what tomorrow?"

Peter shrugged, his gaze shifting around the room. "Mail it."

Megan set papers down and stared at her youngest daughter. "I told you I'd mail it, honey. Your daddy doesn't need to worry about it." She hoped she sounded sincere.

From the skeptical look on Emma's face, it didn't come across that way. "It's been a long time since Papa wrote me, Mommy. I don't think you know the address right. But Daddy knows how to get it to him."

Behind her, Alexis snorted at the comment, while Megan took a step back at the admonition in Emma's voice. Not once had Emma ever accused her of anything, not since she'd come home. Her other daughters, yes. Alexis especially. She constantly accused her of not loving her and Hannah the same as Emma, of not giving them enough time, of not paying enough attention. But Emma had never shown her disappointment like this. It hurt. Really hurt. Even if it was true.

"I'll take care of it, I said." There was an edge to Peter's voice she hadn't caught before.

Megan opened her mouth to say something, but no words came out. It hurt her that Emma distrusted her so much—or was she reading too much into it? The thought left a sour taste in her mouth.

"Is this the one?" Hannah walked into the kitchen with a sheet of paper.

Emma ran over to where Hannah stood and studied the picture. When her chin bobbed up and down, Megan let out the air stuck inside her lungs.

"Where did you find it?" She thought for sure she'd left it on the counter yesterday.

Hannah shrugged. "It was underneath the table in the hallway."

"Totally weird," Alexis piped up.

Megan shrugged. "I must have put it on the table so that I'd remember to mail it." She felt Peter's presence behind her.

"At least we found it. Why don't you go put it in my briefcase," Peter said. When Megan tilted her head to look at him, she caught the wink he gave Emma.

As Emma left the room, Peter leaned his face toward hers and whispered into her ear, "You never meant to mail that, did you?"

CHAPTER FOURTEEN

Jack coasted his old Ford into the parking lot and glanced around. It was still early. Late enough to miss the morning rush of those heading in to work, but early enough to miss the mothers getting out of the house with their noisy kids in tow. Jack tried to stay as far away from small kids as he could. He didn't need any reminders of Emmie. Of her laughter and giggles.

A handful of vehicles littered the parking area, including the boys' trucks. Jack grunted. They'd actually beat him there today. He was usually the first one to arrive. He hoped they'd kept his seat open. He preferred the corner seat so that he could look out across the tables and at the front door, as well as see who drove into the drive-thru area. He knew it was pointless to hope, but maybe, just maybe, he'd see Emmie.

"Wondered when you'd get here; the boys are getting impatient," the waitress at the counter said as Jack entered the store. The tiny bells above the door jingled as it closed behind him.

"Not my fault if they're early." Jack watched her pour him a cup of black coffee.

Jack looked at the far booth in the corner. Both the boys, Doug and Kenny, were slouched over their coffees as they stared at him. His best friends. Before Dottie had passed away, Jack used to make a trip into town once a week just to have coffee with them. Now it was daily.

"I might as well get a honey dip too. Can't let these boys eat alone."

Jack shuffled his way toward the table. "Where've you been? You're late. Dougie and I have been sitting here like two old cows chewin' cud," said Kenny as Jack set his coffee and plate down on the table. They'd saved his chair for him.

"Slept in." Jack grunted. He narrowed his eyes, daring them to say something. He took a sip of his coffee and peered over the rim. Doug looked like Jack felt. With his salt-and-pepper hair all over the place, he looked old.

"You never sleep in."

Jack shook his head. Leave it to Doug to not leave things alone. "I did today."

"Why?" Doug leaned back in his chair and tilted his head down to look over the top of his glasses at Jack.

Jack shrugged and took another sip of his coffee. "Does it matter?" He was getting annoyed. A vehicle drove by, but there was only a single passenger. A man.

"Of course it matters." Kenny piped up with a scowl on his face.

Jack shook his head and scowled before glaring at Doug. He wasn't an invalid or a child. And he wasn't moving. Not now, not ever. He was going to die in that house. It was a promise he'd made to himself back when he was a prisoner of war.

He took a bite of his honey dip but kept quiet as the waitress came over with a full pot of coffee.

"You boys look like you need another cup. Things are a little quiet this morning, and I made too many pots." She refilled Kenny's cup and topped off Doug's and Jack's; then she winked at them before walking away.

Jack jerked his head after her and smiled at Kenny. "I think she has a crush on you."

Kenny's face turned red before he hunched his shoulders. "She's too young."

Doug laughed before slapping Kenny in the shoulder. "Everyone is too young compared to you. Maybe she's looking for a sugar daddy."

Kenny scowled, deepening the lines on his face. "She'd better look elsewhere then."

The three sat in silence while they all nursed their coffees. It was Jack who broke the silence.

"You aimin' to die at my place?" He cleared his throat while Kenny's eyes widened moments before he cast his gaze downward.

"I'm tired, Jack. The quiet at your place is what I need." He shrugged. "And if I die in my sleep while sitting out on your front porch staring at the flowers you planted, then so be it. It's better than dying in my bed with a nurse hovering over me." His voice lowered to a mere whisper, but Jack heard every word. And he understood.

"You're waiting for Emmie to come back, aren't you?" Doug coughed as he broached the one subject neither man was allowed to discuss with him. But Jack let it be.

"Wishful thinking, most likely." Jack wiped at a tear that slid down his cheek.

Doug leaned forward. "Just because she hasn't come in a few days doesn't mean she won't again."

"I know." His chest ached, and he wasn't sure whether it was from holding in his tears or if his heart just couldn't handle the hurt anymore. He rubbed his chest and winced.

"Where's your pills?" Kenny watched him like a hawk. Their fears that Jack would have a heart attack at home weren't too far off. He expected it to happen any day, and was always amazed when he woke up in the morning.

Jack shook his head before standing up and stretching. "I'm fine." He stared down at the boys and asked his original question. "Bingo today?"

The boys played bingo almost daily at the lodge—the retirement home where Doug and Kenny lived. It was an independent-living facility for seniors who didn't require medical attention. Although there was talk of the doctors' wanting Kenny to move to another wing, where there was more assistance than what they got now.

Doug shook his head. "Nah. They have an outing planned instead. Something about a picnic at the beach."

Jack pondered the idea. It had been a long time since he'd last been to the beach. He'd promised Emmie he would take her. Another promise he wouldn't be able to keep.

"There's the races tonight in Hanton. We could go early and play the slot machines." That idea appealed to him. It was something different from the normal bingo game.

Both Doug and Jack nodded their heads.

"Get your beauty sleep then, boys, and meet me at the farmhouse in a few hours."

It would be the first time Jack had been to Hanton since taking Emmie and Dottie to the fair there. But he was a big boy, and it was time to move on with his life. He had to accept that Emmie was never coming back.

CHAPTER FIFTEEN

N ow remember, sunshine: We can't stay long. I have a meeting this morning."

Peter held tight to Emma's hand as she jumped out of the vehicle onto the pavement. She'd dressed up today, wearing a bright-yellow dress with a white-and-yellow headband.

"But Papa's here." A pout formed on her lips as she pointed to Jack's truck.

Peter shrugged. "Sorry, Em, we don't have much time today."

Emma lowered her head and dragged her feet, kicking up loose gravel as she walked.

"But you can still say hi and give him your drawing." Peter shook his head as she lifted her gaze and the brightest smile he'd seen all day appeared.

Emma skipped along, dragging Peter behind her as she headed toward the front doors. Peter caught Jack's eye through the window and gave a slight wave. His stomach clenched. He felt a little hesitant about bringing Emma today, and wasn't sure whether it was from guilt or something else. He was keeping too many secrets from her lately. If he wasn't careful, things could backfire in his face.

Once inside, Emma tore her fingers out of Peter's grip and ran toward Jack. The shuffling of a chair and the excited cries of a girl missing her grandfather filled the restaurant. Peter had to blink his eyes a few times as he watched Emma's arms wrap themselves around Jack's neck as he picked her up and held her tight.

As bad as he felt about it, Peter knew that keeping this a secret from Megan was the right decision. At least for now. She'd never let this happen, Emma holding tight to Jack. She'd do her best to rip her away from the old man. She still hadn't let go of her anger. Maybe once she started to forgive Jack for his part in what happened, she'd be more open, but until then . . .

"Two large, black and mocha, but can I pick up the mocha before I leave?" Peter stood at the counter and gave his order to the woman in front of him. It took him a moment to realize she was staring at Emma and Jack.

Peter glanced over his shoulder and saw Emma sitting on Jack's lap, her hands cradling his face as she chattered away. There was a dazed look on Jack's face, a soft smile as he gave her his full attention. Peter glanced back at the waitress in front of him.

"Um," he glanced down at the name tag she wore, "Claire, might as well add a sprinkle donut to the order. We'll be here longer than I expected."

Telephone to her ear, Megan sat at the kitchen table with a notebook and counted off the list of names she'd written down.

"Mom, I have at least ten kids from her class coming. You can help me with the miniature golf while Dad and Peter supervise the go-kart racing." She kept her voice down, not wanting Alexis to overhear her, even though she was upstairs getting ready for the beach.

"Why are you only telling us about this now? We might have had plans, you know."

The censure in her mother's voice was palpable, and it took all of Megan's strength to keep the fake smile in her voice evident.

"I know, I'm sorry. But I just—"

"You forgot, didn't you? Oh, Megan, how could you?" It wasn't hard to visualize her mother shaking her head while frowning.

"I didn't forget. I just didn't realize it was so soon. Besides, you knew it was coming up, so why would you have plans made?" Why did she have to justify herself? Did they not think she realized how wrong it was for a mother to forget her own daughter's birthday?

There was silence on the other end of the phone for a moment. "You can count on us; you know that, don't you?"

Megan didn't always know that. Their relationship was . . . complicated, to say the least. Megan always felt she had to live up to her mother's expectations, even when she didn't know what they were. When Emma had first disappeared, Sheila expected her to be strong, to not give up hope, and to believe that God would protect Emma and bring her home safely. When Megan fell apart, Sheila's disgust didn't go unnoticed.

"Megan?"

She shook her head and made herself focus. "Thank you. I think it'll be fun."

"What are you doing about the cake?" Sheila was known for her cake-decorating skills. She was on call for many of the churches in town to bake for their functions.

"Hannah's been begging me to let her make the family cake." Like mother like daughter, Hannah loved to bake, and often asked to try new recipes she'd find in the multitude of cookbooks Megan kept in the cupboard.

"No sense in doing that. Let me make Alexis's cake. Did Peter order those golf clubs for her? Why don't I make the cake in the shape of a putting green for her?"

Megan smiled. Alexis would love that. She thanked her mom before hanging up.

She put her elbow on the kitchen table. She'd accomplished a lot in a short time. She'd called friends from Alexis's class and explained the surprise-party idea to them, booked the racetrack, and even managed to coordinate an extra surprise, thanks to the manager. This would be a birthday Alexis would never forget, even if it was pulled together only a few days before the actual event.

Megan checked the time. What was taking Peter so long? He had a meeting this morning with someone wanting to purchase land just outside of Kinrich and said he wouldn't be long. He offered to grab some coffee and suggested taking Emma with him, and if he was only going through the drive-thru, he should have been home at least twenty minutes ago. Unless Emma sweet-talked him into going inside for a donut, something she was apt to do. Lately, it was as if that little girl of theirs had Peter wrapped around her little finger.

Thundering footfalls ripped through the ceiling above her, and a mere second later echoed down the stairs. She rushed to tidy up her lists and managed to turn over the details about the birthday moments before Alexis slid into the kitchen.

"I can't find my bathing suit anywhere." Hands were on her hips as she sported a bright-yellow Big Bird T-shirt and green knee-length shorts.

Megan sighed. It had taken her only fifteen minutes to realize her bathing suit wasn't upstairs.

"Where did you put it last?"

Alexis's brow rose. "If I knew that, I'd be wearing it; don't you think?"

Megan snorted. "If you think it's okay to talk to me like that, we can do a beach day tomorrow."

Alexis thinned her lips but kept quiet.

"Where did you last leave it?" Megan kept her voice calm. This wasn't a battle she was willing to fight. Not today.

Alex glanced around the room before heading to the patio door.

"We all left our bathing suits outside to dry yesterday. Why is mine the only one left out there?"

Megan stood and gathered the sheets of paper. "Maybe because I asked you last night to bring it inside." She opened the cupboard by the kitchen desk area and stuffed the papers into it. She'd finish the planning for Alexis's party later.

"But there are bugs in it now!" In a sudden rage, Alexis turned red in the face as she crossed her arms over her chest and glared.

Megan shrugged. "Guess you should have listened to me last night then."

"That's not fair." Alexis stomped her feet before yanking the sliding door open and heading outside.

Megan watched her retrieve the bathing suit by the tips of her fingers and fling it side to side. Alexis hated bugs. Megan checked her watch again before turning her attention to the sideshow out-side. The child was being thorough, at least, in how she was shaking that tiny piece of clothing.

"If you really loved me, you would have brought mine in, too, instead of leaving it outside," Alexis muttered when she came back inside.

Megan cocked her head to the side. "Excuse me?"

Her daughter stood stoic; arms crossed and lips in a tight line.

"I do love you, Alexis. It's why I told you to bring your suit inside last night. It's not my fault if you didn't." Everything inside Megan screamed. What was she supposed to do? She was blamed for coddling one child and being too hard on the other. No matter what she did, she couldn't win. It was as if Alexis expected—

"I bet you brought in Emma's." She stared defiantly into Megan's eyes.

And there it was. It always came back to Emma. She'd noticed Alexis tore up the stairs after Peter told Emma she could go with him to get coffee.

"Why would I do that?"

Alexis's nostrils flared. "All you care about is Emma. No one else."

Megan lifted her hands up in exasperation. "Are you kidding me?" Her voice rose an octave as she stared down her daughter. How could she think that?

Kathy had warned her that Alex might lash out like this. Megan had thought she was prepared, but some days she wasn't sure how to handle this—be a mother to three different children and meet all their needs. She felt like she was failing them all.

"You know Alex, I can't seem to win with you. What do you expect of me?"

"Love me like you love *her*."

Megan's mouth dropped. Had she failed her daughter so much that she thought she wasn't loved?

"I do love you," Megan whispered.

Alexis snorted. "Actions speak louder than words, Mom. Isn't that what you keep telling us?"

"I . . . Alexis . . ." Megan wasn't sure how to respond to that. "What can I do to show you I love you?" It hurt more than she thought it would to know she wasn't meeting Alexis's needs. She'd tried so hard, made more of a conscious effort ever since that note came home from Alexis's teacher before Emma's return. What else could she do?

"It's the little things, Mom. Like bringing my bathing suit in." Defiant, Alexis stood her ground. She reminded Megan so much of herself.

"Both Emma and Hannah brought in their own suits last night when I asked them to. You were the one who promised you would do it after your show was over." Megan reminded her.

"Oh." Alexis's shoulders deflated.

Megan crossed the room and wrapped her arms around her daughter's rigid body. "I do love you, Alexis. No more and no less than your sisters." She pressed her lips against her daughter's hair and waited for a response, but Alexis refused to bend. With a sigh, Megan let go and stepped away. "Go on up and get ready. Then you can help me pack a picnic lunch if you want." She gently pushed Alexis toward the hallway. "Now, where is your father?" Megan mumbled to herself.

"Right here."

Megan turned and found both Peter and Emma standing in the front doorway. Emma's mouth was smeared with chocolate icing, and she held a box of donuts in her hands.

Megan took the proffered coffee Peter held out and waited for Emma to leave the room. "How long have you been standing there?"

"Long enough."

"And you didn't step in to help me?" She turned her back, placed the coffee on the counter, and leaned down. An overwhelming sense of exhaustion filled her. She could go back to bed and sleep for hours if she could.

"What did you expect me to do, Meg?" Peter came up and stood behind her.

She turned. "Oh, I don't know. Support me, maybe? She's so angry with me, and I don't know how to reach her anymore."

"Have you tried listening?"

Megan's eyes widened as she stared at him in dismay. Not him too?

"Yes, I listened to her. Sure, I could have brought her swimsuit in last night, but to be honest, I didn't think to check that she'd kept her promise to me. So what? How does that turn into me not loving her?"

Peter shrugged. "Why don't you take her out on a mother-daughter date like you used to? You haven't done that with any of the girls since Emma came back."

Megan closed her eyes, sighed long and deep, and then realized something.

"The alarm didn't go off when you came in."

"I figured you'd turned off the system when I left." Peter walked over to the box on the wall by the front door and pushed buttons.

"No. It was on." Megan stood behind him and peered over his shoulder.

Peter glanced at his watch. "Are you sure?" Peter half-turned and leaned forward to kiss Megan on the cheek, but she stepped back.

"What took you so long this morning?"

Peter's eyes widened for a fraction of a second before a smile appeared on his face, but it was enough to catch Megan's notice.

"It's hard to say no sometimes." A sheepish look crossed his face.

"I thought you had a meeting you couldn't miss?"

Peter shifted his feet. "I do. I didn't think the coffee run would take as long as it did."

Megan stepped backward until she stood at the bottom of the stairs. She sat down, pulling her legs up and resting her arms on them. The way Peter's gaze shifted around the room set her on edge.

"It's a five-minute drive there and back. Surely it didn't take twenty minutes for her to eat a donut?" She thought about all the text messages he'd received but wouldn't tell her about and the way he'd been so distant lately with her. "Did you meet someone there?"

"What?" Peter's body went rigid, and he fisted his hands at his sides. "No, she just wanted to eat her donut. Don't make it out to be more than it was." There was an edge to his tone now.

Megan nodded her head. "Okay." It was time to drop the subject. "Why don't you join us at the beach for lunch if you have time after your meeting?"

Peter's stance relaxed, and he pulled out his keys from his pocket.

"That sounds like a good idea. Noon?"

Megan nodded.

Peter stepped forward and brushed a kiss across Megan's lips. "I do love you, you know."

"I know," she whispered.

She watched him as he walked out the front door and waited for the sound of his vehicle to leave before she stood up. Every time she thought they were going to be okay, something else came up between them, and instead of dealing with it, Megan kept backing down. Why? What happened to the woman who faced things head-on, come hell or high water? Why did she back down now? What was she hoping for?

No. She wasn't hoping for anything. She was scared. Scared that Peter would realize their marriage wasn't worth fighting for. He was willing to walk away once, what if he did it again?

Peter loosened his tie as he leaned back in his office chair and sighed. He was half-tempted to kick his feet up on the desk and have a nap. He rolled his neck, groaning at the kinks as they popped, and made a mental note to book a chiropractor appointment.

"You busy?"

Peter cracked open his eyes to see Sam standing in his doorway.

"Swamped," Peter said. He forced a smile onto his face. The last thing he wanted to do right now was talk with Sam, but he beckoned her in with the hook of his finger. "You look like hell." He didn't think he'd ever seen her like this. Gone was the put-together woman men normally drooled over, with her skintight shirts and thigh-high skirts. Dark bags hung beneath her eyes, she wore hardly any makeup, and she'd either just climbed out of bed or was about to go to the gym. Except—he peered at his watch—it was too late in the day for that.

"Thanks for noticing." Sarcasm dripped from her lips, but Peter ignored it. He was too tired to worry about Sam's recent emotional roller coaster. He had enough to deal with at home.

"Did you tell her?" Sam dropped into one of the plush seats in front of Peter's desk. She leaned back and crossed her legs.

Peter shook his head.

"God, you're stubborn." Sam gathered her hair together in her hands and quickly pulled it into a ponytail.

"And you're too insistent. Lay off." He growled.

Of course he was going to tell Megan, but on his terms. Not Samantha's.

Sam's lips tightened until they were a straight line. "I don't like this. She hates me as it is and thinks there's something going on between us. I'd prefer to leave on good terms if possible."

Peter snorted. "Do you honestly care about how my wife feels about us?" He smirked because he knew the answer even before the sly look on Sam's face appeared. The only one Sam cared about was herself. Up till now, that never really bothered him. They had a good working relationship. They understood each other's strengths and weaknesses. While Peter preferred to work with his home-buying clients and creating relationships, Sam was the cutthroat one who went after the larger businesses and local government.

She shrugged. "Not really. But I do care about you, and I see what this is doing to you. You can't keep secrets from her forever. She deserves to know."

Peter took a deep breath and stood. He moved beyond his desk and sat in the chair opposite Sam.

"She will know. Once things are finalized. You gave me condi-tions, and they all haven't . . . been met yet."

Sam leaned forward and placed her hand on Peter's knee. "I only made those conditions to see if you were serious." A sad smile filtered across her face.

Peter placed his hand over hers and squeezed. "I am."

This was what he'd wanted for a long time now, and she'd given it to him on a platter. He cleared his throat and lifted his hand, rub-bing his neck as he stood and paced his office.

If she did this—if she gave in and agreed—it would mean the answer to so many problems Peter faced right now. Problems in his marriage, problems with some clients, and definitely problems for his reputation. He valued Samantha for the very reasons others loathed her: She was good at her job, and it didn't always matter who got in the way.

There was a soft touch on his shoulder. Peter turned and found Samantha behind him.

"Is this really what you want?"

Peter nodded.

Sam squared her shoulders and tilted her head, the gaze in her eyes now steel.

"I'll have the paperwork done this week. I'll even provide the champagne when you tell Megan."

Peter shook his head. "Don't worry about that. But thank you. I know I've asked a lot—"

Sam's brow rose. "You asked for everything. No holds barred. I taught you well." She leaned forward and softly kissed his cheek.

Peter stepped back and clasped his hands behind him. He watched as Sam left his office, lingering in the door with a soft smile on her face.

"No regrets, Peter. It's been a ride . . ."

CHAPTER SIXTEEN

Emma held her hands over her ears. The beach was busier than Megan had expected, filled with the sound of the crashing waves, the noise from the children's park, and the squawking caws of seagulls as they snatched up stray french fries from the parking lot.

Megan reached into the back of her Jeep and pulled out a multitude of beach bags stuffed with beach toys, towels, water bottles, suntan lotion, hats, extra clothing, and anything else she thought they might need. Megan scanned the crowds on the sand and in the water and looked for a place they could put their stuff.

There were so many people here. She'd known that was likely, but seeing the swarming crowds firsthand unnerved her. She wasn't sure she could do this, and she was worried about Emma, who was covering her ears. Maybe it was too much, too soon. They could have gone to the local pool where there would have been fewer people. That might have been better.

A large white van with the local retirement home's emblem pulled into the lot. Megan recognized the bus driver and waved.

"Awesome! The bus is serving ice cream. Can we get one?" Alexis stood beside her and reached for a bag from the trunk.

Megan glanced at the old red double-decker bus and smiled. It was an icon in their town, and she hoped it would never leave the beach. She used to get fries and chocolate soft-serve ice cream from it as a teenager. It looked a little worn around the edges, and the Double Decker Fries sign needed a fresh coat of paint, but the smell wafting through the air was the same. She wondered whether they still sold the greasy but delicious corn dogs; she hadn't had one of those in eons.

"Sure. Why don't we go snag a spot on the beach first and then grab some ice cream." She high-fived Alex, whose grin stretched from ear to ear.

Megan glanced at Emma again. Hannah stood beside her, holding her hand as she pointed toward different sights along the beach. She'd begun to notice Hannah's protective attitude toward Emma in the past few weeks. Instead of being out playing with her friends, Megan would find Hannah in the same room as Emma, playing ponies or drawing pictures. It was as if she didn't want to let Emma out of her sight, a familiar feeling for Megan. All she'd done was turn her back two years ago, and she'd forever regret that small act.

She'd chosen this side of Station Beach hoping that it would offer more in terms of entertainment for her kids. Tiny Tots park was just above the beach area, with children running around and playing amid the slides, swings, and teeter-totters. In the distance was the old lighthouse rumored to be haunted by a former keeper who played the bagpipes while the sun set.

She had the kids follow her down to the pebbled beach, and they found a small section of grass on which to place their bags and towels. She instructed the girls to lay out their towels and set up the umbrella to block the sun, and then led them back to the bus, where they stood in line to order their ice cream.

Megan held Emma's hand while Hannah stood on her other side. Emma's eyes lit up. Sadness washed over Megan as she thought about everything her youngest daughter had missed. By this age, the other two girls had practically lived at the beach with Megan, and they would have thought nothing about the swarms of kids playing around them. In fact, her girls would have by now seen several of their friends from preschool or the neighborhood and been begging to go play with them. But not Emma. She'd been so sheltered at the farm; Jack and Dottie had rarely taken her anywhere. It angered Megan that her daughter had missed so much, but at the same time, she had to thank God—because it could have been worse. At least Emma was alive.

After ordering their ice cream cones, Megan walked the girls back over to their towels. She thought she'd have been more relaxed than she was. Once upon a time, the beach had been her second home. Peter had once suggested putting a pool in their backyard before they had kids, but Megan rejected that idea. She loved the beach: the feel of the sand between her toes, the sun kissing her skin. She loved closing her eyes while lying back, listening to the waves as they crept along the shoreline. She never wanted to give that up. But instead of finding the sounds relaxing today, Megan was tense, on edge. Was it safe? Could her children play here and not disappear?

She was being irrational. She was allowing her fears to ruin her day. So instead of giving in and taking the kids home, Megan made sure there was a smile on her face as her sunglasses hid the unease in her eyes. But when she caught Hannah's look, she knew she'd done a poor job masking her fears.

"Want to build a sand castle with me?" Hannah squatted down next to Emma, who had chocolate ice cream dripping down between her fingers. Emma's eyes lit up at the suggestion, and Megan dug out the sand buckets and tiny shovels.

"Alexis, why don't we have a contest? We'll be in teams." Megan handed the buckets to the girls. Alex frowned while she searched the beach area.

"Hailey and Taylor are here. I'd rather go hang out with them." Alexis waved at her friends, who waved back. The girls stood knee-deep in the water directly in front of them.

"You're gonna ditch your family for your friends?" Megan pretended to be hurt, but winked before Alexis could argue back. She didn't need another blowup today.

Hannah stood up. "It's okay, Mom. Why don't you relax? Emma and I will just build our castle together. There's an empty spot." She pointed just off to the right of their towels. "You can watch us the whole time."

Alex dropped her bag and ran down the beach. Megan started to call out to stop her, but when she realized who Alexis had run to, she relaxed. Hailey and a bunch of other kids from school all gathered at the water's edge. She was glad Alexis had friends to play with here. Megan caught the eye of Barb, Hailey's mom, who waved at her from down the beach. Megan waved and smiled back. It had been a while since she'd last spoken to Barb. Back when Alexis and Hailey had been younger, they used to do playdates on a regular basis.

Megan sat down on her towel while she watched Hannah lead Emma over to a spot on the beach where they could build their sand castles. It felt odd to be sitting there not joining in on the fun, but she'd let Hannah take the lead for a few moments. She knew she should be encouraging Hannah to go play with her own friends instead of watching over Emma; the two older girls needed to retain a sense of freedom, and Emma needed to learn it. But since she'd come home, Megan had kept Emma close at all times. She did notice the way Emma's gaze continued to drift her way, as if to ensure she was still there. *I'll always be here, Emma. I'll never leave you again.*

She reached inside a bag and brought out a book she'd wanted to read for a while. It was the story of two babies switched at birth. Peter had given her the book for her birthday, knowing it was by her favorite author, but this was the first chance she'd had to crack the book open. She had been tempted to bring her e-reader to the beach, but she loved the feel of a real book between her hands.

The sounds of children's laughter, seagulls squawking overhead, and the waves crashing against the shore blurred together. Every few minutes she'd raise her eyes and blink against the sun as her eyes refocused, wave at Emma and Hannah, and then search the water for Alex. Little by little, she allowed herself to relax. She remembered what it was like for her as a child at the beach. Carefree. Safe. She wanted her girls to feel the same way. If she hovered like she wanted to, they wouldn't. And there was no reason to. She noticed a few officers on bikes patrolling the pathways and lifeguards sitting high on their platforms. Everything was going to be okay. Slowly, Megan let herself get lost within her story.

So when she glanced up again from her book a while later and couldn't find Hannah or Emma sitting in the spot where their sand castles had continued to grow, she didn't immediately panic. She shielded her eyes and looked around the area where the girls had been, certain they were nearby. Except they weren't. She searched for Alexis and found her with her friends, splashing water at one another without a care in the world. Megan got to her feet and turned, looking at the park behind her. Scores of young children crowded the park area, running up and down the jungle gym, swinging and playing on the teeter-totters. Too many kids for Megan to see

Hannah or Emma. Besides, she would have known if they'd run past her in that direction. Hannah would have said something.

"Emma." Megan called out, circling her small area, hoping that her girls were close by and she just hadn't spotted them. But she couldn't see them anywhere. Their castle sat alone, the shovels resting on the sand as if waiting for the girls to come back.

Megan grabbed her cell phone and rushed across the sand and stood by their castle. "Hannah!" Her throat tightened as she struggled to keep the panic that was overwhelming her from being noticeable. Her girls had to be here. They had to be. They wouldn't have gone far. Her hands shook as she dialed Peter's phone number. "Emma!" This time she raised her voice, not caring if she sounded like a hysterical mother. She was not going to lose her child again. She brought the phone up to her ear. "Pick up, Peter. Come on, pick up the damn phone."

Her entire body was on edge, and a heavy weight settled in her chest as she struggled to breathe. In. Out. In. Out. She continued to scan the area, searching for Emma's cute pink bathing suit with a bow at the back and Hannah's bright-orange one. Maybe they were by the water, filling their buckets with water. She looked but couldn't see them. At all. They weren't anywhere.

"Emma!" Megan screamed as loud as she could for her daughter, her throat raw.

A hand landed on her back, and she dropped her phone before whirling around.

"Megan, what's wrong? Why are you screaming? Where are the girls?" Peter stood there, eyes wide as he waited for her to answer.

She was so grateful she wasn't alone this time, not like when Emma had wandered out the front door and out of their lives two years ago.

"I can't find Emma, Peter. I can't find her. She's gone." Megan raised her hands to her mouth as reality crashed into her. "I lost her again."

CHAPTER SEVENTEEN

Megan clutched at Peter's arm. Hysteria welled up inside of her while Peter remained calm, solid as a rock.

Part of her was waiting for him to blame her, for asking why she didn't keep an eye on their daughter.

"She was just there. I swear it. She was just there—"

"Maybe they saw some friends and went to say hi?" Peter scanned the area while rubbing her arms with his thumbs. "It's okay, Megan. We'll find her."

"What friends? Emma doesn't know anyone, and Hannah knows better than to just take off." She searched for one of the patrol officers she'd seen earlier. "I can't believe I lost her again. Oh my God, Peter, what if—"

"Stop! You didn't lose her. It's not your fault. They have to be around here somewhere, Meg. Think. What were they doing the last you saw them?" He turned her so that she faced him and tilted her head up until she looked him in the eyes. The moment she did, she felt the heavy brick that rested against her heart lift and her breathing began to return to normal. His calm look reassured her. Nothing in his eyes showed that he blamed her for this. Nothing.

"They were building a sand castle." She pointed to the display at their feet.

She noted the way Peter took in the discarded shovels and the lack of buckets. She stared at the water's edge, desperate to see them. It was as if they'd vanished.

Except for the voice calling her name.

"Mom. Mom!"

Megan's heart stopped at the sound of Hannah's voice. She was walking toward her with Emma and another small girl in tow. Behind them was an adult, hopefully the other little girl's mother.

"Do you know who the girls are with?" Peter reached for her hand and squeezed. She held tight and didn't let go. She wanted to run toward Hannah and Emma and scoop them into her arms, but she couldn't. The look on Emma's face shocked Megan. She wore her brightest smile, and her eyes glowed with happiness. She swung hands with the little girl beside her as they skipped together in the sand.

"I have no idea." Megan shook her head. She'd never seen that little girl before. Nor the woman who now stood in front of her.

"I'm so sorry! I heard you calling for Emma, and I realized the girls never told you where they were." The woman, wearing a bright-red bikini with her hair in a ponytail, stood there, an apologetic look on her face as she wrung her hands together. "I'm so sorry," she repeated. "I can only image what you must have felt when you realized the girls weren't there anymore."

Megan squatted down and looked Emma in the eye, mesmerized by the glow. She'd only seen that look once since she'd come home—the day they retrieved her from the farm, when Emma first saw her standing there, waiting for her.

"Why did you leave without saying anything?" Megan asked Hannah, who lowered her chin until it almost touched her chest.

"Oh, that's our fault," the woman interrupted. "Marie noticed Emmie and started screaming her name. The girls ran toward each other and—"

"Emma. Her name is Emma." Megan, her voice tense, corrected the woman. A chill passed through her body and settled deep in her heart.

"I'm sorry?"

Megan stood up and crossed her arms over her chest. "Her name is Emma. You called her Emmie."

The woman shook her head before her eyes widened and she covered her mouth in shock. "I'm so sorry. I never thought. We knew her as Emmie."

Megan's cold heart thawed.

"How do you know our daughter?" Peter's voice was controlled, but Megan caught the hesitation. They both knew their lives were about to be changed in a way she wasn't sure they could handle. This was the first time they'd come in contact with anyone who knew Emma while she'd been living with the other couple.

The woman gazed down at the girls. "Jack is our neighbor. Before"—she lowered her voice—"Dottie got sick, Em . . . Emma would come over and have playdates with Marie and the other children."

Megan's brow furrowed. "Other children?"

The woman nodded her head. "Yes. I run a home day care. I'm sorry; I'm Sherri, and this is my daughter Marie. She and Emma were . . . are friends."

This surprised Megan. Friends. She thought Emma had been isolated, alone with the woman, with only Daisy as her playmate. But she had friends. Other kids she could play with, interact with. Have a life with. Why didn't Emma ever mention Marie or the other kids?

She turned her attention to Emma, who faced the little girl. Marie. The girl's attention was focused keenly on Emma's face, watching her mouth while she spoke. Megan noticed that Emma spoke slower to her, more precisely, and she touched her a lot. They held hands, touched arms, fingered each other's hair.

"Marie is partially deaf. But it never seemed to faze Emma. They were friends right away." Sherri moved to stand behind her daughter and placed her hand on her head. When Marie glanced up, Sherri told her to say hi. Marie only smiled shyly.

"This is my friend, Mommy." Emma gave Marie a hug while she introduced them.

Peter squeezed Megan's hand, and she looked over at him. He obviously caught the difference in Emma too.

Megan held out her hand. "It's nice to meet you, Marie." She smiled at her and waited for the little girl to shake her hand.

"I miss Emmie." Marie gripped her hand and shook hard. Megan didn't have the heart to correct her.

Peter cleared his throat. "Well, that just won't do, will it?" He bent down and winked at Emma. Megan's breath caught in her throat as she realized what he was about to do. "We'll have to make sure you guys get to play together more often. Friendships are important."

Marie's head dipped low as she nodded in agreement. Emma beamed, threw her arms around Peter, and held on tight. Megan looked up and caught the smile Sherri gave her.

"She's really all right, isn't she? I was so worried."

Something registered in Megan's mind. A phrase Detective Riley had said a couple of times. *If it hadn't been for the neighbor . . .*

"You were the one who told the officer about Emma, weren't you?"

Sherri nodded. She cocked her head and stepped to the side, away from the girls. Megan noticed that Hannah moved her body so that she stood between Emma and Megan, almost as if she were also trying to shield her sister from overhearing their conversation.

"Dottie had just had her stroke, and Jack needed to go to the hospital. I offered to have her stay overnight with us. It was Marie who noticed Emma's image on the flyer that came in the paper that day. When the officer came to the house asking about Jack, I knew I had to say something. The resemblance was too much to ignore. I'm so sorry that I didn't notice right away. I should have. The signs were all there, now that I look back. Of course, Matt, my husband, tells me there was no reason to suspect anything."

"Signs? What do you mean?"

Sherri shook her head. "Nothing major, just little things. Dorothy was overprotective of Emma. It took me a lot to convince her to let Emma come and play with the kids I take care of. Emma was very sheltered." Sherri shrugged her shoulders. "She didn't recognize some of the kids' programs on the television, so I knew she didn't watch much. I wasn't sure, though, whether some of the issues were due to Dorothy's dementia or whether she was just an overprotective grandmother."

Megan bit her lip. "She wasn't Emma's grandmother."

Sherri nodded. "I know. I'm sorry."

One question continued to plague Megan, and finally she could have it answered.

"Was she happy, though? I mean . . ."

Sherri reached out and touched Megan's arm. A tender smile covered her face. "Yes. Quiet and seemed okay to play by herself, but yes, she was always a happy girl. And she loved Daisy. Does she still have her?"

Megan nodded, thinking about the dog Emma refused to let out of her sight for the first few weeks after she came home.

Sherri sighed. "Oh, good. I think that dog was her lifeline. She used to talk about how much she missed you, you know? She talked about you as if you were in heaven, especially toward the end, right before you came and got her."

Megan's face blanched. "She thought I was dead?" Of course she did. Megan knew that. Or thought she did. But to hear it confirmed . . . it hurt. Really hurt. The emotional trauma her daughter must have experienced. How did a child that young recover from believing her mother was dead?

"She used to draw you pictures all the time. Does she still do that?"

Peter stood and placed his arm around Megan. It was amazing how the body reacted to shocking news. The sun beat down on her, and she was sure she'd be as red as a lobster tonight, since she forgot to put sunscreen on, yet shivers ran down her body as if a cold northern wind blew directly on her.

"That much hasn't changed. Emma still loves to draw," Peter replied for her.

Megan had so many questions. She felt as if she too had been given a lifeline. An insight into her daughter's life while she lived on the farm. All those questions that plagued Megan in the middle of the night—Where had Emma slept? Did she cry herself to sleep? How did the other woman discipline her?—now she might have at least some of them answered.

"Listen, I'm sure you have lots of questions. Why don't we schedule a playdate for the girls, and I'll try to answer as much as I can."

Megan nodded, a smile slowly growing on her face as she stared into Sherri's eyes and realized this woman understood. "That would be lovely."

"Ms. Sherri?" Emma had turned and was tugging on Sherri's arm. Megan could see the questions in Emma's eyes, and for a split second, she wished she could stop time. She wasn't sure what Emma was going to say. "Ms. Sherri? Did you know my grandma is in heaven?"

Megan listened to the quiet chatter coming from the family room while she wiped down her kitchen counters. Peter was outside cleaning up the barbecue from dinner, and Megan was just waiting for the coffee to finish before she joined him outside.

She swirled the cloth in a circular motion on the counter, letting her thoughts drift back to this afternoon. Meeting Sherri had been a godsend. Sherri had managed to deflect Emma's questions, and they scheduled a time to meet the next day. A bubble of excitement welled up inside Megan.

The rest of their day at the beach had been relaxing. Peter stayed longer than he'd intended, and it was nice. He'd kicked off his shoes, rolled up his pants, and dug into the sand with the girls as they worked on their sand castle. Megan lay back on the towel and soaked in the sun, letting its warm rays seep into her bones. She even drowsed for a bit before Peter nudged her, needing to return to the office. They'd stayed at the beach for as long as they could before it was time to race home and start dinner.

Emma had loved the beach. She asked the entire way home when they could go back. Megan couldn't keep the smile off her face. There was a twinkle in her daughter's eyes that she hadn't seen before. She wanted to believe it was due only to her time at the beach, but deep down Megan knew it was also from seeing Sherri and her daughter again.

The smell of coffee filled the air. Megan sniffed, loving the aroma. At the same time, Peter opened the screen door and poked his head inside. "Is the coffee done?"

Just as she was filling their cups, a large crash sounded in the family room, followed by a sharp wail from Emma. Megan set the coffeepot down and rushed to see what was wrong.

Alexis stood in the middle of the room with her hands on her hips. She was scowling at Emma, who sat huddled against the couch, her knees tight against her chest while she rocked back and forth. She raised her face, and Megan caught sight of the tears in her eyes. Emma pushed herself up from the floor, launched herself at Megan, and wound her arms tightly around Megan's legs moments before she buried her head and sobbed.

Bewildered, Megan automatically rubbed Emma's back and stared at her middle daughter. "What's going on?"

Alexis shook her head, as if disgusted with what she just witnessed.

On the floor at their feet were scattered toys. Little pony pieces and dollhouse furniture lay in disarray.

"Alexis, I asked you a question." Megan lowered her voice but continued to rub Emma's back. Her youngest daughter's sobs had quieted, but her strong grip remained.

"Nothing." Alexis lowered her head.

Megan snorted. "Really? So why is your sister crying?"

Alexis threw her arms up in the air. "Because that's what she always does when she doesn't get her way. She freaks out."

Megan's brows rose. Since when did Emma freak out like this?

"I knew you wouldn't believe me." Alexis dropped to her knees and began to pick up the scattered toys and toss them into a bin they had brought down from Emma's room.

"I never said I didn't believe you. But what happened?" Megan reached for Emma's hands and pulled them away from her body. She gently touched Emma's chin and raised her face.

"Emma?" It didn't take a rocket scientist to figure it out.

Emma only shook her head. Megan brushed her fingertips across Emma's cheeks.

"She wanted to play a different game, and when I said no, she threw a fit and wrecked the house I'd built. She's such a baby." Alexis glared at her younger sister before picking up the now-filled toy bin and dropping it on the coffee table.

"That's not true." Emma glared at her older sister.

"Are you calling me a liar?" The shock on Alexis's face almost seemed real.

If there was one thing she knew about her daughters, it was that Alexis had a quick temper and was more prone than Emma to outbursts like what had just happened.

"No one is calling anybody in this room a liar." Megan planted a light kiss first on Emma's forehead and then on Alexis's. "Can we just try to play together? Please? Without any fighting or arguing?" She waited for the brief nod from Alexis before she noticed Peter standing in the doorway holding the coffee cups in his hands. He held one out to her.

"Crisis averted?" he asked as she brushed by him. Megan shrugged her shoulders before sipping her coffee and heading to the sliding doors.

"Coming outside?" she called over her shoulder. Peter still stood in the doorway, his back toward her as he watched the girls.

Emma walked out of the room carrying the bin of toys, while Alexis dropped onto the couch and reached for the remote control.

"Where's Hannah?" Peter glanced over his shoulder at her. If she wasn't shadowing Emma, then she could probably be found in her room listening to her music or reading a book. She said as much to her husband before she went on the porch and settled onto the porch swing.

The gentle breeze in the air felt refreshing against her skin. Her chest and shoulders were probably burned, since she'd forgotten to apply sunscreen. No, she laughed to herself, she just hadn't bothered.

Peter stepped outside and headed her way. He eased down on the seat beside her and held the coffee between his hands. She caught sight of his wedding ring and thought about their marriage. The odds had been stacked against them. Families torn apart by a kidnapping rarely stayed together. She was very thankful they had made it this far. Their life wasn't perfect, and their marriage was still shaky, but there was hope for them.

"Did you find her?" Megan asked.

Peter nodded his head. "She was on the phone with one of her friends. She'll probably come down soon asking if she can play over at their house tomorrow."

Megan cocked her head. "Which one?" It was nice to see Hannah interacting with friends again.

Peter shrugged. "Not sure. You should let her, though." He took a sip of his coffee.

Megan rubbed the back of her neck. "I wanted to thank you for not getting upset with me earlier today when I freaked out." It meant a lot to her that he didn't blame her for taking her eyes off Emma. More than she imagined it would.

"Why would I have been upset?"

"Because I wasn't watching the girls like I should have been." Megan raised her mug to her lips.

Peter huffed and reached for her hand. "You can't watch her every moment of the day. I know you feel like you have to, that you're worried she's going to disappear again. I worry too. But at some point, we have to let her . . . just be a kid."

Megan squeezed his hand. "I don't know if I can. All I did was turn my back, and we ended up living in hell for two years, not knowing what happened to her. I'm not sure I can stop watching her. I need to make sure she's always here, safe."

"I trust you, Megan."

Megan choked up at his words. Part of her didn't feel worthy of his trust. She didn't trust herself.

"What's going on with you and Alexis lately?"

Megan struggled to follow his line of thinking. What was with the change in subject?

"I don't know. Maybe you should ask her."

"I have. But I'm asking you." Peter unwound his fingers from hers and wrapped them around his coffee mug.

"I don't know, Peter. If I did, don't you think I'd be doing everything I could to fix it?" Why did she get the feeling this conversation wasn't going to go well?

An uneasy silence settled between them. Peter leaned forward and rested his elbows on his knees. His head hung down before he glanced up and studied her.

"I actually don't think you would."

Megan was jolted back at his words. Was he serious? How could he say that?

"I think it's easier for you to ignore what's happening right in front of you. It's what you've done for the past two years. You get so focused on one thing that you lose sight of everything else."

Megan's lips widened in surprise. "That's rich, coming from you. You're hardly ever home, so how would you know?" Anger boiled inside of her. How dare he accuse her like that?

Peter sat back and sighed. "You're right. And I plan to change that. But Alexis talks to me, so I do know."

"Know what? That I'm a horrible mother? That I ignore her and give all my attention to Emma? That I'd rather put a Band-Aid on the rift growing between us than sit down and deal with it?" She leaned back and closed her eyes.

The swing they sat in moved, and Peter's knee bumped into hers. She peered at him beneath her lashes, expecting to see something other than the compassionate look he gave her.

"No, Meg, you're the best mother I know. We just have a very sensitive daughter who is feeling neglected. And we're both at fault. I think we assumed that our family would be completely healed with Emma being home. And that hasn't exactly happened yet."

No, they weren't healing the way they should be. Megan knew that. Maybe it was because she thought it would happen in time and was too focused on helping Emma. That was her fault. The family wasn't on the top of her priority list, and that was where she was failing as a parent.

"You ever feel like no matter how much you try, no matter how much you change, it's never going to be enough?" She cleared her throat and wiped away the tears that trickled down her face.

Peter wrapped his arm around her and pulled her close.

"All the time." He leaned his head against hers. "Maybe it's because we're both trying to do it on our own instead of together."

That was the problem. They weren't together in this. Instead of standing beside her and dealing with the attitude she was getting from Alexis, he stood there and watched, and then blamed her for not caring enough to actually deal with the issues. She wasn't blind.

She saw how angry her daughter was, how hurt she felt. She was just at a loss on how to handle it anymore. Nothing she did was good enough.

But instead of telling Peter this, Megan kept quiet. Just one more battle she wasn't ready to face. One more battle she wasn't ready to lose.

Maybe, if she left it alone and gave it more time, the issue between them would heal itself. Wishful thinking, but right now, that was all she had enough strength for.

CHAPTER EIGHTEEN

Megan rushed around the house, cleaning an already spotless kitchen, entranceway, and family room. When Sherri arrived, they sat outside on the back deck and let the kids play.

There was an awkward silence as the two women sat at the patio table. Hannah and Alexis were at friends' houses, and the women's eyes were on Emma and Marie, who played with Daisy on the grass. The peals of laughter coming from both girls filled the backyard. Megan wished she could bottle and keep that sound forever.

She caught the sidelong glances Sherri gave her, but she wasn't ready to start the conversation. Megan crossed her legs and rubbed her fingers. She was thankful that the woman was waiting for her to be ready, except Megan wasn't sure she ever would be.

"Your daughter is beautiful." Megan finally broke the silence.

Sherri nodded. "Thank you. She's a real treasure."

Megan poured fresh iced tea into their glasses. Her hands shook. Here was the one person who could answer the multitude of questions she had, so why couldn't she think of even one?

"I'm sure you have so many questions to ask and you're not sure where to start." Sherri raised her glass and took a sip.

The compassion in her eyes was almost Megan's undoing. She gazed out at the girls and watched how they played.

Megan cleared her throat a few times and then rubbed at the base of her neck. She asked the one question that meant more than the world to her: "You mentioned at the beach that Emma was quiet . . ."

Sherri's shoulders relaxed as a smile crossed her face. "Very, but every time I saw her, there was a smile on her face."

Megan cocked her head. "But how quiet? Did she talk much or was she just shy?"

When Sherri pursed her lips, there was a tightening in Megan's heart. This was it. This was the bad news she'd anticipated. This was the nightmare she didn't want to know but needed to hear—that Emma hadn't been fine during those two years when she had been kidnapped.

"She was lonely. I try to stay tuned to children's moods. Emma always had a smile on her face and a light in her eyes, but you could tell she was sad. I thought it was her lack of friends, so I would ask Dorothy all the time if Emma could come over and play. But now . . . now, when I look back, I know she was missing you. I wish—we didn't move in until last summer—but I wish I had realized sooner what had happened." Sherri reached out and covered Megan's hands. "I'm so sorry."

Megan shook her head. "Don't apologize. Please. You were the one who made it possible for Emma to come home to us. And you gave her a friend. Please don't ever apologize." Tears gathered in her eyes as she squeezed Sherri's hand. She owed this woman the world.

"The girls get along really well," Sherri said. "You almost wouldn't know they haven't seen each other for a while."

Megan leaned back in her chair. "Did you spend much time with the family who took Emma?" She wasn't sure if she really wanted to know whether they were the monsters she'd made them out to be.

Sherri scooted her chair back and crossed her legs. "Not much. I invited them over for some homemade iced tea once, but I don't think it was one of Dorothy's good days, and with all the kids running loose in my home, I'm afraid our visit was cut short."

"So you didn't see them much?"

"Oh, no, I saw them lots." Sherri pulled her hair into a ponytail before taking another sip of her drink. "Dorothy was always out in her vegetable garden, and Jack could usually be found puttering around their yard. Emma was always outside, especially after Daisy arrived. I don't think she watched much television at all." She frowned. "Not like my own daughter." Megan was startled by the intense look in Sherri's eyes.

"Megan," she went on, "they loved her. You could see it. I rarely ever saw her cry, and I never heard a harsh word spoken to her or saw them discipline her. I know Jack . . ."

Megan's look silenced Sherri. She didn't want to go there. She didn't want to discuss those people with Sherri. All she cared about was Emma and whether she'd been okay.

She took a deep sigh and let the tension in her shoulders release. The sounds of the girls' laughter washed over her, and Megan realized that she needed to look beyond the last two years and toward the future. She had to stop holding on to the hurt she nursed deep in her heart.

"Thank you." Megan smiled at Sherri. "You brought my daughter back to me, and you . . ." Megan took a deep breath and let it out slowly, "you've eased my heart. My number-one concern has always been that she was unhappy or treated poorly. I might never forgive them for what they did, but I can be thankful that they loved her in their own way."

Sherri just smiled at her before leaning forward and resting her elbows on her knees. "I wonder what those two are whispering about."

Megan turned her attention back to the girls. They were huddled close together. Marie's eyes were wide and a smile grew across her face moments before she reached out and swallowed Emma in a hug. The girls rocked back and forth for a few moments before Daisy got involved and jumped all over them.

A sense of peace settled in Megan's heart. Seeing her daughter act as any other little girl proved to her that despite everything, she really was okay. Inviting someone over from a past Megan knew nothing about was okay. It didn't hurt and didn't push her daughter back to a time she wished they could forget. Instead, there was laughter in her daughter's voice and life in her eyes.

If having secrets with her little friend was the result of this, then yes, it was okay.

CHAPTER NINETEEN

Some days, Megan wished Laurie lived closer. On hot days like today, it would be nice to just hop over the fence and take a dip in her pool without having to pack things up and drive everyone over in the car. A few weeks ago, Laurie suggested she leave towels, sunscreen, and pool toys in her deckhouse instead. It made sense, since Megan and the kids practically lived there during the summer days.

Hannah sat in the front seat beside Megan, holding a tray of iced coffees and smoothies. The street Laurie lived on was full of potholes, forcing Megan to carefully weave her way. Laurie lived in the older section of Kinrich, where the Victorian homes were either falling apart or being renovated. Her street was scheduled to be repaved in the fall, but that didn't help Megan much at the moment.

"Does Laurie have visitors today?" Hannah asked.

"I hope it's someone with kids." Alexis leaned forward and yanked on Megan's seat.

Megan pulled up to the curb and saw a two-door car in Laurie's driveway that she didn't recognize. She followed the girls up the walkway and to the side of the house; then she slipped the lock of the wooden gate open and let the girls pass her by as they headed toward the pool.

Laurie's backyard was gorgeous. If anyone had a green thumb, it was her best friend. Compared to her own house, where chaos reigned, Laurie's historical showplace home, with its award-winning English garden, was a peaceful oasis. Megan would be lying if she said she didn't envy her best friend's life. Laurie did bookkeeping part-time out of the comfort of her home, with the ability to make her own hours. Megan loved being a stay-at-home mom and taking control of the Safe Walks program, but there were times she missed doing the books for Peter and working alongside him as they built up his real-estate business.

"Can we go in, Mom?" Alexis was in the process of flinging her flip-flops to the side and stood poised on the edge of the pool, ready to dive in.

"First, I need to let Laurie know we're here. You know the drill, guys." Megan lifted Emma's shirt and wiggled it over her head. Emma threw it on one of the white wicker chairs by the pool and dipped her toes in the water. Hannah rummaged in a bin off to the side of the pool and pulled out water toys and Emma's water wings.

Megan slipped off her flip-flops and pushed open the sliding door into Laurie's spotless kitchen. With a quick glance over her shoulder to ensure none of the girls were swimming yet, she headed into the house.

As she rounded the corner from the kitchen to the front hallway, the smile on her face fell until her mouth gaped open. If Laurie's eyes had been open, she would have noticed Megan standing there in shock, but they weren't. Her eyes were closed and her lips were joined to the one man who had stood by Megan's side while Emma had been missing.

Megan's heart stopped for what seemed like an eternity as she watched her best friend wind her fingers through the black curly locks of Riley Thompson's hair.

Images flashed through Megan's mind of a similar scene. Except she stood in Laurie's place, with her own fingers threaded through Riley's hair as his lips hovered over hers . . .

She should call out to Laurie and Riley and let them know she was there. She should make some noise, clear her throat, or do something else. Anything else. Anything that would disrupt the scene she couldn't ignore.

"Laurie," Megan finally managed to whisper while clutching the bag in her hands tight. She knew her cheeks flamed bright red as she bit her lip, waiting for that awkward moment she knew was about to occur.

Time stood still as Laurie unwound her fingers from Riley's head and shoved herself away from him. She blinked a few times before she looked up.

Megan wasn't sure who was more embarrassed.

"Meg . . ."

"Um, I just wanted to let you know"—Megan pointed behind her—"that we were here, but um . . ." She swallowed before taking a step backward. "I think we're actually going to leave."

The silence in the room was overwhelming. Riley cleared his throat and took a step toward Megan, who in turn took another step back. She struggled to grab hold of the handle to the sliding door.

"Megan, don't go . . ." Laurie called out behind her.

"Girls, change of plans. Let's go get some ice cream." She slipped her flip-flops back on and grabbed the purse she'd laid down on the patio table. Ignoring the drinks she'd placed there earlier, Megan slipped her purse onto her shoulder, her knuckles turning white around the strap.

"But—" Alexis planted her hands on her hips and was about to argue but stopped. Megan wasn't sure why, but she was thankful for whatever it was that made her girls reach immediately for their things and follow her without question back to her vehicle. It was all she could do to breathe and not allow the wash of emotions to drown her.

"Megan, stop. Please?" Laurie called to her from the front porch, wringing her hands as Megan struggled to process what had just happened.

"Are you okay?" Hannah slipped her hand into Megan's as they neared the Jeep.

Megan bit her lip and nodded. She opened the doors and waited for the girls to climb inside before she made her way to the driver's side. She kept her eyes down, refusing to look back at the house. She didn't want to see the look in Laurie's eyes right now, didn't want to hear any excuses. And she certainly didn't want to know if Riley stood beside her.

She wished the last five minutes of her life had never happened.

❦

When the bedroom door clicked shut, Megan sank to the floor. She drew her knees up to her chest, buried her head in her arms, and gave in to the sobs she'd held back for the last forty-five minutes.

The memory of her best friend's arms wrapped around a man Megan had once desired tore her apart. A heaviness settled over her as memories flooded of her own infidelity. No matter what anyone else said, she'd betrayed her husband with that one kiss. She knew it. Riley knew it, and even Peter knew it.

She would never forget what had happened that day. It had been right after the first anniversary of Emma's disappearance. She'd just dropped off a new flyer with a different image of Emma to be printed at the downtown photo shop. She stopped in at the library and grabbed a few books she'd placed on hold for Hannah and Alexis and decided to wait at a nearby park for the flyers to be printed. She sat on one of the park benches and browsed through a home decorating magazine she'd picked up earlier until she heard the laughter of children nearby. Two small girls were playing in the fountain that sat in the middle of the park, splashing each other while their mothers stood by. Megan smiled and was about to return her attention to the magazine when something caught her eye. Another little girl with blonde curly hair.

Megan still recalled the way she dug her fingernails into the palm of her hand and forced herself to count to ten, just like Kathy had told her to do. It took everything in her not to rush over to see if it was Emma. She'd done that too many times to count, and it never ended well. But when the little girl looked her way and a wide smile covered her face, nothing could have held Megan back from rushing over to her. She could have sworn that little girl was her daughter . . . until she got closer and realized the curly blonde hair was the only thing Emma and this little girl had in common. But by that point, the smile had disappeared from the girl's face and, instead, she stared at Megan in horror.

Megan would never forget that look. Never.

She rushed away and drove straight to Peter's office, only to find out he was out with *her* for the afternoon. When she arrived home, she found Riley waiting in her driveway. All it took was one look; once inside, she found herself bawling like a baby in his arms instead of confiding in her husband.

Maybe it was the way he stroked her hair or rubbed her back. Maybe it was the fact that he didn't condemn her for thinking that that little girl was Emma or berate her for scaring the little girl.

Or maybe it was just the fact that he was there when Peter was not, and all Megan needed was someone to lean on.

Either way, one second Megan was crying against Riley's chest, and the next, his lips were on hers and she found herself lost in the moment.

It was one kiss, but the ramifications were endless. For both of them.

Peter had walked in shortly afterward, when they stood there staring at each other trying to understand what had just happened. No words were said, but they all felt the tense undercurrents. To this day, Peter had never confronted her about it.

Megan's shoulders heaved as she acknowledged the wide range of emotions flowing through her. Maybe that was their problem. The many things she and Peter had left unsaid to each other were eating away at them, tearing them apart, and no matter how hard they worked at rebuilding their marriage, some things couldn't be swept under the carpet. She was ashamed at herself for allowing the silence to grow between them, for thinking it would go away if it were ignored. Like everything else in her life.

She was also angry with herself for feeling betrayed—and at Laurie for betraying her. It didn't make sense for her to feel this way. And yet she did. While she might not have slept with Riley, there had been an emotional connection, and sometimes that could be stronger than a physical connection.

Megan leaned her head back against the door. She loved Peter. With all her heart. But he hadn't been there when she needed him the most, and that pain, that memory of feeling so . . . alone, seemed like it would never go away. But she couldn't forget what it felt like to have someone else in her corner, someone who *did* believe in her. Someone who encouraged her to never give up instead of suggesting they hold a memorial service.

Megan's jaw clenched. Peter had given up. Megan sucked in air, drawing it deep into her lungs. Everyone else gave up, but she never did.

Using the wall for support, Megan climbed to her feet. She needed to leave all that in the past. Her counselor had urged her to learn to forgive. And she had, or so she thought. But there was a difference between forgiving and forgetting. Forgiving was something she could learn to do, but forgetting? That would never happen.

She climbed into the corner armchair in her room and reached for the knitted throw. A cold chill permeated her bones, and once the blanket covered her, she nestled beneath its heavy weight despite the warm wind blowing through the window.

Was it wrong of her to feel betrayed by Laurie? Of course it was; it had to be. But why didn't Laurie tell her? Why didn't she come clean that night at the bakery instead of keeping silent and pretending it was nothing?

Megan's shoulders dropped. Laurie didn't tell her because she knew how Megan would react. Did she blame her? No. The look in Laurie's eyes when she realized Megan was standing there haunted her.

But Laurie should have come clean.

That was what hurt the most. Not that she and Riley were involved, but that Laurie had hidden it from her. Perhaps if Laurie had told her ahead of time and given her time to process what it would mean to Megan and their friendship, then maybe seeing them in such a tender embrace wouldn't have affected her as strongly as it had.

Or maybe it would have. But it would have been nice to know. She wasn't sure what to do now. Confronting Laurie didn't make sense. She'd only be admitting something that wasn't true: that she was jealous when she wasn't. She had no right to be. And telling Peter would be awkward. He wouldn't just hear the words; he'd be looking for a hidden meaning or emotion, wanting to see whether she still had feelings for Riley. Needless to say, bringing him up to Peter wouldn't be smart.

Megan breathed in deep and exhaled. She should be happy for her best friend. It had been too long since Laurie had been involved in a relationship. This was a step in the right direction.

But as Megan folded the blanket over the back of the chair, she couldn't help but wish that Laurie would wake up and see how awkward this would be if their relationship continued.

She winced when she realized how that sounded.

CHAPTER TWENTY

Peter squirmed in his seat—he was uncomfortable sitting at the corner table at the donut shop, where everyone and anyone coming through the drive-thru could see him.

"Worried your wife's going to drive by?"

Peter almost dropped his coffee mug as he was raising it to his lips. Instead, the dark liquid spilled over the sides. He wiped it up, never glancing at Jack, who sat across from him, and struggled to respond without giving too much away.

"Don't bother trying to deny it. No man parks in the back corner of the lot if he doesn't care about being noticed." Jack chuckled before picking up a green crayon and filling in a tree outline in the new coloring book he'd bought Emma.

Peter knew his face flushed.

"You haven't told her yet."

Peter glanced over in time to catch the small shake of Jack's head. He shrugged. Jack didn't know Megan; he didn't understand the battle he'd be in if she found out about these little dates. He was actually surprised she hadn't by now. He thought for sure she would have figured something was going on and would have called him on it.

"Take it from one who knows: Keeping secrets from your wife always backfires. Somehow, she'll figure it out. It might be a look on your face, or something Em here says, but trust me, when she does, there'll be hell to pay."

"Papa!" Emma's brows knotted together She shook her crayon at him, and it was all Peter could do not to smile. Apparently, it was the same for Jack.

"Okay, princess. I'm sorry." He rubbed the top of her head and winked at Peter before his face paled.

"Are you okay?" Peter leaned forward. The look on Jack's face was vaguely familiar. Peter's own father had passed away from a heart attack, so he knew the signs. Tiny beads of sweat dotted the top of Jack's head and forehead as his face grew white.

Peter pushed back his chair, but Jack held up his hand. His nostrils flared before his color returned.

"Daddy?" Emma sat back, her crayon clutched tight in her fist as her head rotated to look at Jack, and then Peter, and back to Jack.

"It's okay, sweetheart. No need to worry." Jack's hoarse voice seemed to calm Emma down. She rose up to sit on her knees and placed her hand over his chest.

"Is it your heart again, Papa?" She frowned at him. "Grandma said you have to be careful. Maybe you shouldn't color with me." She leaned forward and planted a kiss on his lips before she rested her head on his chest.

Peter sat back down in his chair as Jack stroked Emma's hair. There was so much to take in right now: Jack being sick, and Emma not only knowing about it but calmly accepting it. This obviously wasn't the first time something like this had happened. "How bad is it?"

Jack shrugged. "Doctor wants to do more tests."

And? Peter mouthed the word, not sure that this was something Emma should be hearing.

Jack only shrugged.

Peter swallowed and almost choked. It must be bad. He couldn't imagine being so calm about something so serious.

"What does your doctor say?"

Jack raised his coffee mug and took a sip. "What do they know? I've got a little girl here to watch grow up. I'll go when I'm ready to go."

"And you're not ready." Emma piped up. She pushed off Jack's chest and sat back down in her chair, engrossed in her drawing once again.

Peter still couldn't believe how calm Emma was about all this. He would have expected her to be more stressed about Jack being sick, but she was as unfazed as if this were an everyday occurrence. Maybe it had been. Peter winced at the thought. He hated that his little girl had known so much grief in such a short time.

"There you go; the boss has the final say," Peter said. Jack's hand shook slightly, and Peter tightened his lips. Maybe he should insist Jack go to the hospital.

"Do me a favor?"

Peter glanced down at the hand covering his own. It was wrinkled and spotted with age. Jack's fingertips were rough as they grazed his knuckles. He glanced up to see concern in the other man's eyes.

"Tell her. Even if it means I don't see Em again for a while. Your wife needs to know. Keeping secrets, especially something like this, isn't good for a marriage. It'll destroy you both, and nothing is worth that. Not even this." Tears gathered in Jack's eyes before he blinked them away.

Peter winced. He was right. He needed to tell Megan. But he wouldn't let her take Jack away from Emma. Not again. Not now.

"On one condition," Peter said.

A steel gaze met his own, but Peter refused to back down.

"What's that?"

"You remember you're not alone anymore. You've got a grand-daughter to live for now."

Jack turned his attention from Peter down to the little girl beside him.

Peter knew the effect his words would have. He knew there would be ramifications, but it was worth it. He'd have to make Megan see that these meetings were necessary. That it wasn't only Emma's emotional well-being at stake. And if she didn't agree? He knew he'd have to stand firm in his decision.

He had just given Jack his family back.

CHAPTER TWENTY-ONE

Megan's mom and dad had dropped by on the pretext of picking Alexis up to take her out for ice cream, something they did for all the girls on their birthdays. Daniel had wanted to check the latest baseball score on TV and sat down in the family room with Peter, while Sheila drank a cup of coffee in the kitchen with Megan. They had one hour before they all needed to be at the small amusement park where Megan had booked Alexis's birthday party.

Emma sat curled in an overstuffed chair in the far corner of the family room, playing with some of her ponies. She'd originally been out in the kitchen with Meg and Sheila, but slowly she'd ventured into the family room.

"Emma, why don't you come and sit by your old Papa?" Daniel patted the couch beside him during a commercial. Peter caught the deer-in-headlights look on Emma's face as she raised her head and stared at Daniel.

"Come on, sweetheart. I won't bite." Dan's smile faltered when he saw the look in her eyes.

Emma sat frozen in her chair.

"Not yet, huh? Well . . . I'll just go see what your grandmother is doing." Dan's shoulders slumped before he pushed himself off the couch.

Peter gave him an apologetic smile before he too stood and went over to crouch in front of Emma.

"What's wrong?" He lowered his voice and reached a hand out to place on top of hers. Although ever since coming home she had been somewhat reserved when Megan's parents came by, she was usually friendlier than this.

Emma's lip quivered. "He's not my Papa," she whispered.

Peter sat back on his heels. He should have expected this, should have realized why, in all the times Dan and Sheila had stopped by and tried to connect with Emma, she pulled away. Why she struggled with getting close to them.

Why did they not think about this? Emma didn't even remember them, so to throw her into a relationship with them, expecting her to trust them . . . how many times did they have to hurt their youngest daughter before they realized it?

"Do you remember our talk the other day about nicknames for people?" He watched as Emma bit her lip before she nodded.

"So how about we call Mommy's daddy another name? Like Grandpa or Grandpa Dan? I used to call my grandpa Pops."

The tension in Emma's body released, and she picked up one of her ponies. "Can everyone have their own special nickname?"

Peter nodded. He had a feeling he knew where she was going with this.

"Mommy won't be upset?"

Peter relaxed his shoulders as he casually looked over them into the kitchen. Dan stood at the kitchen table beside Sheila, but his gaze was fixed on Emma.

"No, sweetheart, she won't be upset."

Emma cast her eyes downward as she fiddled with the pony in her fingers. Peter stood up, leaned down, and placed a small kiss on the top of her head; then he held out his hand.

Dan continued to watch them. Peter understood what his father-in-law must be feeling, because he'd been there. He'd been faced with a problem that he couldn't solve.

He led Emma out into the kitchen and released her hand. Daniel squatted down beside her. Both Megan and Sheila stopped their chatter at the kitchen table.

"Is something the matter, honey?" Dan asked.

Emma stared Dan in the eyes as she straightened her shoulders. "Can I call you Grandpa?"

Peter watched Dan carefully and noticed his shoulders bunching, and the puff of his chest. He heard the slight gasp from Sheila and caught the way Megan's hand reached across the table and clamped down on Sheila's hand. He knew from the look in Megan's eyes that she understood Emma's question, even if Sheila and Dan didn't.

"Of course you can, sweetheart. That's what I am, your Papa." Dan lifted his arms and held them out, but Emma's shoulders sank, and she looked down at her hands.

"No. Not Papa. Grandpa." She tentatively raised her eyes as if worried about the reaction she'd get.

Dan's arms lowered.

Sheila twisted in her seat, and before she could say something, Peter cleared his throat. "That's right, Emma. Remember, we talked about nicknames? Grandpa will work."

Peter caught Megan's sharp glance but ignored it. That wasn't a conversation he wanted to have right now.

With a deep nod of her head, a slow smile crept along Emma's face before she stepped toward Dan and touched his hands.

"Let's go watch baseball, Grandpa Dan." She pulled his arm and led him into the living room.

"Well," Sheila muttered, "how am I supposed to tear that man away from that sweet angel to take Alexis out for ice cream?"

Peter glanced at the watch on his wrist. "Give him ten minutes and then go. That will still give you time to enjoy your cone while we head out and get everything set up."

Sheila shook her head. "Do you honestly think ten minutes is going to be enough for him? He's been waiting two months for her to warm up to him. No, he's not going to want to leave her side now."

Peter turned to head back into the living room to finish watching the game, but he didn't miss the whispered words from his wife.

"That's exactly how I feel every day."

Squeals of laughter amid the roaring engines of go-karts greeted Megan as she opened the Jeep door. Excitement bubbled inside of her as she thought about Alexis's reaction when she pulled up. A large sign strung across the front entrance said *Happy Birthday, Alexis.* Perfect. Absolutely perfect.

"She's going to hate you for that." Peter hefted a large plastic bin into his arms while she slammed the trunk door closed.

"I know." Megan couldn't stop the smile from growing on her face.

An older woman waited at the front door for them. She had short-cropped gray hair and wore a bright-yellow top with the company logo on the front. Her cheeks were rosy as she waved wildly at them.

"There you are; I've been waiting for you to arrive. I'm Wilma; we spoke on the phone. Bob, my husband, is out back supervising the go-karts and will be ready for your group when they all show up." Wilma led them into a large room where there were several tables set up, balloons and streamers, and trays of pastries. "I hope you don't mind about the sign and the little extras we did in here. We've been following the story of your family in the news and, well, we wanted to help make this birthday party as special as we could." Wilma's nonstop chatter continued as Peter set down the bin and glanced around in surprise.

"You do realize this birthday isn't for our youngest daughter?" The surprise in Peter's voice was evident. Megan couldn't believe all the work this woman had put into this room.

Wilma waved her hand. "Oh, sugar, I know that. But that little girl has missed out on so many things with her family that, well, Bob and I just wanted to make this a little extra special."

Megan grabbed a cookie off a tray and knew right away from the design who'd baked it. "Jan helped, didn't she?" She handed the cookie to Peter and went to give the woman a hug. "Thank you," she whispered into her ear. She'd never met Wilma personally; she'd seen her at a few charity events and such around town, but she knew that today she'd made a new friend.

"Now, let me take that cake, and I'll put it over here along with the extra cupcakes." Wilma reached her hands out for the cake Peter lifted out of the container. "Oh my, is this one of Sheila's?"

Megan smiled. "Doesn't it look amazing? My mom outdid herself this time." Sheila had created a putting green cake, complete with a fairway and a girl swinging a golf club. It looked fabulous. Sheila liked to make feature cakes, but Megan hadn't been expecting something this elaborate.

"It looks like you're ready to feed a classroom full of kids in here!" Megan couldn't get over the amount of cookies, bars, cupcakes, jars of Twizzlers, suckers, and bubble gum.

A large smile bloomed across Wilma's face. "Once I got started, I just couldn't stop! I saw a page in a magazine where there was a table full of baked goods and jars full of candy, and I wanted to try it out."

"Well, it looks amazing." Peter placed his arm around Megan's shoulders as he gave the room a once-over. "How many kids are coming?"

Megan pulled out a list she'd stuffed in her pocket and showed it to him. "I had ten confirm and four I couldn't get hold of."

Lifting a cookie to her mouth, Wilma nodded her head. "Even if they all come, we'll have enough. I made extra goodie bags as well, just in case. There's nothing worse than finding yourself unprepared."

When she'd called Wilma to make the arrangements, the woman had promised that it would be a carefree day and that she'd look after all the details—goodie bags, setup, and teardown included.

"What about that special surprise?" Megan checked her watch. The kids were due to arrive shortly. Sheila said they'd come a bit late to make sure everyone was there ahead of time.

"All covered," Wilma confirmed.

Peter cocked his head. "Surprise?"

Megan's face grew warm. This was as much a surprise for Peter as it was for Alexis. "Wilma mentioned their son is a pro, and . . ."

"Our son Stevie, why, he's been playing golf all his life. He just finished qualifying for the Q-School for the PGA Tour and will be starting in November. He's home for a few months to visit," Wilma remarked. "When your wife mentioned that your daughter loves to golf, I thought it would be nice to have Stevie come by and give her a lesson or two." Wilma shrugged her shoulders, but she couldn't hide the pride in her eyes.

Megan watched Peter closely. His brows rose as he turned his attention from Megan to Wilma.

"You don't mean Stephen Brown, do you?" he asked.

Wilma's head bobbed up and down. "I sure do." Peter's jaw dropped. "We've set it up so that miniature golf is the last game you'll play, and he'll be there to meet Alexis."

The look Peter gave Megan made her heart quicken. It had been a while since she'd done something for him. She only hoped he understood this was her way of showing him he was still important to her. Sometimes, the words were harder to say.

"Thank you," Peter said, before leaning down and giving her a quick peck on the lips. She shrugged her shoulders as if to indicate it was nothing, but they both knew it was something. Peter had been watching Stephen on the news. He'd first seen him on a television show for golfers who were trying to become known. Peter would tape the shows and watch them repeatedly, while Megan sat beside him reading a book. She wasn't into golf like he was, but knew how special this would be.

"All right, you two lovebirds, your guests should be arriving soon. How about we meet them at the front door and all wait on the steps for your daughter?"

Megan lagged behind and looked out over the parking lot.

"Where's your sidekick?" Peter grabbed hold of her hand and tugged.

"Laurie? I don't know." She pursed her lips. "Maybe something came up." Megan muttered.

Peter snorted. "Doubtful. You know Alexis is her favorite. Have you tried calling? Maybe she's out shopping for the perfect gift and

lost track of time." He followed Wilma, pulling Megan along with
him.

She reached into her pocket as she stumbled up one step and
pulled out her cell phone to check if Laurie had responded to any
of her earlier messages. She knew they were going to have to deal
with what happened, but they'd been friends forever. Surely, Laurie
wouldn't let a man come between them.

Or would she? And if that's what was happening, was Megan
ready to accept it?

CHAPTER TWENTY-TWO

That. Was. The. Best. Birthday. Ever!" Alexis flung her arms around Megan's waist and squeezed tight.

Megan squeezed back. From the moment Dan and Sheila drove into the parking lot and Alexis leaned out the window and screamed, she'd been hugging both Megan and Peter.

After the party, they'd headed to the local pizza restaurant. They'd all eaten too much pizza, and the girls drank too much pop. Megan was wiped out, and other than Alexis, who was still bouncing off the walls with excitement from the day, she had a feeling everyone else was too.

"All right, squirt." Peter dropped her new golf bag and clubs and the container he carried onto the floor. "Why don't you go put this away?"

Alexis released Megan and high-fived Peter before lifting her new bag onto her shoulder and heading into the garage.

Hannah trailed behind, holding Emma's hand. The girls had all had a blast and were loaded up on more sugar than their bodies could handle. Looking at Emma, Megan thought for sure her youngest was about to crash. Her eyes were dull, her shoulders drooped, and her footsteps lagged. Hannah had been like a mother hen all day, watching over Emma even after Megan tried to convince her to do stuff with the other kids.

Today, the focus was on Alexis, and it had seemed to do her good. Her middle daughter was on cloud nine. She had been awestruck when she met Stephen, and when he offered her three free golf lessons, she went through the roof, squealing like a piglet. Megan loved it.

"Want to cuddle in bed, Em? I can read you a story until you fall asleep." Hannah's soft voice caught Megan's attention. She turned to find Emma sitting on the bottom step while Hannah hovered over her, stroking her hair and rubbing her arm. Megan knelt down.

"What's wrong, honey?"

Emma shook her head and didn't look up. Instead, she dropped her head into the nook of her circled arms that rested on her knees and sighed.

Megan felt her forehead. Emma had been out in the sun all day, and even though she'd worn a hat and kept a water bottle nearby, it wouldn't be too surprising if she'd gotten a little bit of a sunburn.

"I bet a nice cool bath would feel good right about now," Peter said.

Megan nodded. It was days like these when having a backyard pool would come in handy. A nice dip in the evening to cool off before bed—nothing could be better.

"Come on, Emma. I'll help get the bathwater ready. Is that okay, Mom?" Hannah held out her hands to help Emma up.

Megan wrapped an arm around Hannah's shoulders. "Sure thing, hon. Why don't I grab you both a nice cold drink of water, too, and then come up to check on the bath."

Hannah pulled away. "I've got it."

Megan studied her eldest daughter. There'd been an authoritative tone to her voice that she didn't like. Megan wasn't blind to the ways the older girls handled Emma. Hannah was protective, while Alexis was dismissive. She'd thought they would grow out of it until they were a cohesive group, or as cohesive as three sisters could be. Was she wrong?

"You know what, Hannah? Let me take care of Emma, okay? Why don't you go relax and see if that episode of *Heartland* taped." Megan placed her foot on the bottom step and angled her knee in between her two daughters.

Hannah shook her head. "No, I can take care of her." There was a wildness to her eyes that unsettled Megan. She wrapped her arms around Hannah and held her close.

"I know you can, honey. You always do."

She saw the protest building in Hannah's eyes, and she pulled back and held up her finger to stop whatever words Hannah was going to utter. "Listen, you've been such a huge help for me with Emma since she came home, but it's summertime, and you should be out playing with your friends instead of trying to keep Emma entertained during the day."

"But, Mom—"

Megan shook her head. "No, honey. This is all my fault. Ever since Emma came home, you've stuck to her side like glue, and I've let you."

Hannah's lips trembled. "I'm just trying to help. To make sure she stays safe."

Megan's heart sagged. "Because you feel it's your fault she wasn't safe in the first place?"

Hannah nodded.

"Oh, honey," Megan's chest constricted at the depth of her daughter's pain. "That wasn't your fault. Nothing that happened that day was your fault." Megan reached up to touch her daughter's cheek.

"I need you to believe me. When we lost Emma, it wasn't your fault at all. And keeping Emma safe now isn't your job; it's mine. Mine and your dad's." She wasn't sure what it would take for her eldest daughter to believe that.

"I'm so sorry, Hannah, that I let you live with the guilt of losing Emma. It was never your fault." Tears misted in Megan's eyes as she watched her daughter take in her words. Did she believe her? Was it too late?

"I need to be with her, Mom." Hannah's voice quavered as she gazed down at Emma.

"I know." Megan said. She rubbed Hannah's arm for a few moments before she let go.

Hannah stepped back, but not before she bent down and laid a kiss on the top of Emma's head. It broke Megan's heart to see her daughters like this, knowing that it was partially her fault. No, if she were honest, she'd admit it was all her fault. Hannah wasn't old enough to take on the role of mothering a five-year-old, and yet that was exactly what was happening.

Megan bent down and gathered Emma in her arms. She wanted to cry when Emma rested her head against her shoulder but kept her eyes closed. She should have kept a better eye on her youngest daughter.

"You just don't trust me," Hannah whispered before she walked away.

Megan heard her, but instead of turning and calling out to her eldest daughter like she should have, she pretended she didn't hear. It was hard, but she needed to concentrate on Emma at the moment. When she tucked Hannah in tonight, she'd talk to her about the whole trust issue.

Hannah wasn't the one she didn't trust. It was herself.

❧

Jack looked at his house, at the white porch and dirty windows. He needed it to become his home again. Jack stood and straightened his back. With Emmie back in his life, he had a whole new reason for living.

He wasn't going to give her up again. Not this time.

The old house creaked around Jack as he puttered around, picking up piles of things he'd long forgotten about. He'd let the housework lapse, and if he had to look deep, he knew he was reacting to all the changes in his life instead of acting.

The loneliness was starting to get to him. Talking with Dottie today reminded him of that. And if he didn't smarten up, he'd soon regret it. He had a lot to live for, even if his old heart didn't want to accept that. He didn't care what the doctor said at his last appointment. He'd live to be one hundred if he had his way. What did his doctors know? Nothing. Not the important stuff, anyway.

He tapped his heart twice with the palm of his hand. "You're living for Emmie now, you hear?"

That was all that mattered anymore. Just his little girl.

He stood at the base of the stairs from the kitchen and looked up. Maybe he could pack up some of her favorite books she'd left behind, or maybe one of the stuffed animals, and make sure he had them with him the next time he saw her. She might like that. Jack heaved his body up the stairs, his grip on the handrail firm.

There were a few old suitcases high on a shelf in his closet. He could always use one of those to put Emmie's things in. He should probably also use a few of them for Dottie's things. He was running out of boxes, and he didn't need the extra luggage anymore.

When he stepped into his room, the amount of clutter hit him. He'd been hesitant to get rid of anything, especially when it reminded him of Dottie. Memories attached to everything in their room. The sagging bed they'd shared for so many years sat in the middle of the room between the two windows. On either side were small tables he'd built years ago. The worn paint and dents were marks of love, Dottie always said. Then they both had their own dressers on opposite walls, and one main closet. Dottie's dresser was full of rarely used perfume bottles, a candle, a comb, and a pen, while his held only a shaving kit and a couple of receipts. Dottie loved her walk-in closet, even though only one person could stand in there at a time. Beside the closet was a small bookshelf, another project he'd labored over in his shed one year as a birthday gift for his sweetheart. Dottie's favorite books and most of her journals were all lined up there.

Little by little, he'd start to pack up Dottie's things. He knew she'd want him to donate her clothes, but some things he couldn't bear to part with. Her journals were one of those. Her clothes were another.

Like the soft cream-colored cardigan he'd bought her one year for Christmas. He picked it up from where it lay across Dottie's pillow and caressed it with his fingers. Some nights he just needed to not feel so alone.

Standing in their closet, Jack looked over the items Dottie had stacked on the floor. Bags full of wool, shoe boxes, and her fancy shoes she liked to wear to church. The top shelf was jam-packed with purses. Jack's eyes widened as he counted how many there were.

He caught sight of a soft pink color in among the mixture of black and brown purses. For the life of him, he couldn't remember Dottie ever having a pink purse. He grabbed a handful of the purses by their handles and dropped them on the floor by his feet. Just one more mess he'd need to clean up.

With enough cleared away, Jack could see that it wasn't a pink purse hidden away, but instead something like a blanket sticking out of a shoe box with a lid only half closed.

He reached up, his arm swiping another couple of purses off the shelf, and grabbed hold of the material. Why that woman shoved it so far back he had no idea. With the edge of the blanket between his fingertips, Jack tugged, expecting it to come easily, and was a bit surprised to meet with resistance. He pulled harder until the box edged forward enough that he could grab it with both hands.

"What did this woman think she was doing? Filling a box with—" Jack stopped when he pulled off the lid and saw a note pinned to the blanket.

He rubbed his eyes, sure that he'd read the note wrong.

Dear Mary,
This blanket is for my granddaughter. One day I hope you'll let me see her.
Love,
Mom

Megan arched her back and groaned as she wiped a cool cloth over Emma's head once again. Peter rested his hand against her shoulder blades and pressed hard. He'd just returned with a clean bowl for Emma's vomiting. For the past hour, she had been throwing up, and they were now at the point where even the little bit of water Megan managed to get her to sip wouldn't stay down.

Her poor little girl probably had heat exhaustion, and it bothered Megan that there was nothing she could do. She'd given Emma a cool bath, had her drinking fluids, and knew she just needed to sleep. But if the vomiting kept up, they'd have to go into the emergency room.

"She's going to be okay," Peter whispered beside her.

Megan reached her hand up and laid it over his. "I know. I just . . . feel helpless."

Emma whimpered, and Megan's first response was to reach for the bowl at her feet.

"I want Papa," Emma groaned as she grew restless beneath the covers. Megan pulled the cover down and freed Emma's hands.

"Shhh, it's going to be okay, honey. Just try to go to sleep, okay?" Megan whispered as she stroked Emma's hair.

Since coming home, this was the first real time Emma had been sick. While it broke her heart knowing that if she'd only paid a little bit more attention, Emma would be okay, there was no place Megan would rather be than right here, stroking her daughter's hair.

"I want Papa, please?" Emma's weakened voice begged.

That hurt, knowing her daughter wanted someone else at a time when all she should want was her mommy. Anger burned in her heart once again toward the one man who'd stolen so much from her.

"Daddy?" Emma opened her eyes.

Peter sat down on the bed behind Megan and reached for Emma's free hand.

"I'm here, Em. I'm here. Just go to sleep, okay, baby?" Peter's voice broke.

Megan leaned back into him and relaxed. She wasn't alone. She didn't know what she'd do if Peter had actually left, before they found Emma.

"Can we go see him, please? Tomorrow? Please, Daddy?" Emma's voice grew stronger as she continued to beg Peter for something they both knew couldn't happen.

"Shhh, just go to sleep, Em. We'll talk about it tomorrow, okay?" Peter released her hand and was about to stand up, but Emma reached out and grabbed his arm.

"Promise, Daddy. Promise we'll go on our date with Papa tomorrow. Promise." Megan sat back, alarmed at her daughter's persistence. Peter glanced at Megan before looking around the room. He started to pace across the floor, his nervousness apparent, as if he were unsure how to respond.

Megan waited for Peter to correct Emma, but he didn't. The tension in the room became unbearable.

"As long as you're feeling better, honey, of course you can go on your date with Daddy."

The smile on Emma's face grew and her body relaxed at Megan's words. Megan didn't miss the quiet gasp from Peter, however, before he left the room.

"Peter," she called out. He halted at the top of the stairs, just outside of Emma's room, his back rigid as one hand rested on the railing. "Peter," she called again, wanting him to turn and look at her. Except he didn't. He disappeared from view.

Megan's lap grew damp as the dropped wet cloth soaked into her shorts. She picked it up and leaned across Emma's body. As she gently stroked her daughter's forehead with the cloth, she waited to see whether Emma would open her eyes again. She wanted to ask her about the dates she'd gone on with Peter. Neither one had ever given any details about those times, and she'd never thought to ask how they went. Maybe she should have.

But Emma's eyes remained closed and her breathing evened out. She was finally asleep. As if the promise Megan had made were all Emma needed.

She should be thankful Emma was sleeping. So why was her stomach in knots? Why did she suddenly get the feeling that something was going on behind her back, something that was about to change her life in a way she wouldn't like?

CHAPTER TWENTY-THREE

The creak of the porch swing joined the chorus of sounds cascading around Jack as he applied a little bit of pressure to the pad of his foot to keep the momentum of the swing going.

Nothing better than relaxing on his front porch during a warm summer day. All he needed was a sweating glass of iced tea at his side and life would be perfect. Well, almost perfect. Jack avoided glancing down at the box beside him.

He'd spent the last few hours tending his front yard, anything to keep him busy. The grass was all cut, the bushes trimmed, and his flower beds were looking better than ever. Dottie's little tree in the middle of the yard was flourishing despite the heat. All was right with his world. Finally.

With his head leaned back and his eyes closed, Jack reached for the handkerchief he'd laid on the cushion beside him and wiped the sweat from his forehead. A low buzz off to his right had him peeking his eyes open, and he caught sight of the fattest bumblebee he'd ever seen hovering over the box he'd brought outside but tried to forget.

"Shoo, now. There's nothing there for you." Jack waved his hand at the bee.

He eyed that box with misgiving. Pandora's box, thanks to Dottie herself. If he opened it, his world was about to be altered in a way he wasn't sure he was ready for. He had half a mind to bury the box back in Dottie's closet and worry about it another day. Except he wouldn't do that. He'd never run from a battle in his life, and he wasn't about to now.

"Oh, Dottie-mine, what have you done?"

Jack shifted in the seat until he was upright before lifting the box onto his lap. He noticed that his hands shook as he lifted the lid, and he swore. There was nothing in here he couldn't face. Nothing in here that would kill him. Maim him, yes, but kill him? No. Not now.

He pulled out the blanket that haunted his nightmares. He avoided the note, folding the blanket into quarters until the note was hidden. It was possible Dottie had made this blanket for a future grandchild she prayed Mary would have. Possible. Not likely, though. He knew Dottie better than that. There was nothing extra special about this wool. In fact, he'd boxed up more than a dozen baby hats and socks his wife had knitted in the same color.

There wasn't much in the box after the blanket was taken out—an opened letter and a soft pink journal. Jack pulled both out and set them on his lap. He opened the journal first and tried to think whether he'd ever seen Dottie write in this one before. It wasn't until he opened it and leafed through the empty pages that he realized he'd never seen it. There was writing on the first page and that was it.

To my granddaughter,
Yes, I know you're not even born yet and that you may turn out to be a boy, but I don't think that will happen. Daughters have always

been the firstborn in our family, and there's no reason why your mother's child would be any different.

This journal is for you, from me. I'm older than I'd like to admit, and I know that I might not always be around to share stories or tidbits of wisdom with you. One day, maybe when you're older, your mother will give you this journal and can explain to you why this is my keepsake for you. I hope your mother will read it first and realize just how much I love her.

You'll be born into a world that is very different from the one I was born into, but we women have to stick together.

The moment your mother told me she was going to have a baby, I knew you were a gift from God. A second chance for this old woman to maybe do things a little bit differently. Maybe even this time to do it the right way.

Always listen to your mother, little one. While you might not always understand or agree with her decisions, trust me: She loves you more than life itself. That is the one gift all mothers can pass along—love.

Love forever,
Your grandmother

Jack's eyes smarted as he laid the book back down in his lap. So there had been a grandchild. Dottie hadn't been mistaken. A small seed of hope sprouted in Jack's heart. Was it possible that Emmie was really his granddaughter after all?

He picked up the letter, noticing the sender. Mary. Offhand, he could recall only three letters coming from his daughter after she ran away, and they were all addressed to him.

He pulled the letter out and a vise squeezed around his heart. He missed his daughter more than he thought possible. In the past, there had always been a hope that she'd come home, that they could mend whatever broke them apart as a family. He'd thought the silence for the past two years had been due to her stubbornness. Never once had he thought she'd been dead. Never once. Knowing for sure that she was dead, that he'd never see her again, never hear her voice . . . there was a finality about it that he couldn't process. He should have been able to mourn her properly, with Dottie. Instead, he had to mourn both wife and daughter at the same time, and it wasn't something he could handle. Not properly, anyway. It was no wonder his heart wasn't doing very well. The grief, the sadness, they ate away at him day and night. The only bright spot in his day now was Emmie.

His vision blurred as he read over the letter from Mary to Dottie. He wanted to stop, to not let the words sink in, but he couldn't. How could Dottie not tell him this? How could Mary keep this a secret from him? How could he not have known? Surely, there would have been signs? Clues? He checked the date and struggled to remember whether he'd visited Mary around that time. But he couldn't remember. How could he not remember?

Dear Mom,

I'm sorry. I know you see this blanket, and I can only imagine the thoughts going through your head.

There's only one way to say this. You were the one who taught me to "make it plain." I gave birth to a beautiful little baby girl, but she came too early. Preterm is what they said. What they didn't say was that it's all my fault.

Can you keep this blanket and put it away for me? One day I'll need it, even if it's just to remember her by.

I named her Emily.

Before you say it, I know this was my fault. I tried. I really tried. But I'm not strong, not like you are. I didn't think the drugs would do this. Or maybe I did. Maybe I didn't want her enough to stop using them. I don't know. What I do know is that I gave in and she paid the price.

She was tiny. The nurses let me hold her. She would have fit in Dad's hand. She had all her fingers and toes and a tiny little nose. She was perfect. And for once, I understood a little bit of what you told me, about that love. It's been a while since I've said it, but I love you, Mom.

Please don't be disappointed in me. I'm disappointed in myself as it is. And please, please don't tell Dad. I know you promised not to tell him about my being pregnant until I was ready. I don't ever want him to know now.

Mary

Jack read and reread the letter from his daughter to his wife. He didn't think it was possible for his heart to break again, but he'd been wrong.

⚜

A line had formed outside Brewster's Bakery that snaked around the corner. It was like this every week. Everyone wanted to take home Jan's homemade cinnamon buns, and she made extra batches once a week. But once she sold out, that was it. There were always two line-ups on days like this. One to order cinnamon buns only, and one for dine-in. Megan chose the dine-in line and almost stopped cold when the smell radiating from the open door hit her. She breathed in the sweet aroma of fresh-baked cinnamon buns as she made her way into the store.

"Well, hey there, sugar," Jan called out as Megan wove her way around the crowded tables and wedged herself in until she found the last empty barstool in the far corner. She reached for the freshly poured coffee Jan set down in front of her, buried her nose inside the cup, and breathed in deep.

"What is this?"

A large smile bloomed across Jan's face.

"Caramel pecan pie. A new shipment came in with an assortment of flavored coffees. It's my little piece of heaven."

Megan glanced over her shoulder. "I think their little piece of heaven is your cinnamon buns." She shook her head at the long line.

"How was the party yesterday?"

"Best day of Alexis's life, or so she says. Emma got heatstroke, though; she's home right now with Peter." Megan knew worry lines creased her forehead. It was Peter's idea that she go out for coffee this morning. She'd stayed by Emma's side half the night. When she left her, the fever had broken and her daughter had been sleeping just fine. She glanced back at the line. "Have you thought about selling those buns in grocery stores?"

Jan shrugged. "No. But I was thinking of opening up another store in Hanton in the fall."

Megan's eyes widened as she sputtered the coffee she'd just sipped. She'd been bugging Jan for years to open another shop.

"Thought maybe you could help me?"

Megan thought about that for a moment before she shook her head. "I'm not sure I could handle driving to Hanton every day." It was too far away from the girls.

"Not there. Here. You could help me manage this place."

Megan wasn't sure what to say. With the kids back in school in the fall, she wasn't sure what she'd do with her time, and it would be nice to use her professional skills again. With a degree in business, she used to work beside Peter in the office, taking care of the day-to-day grind. But this was a huge change. More than just helping Peter with the books or taking on a few more clients and working from home.

"Think about it; that's all I ask."

Megan nodded. She'd think about it. As Jan walked away, Megan glanced around the bakery and thought about what it would be like if she worked here. There would be long days with tired feet, but she knew there would also be a sense of accomplishment she didn't have lately. Sure, when the walking program took off, that made Megan feel worthwhile, but it ran so smoothly now . . . so smoothly that she really wasn't needed anymore.

She finished her cup of coffee and smiled when Jan set down a box of cinnamon buns and a to-go mug in front of her.

"Just think, you would get first dibs on all the baked goods . . ." Jan's eyes twinkled as she waved Megan's cash away.

"Bribery will get you nowhere with me."

Mock surprise filled Jan's eyes. "Who said I was bribing you? These are for Peter."

Megan chuckled as she leaned forward and hugged her friend across the counter. She wove her way through the crowded tables and caught sight of Shelly Belle before bumping into someone. Megan held her to-go mug up high as it sloshed over the little opening in the hole.

"Sorry," she said, before glancing up and realizing Riley stood in front of her. A slow flush crept along her neck as his hands gripped her upper arms to help steady her.

"Hey, um . . . I just left a message on your cell." Riley sidestepped out of the way and brought her along with him.

"You did?" Megan furrowed her brow. Her phone hadn't rung. She reached inside her purse for her phone, only to realize she'd left it at home to charge.

"If this is about you and Laurie . . ." She so did not want to talk about this. Not here. Not now, and especially not with him.

Riley scowled before shaking his head. "No, but, uh—"

Megan held up her one hand. "No. It's okay. It's cool. I was just caught by surprise. I had no idea about you and her." Which hurt most of all. Out of every available woman in their small town he had to pick her best friend. Nothing like rubbing her poor judgment in her face. If whatever happened between him and Laurie became serious, how long would it take before the memory of their kiss faded away?

Riley sighed. "She was going to talk to you. Is going to talk to you. She, ah . . ." He gazed around hopelessly as he struggled to finish his sentence.

Megan swallowed her coffee and decided to take pity on him. She reached out and briefly touched his elbow.

"It's okay."

Relief eased the scowl on his face. "Good. Good. Listen." He smiled at her. "I just wanted to let you know the restraining order against Jack has been lifted."

Megan took a step back. What? What did he mean it had been lifted? That was the one concession she had made instead of insisting charges be brought against him. That man was to have no contact with Emma. She had let his first few letters pass through because Emma wanted to send him pictures, but he wasn't to call her, see her, or anything else.

Riley must have seen the confusion on her face.

"I promised Peter I'd let him know once it was taken care of."

Megan's breath caught in her chest, constricting it until she saw tiny flashes of dark circles cloud her vision. *Oh my God . . .*

Peter. Peter had done this. Why? Emma's request to Peter last night now made sense.

"Meg, are you okay?" Riley's touch centered Megan, forcing her to let out the air stuck in her throat. She counted to five, breathing in deeply and releasing just as deeply, exactly like Kathy had told her to.

She forced a small smile onto her face.

"Thanks for letting me know. I'll be sure to . . . tell Peter." She held up the bag containing the cinnamon buns. "I'd better get these back to the house while they're still warm. Thanks."

She pushed past Riley, ignoring him calling her name behind her as she wiggled her way through the crowded front door. She kept her gaze focused on the ground, steadying herself until she made it back to her vehicle.

Even then, she wouldn't give in to the rage growing inside of her. She'd talk to Peter first. Have him confirm why he'd do something she was so dead set against. Explain why he'd think it was okay to take away what little protection was left around their daughter without talking to her first.

And if she didn't like his answers, then he wasn't going to like her reaction.

CHAPTER TWENTY-FOUR

February 28

Secrets. They can kill a marriage or make it stronger. I've always believed that.

The worst secrets are those that eat at you inside, when you know you need to be honest and face the consequences but are too afraid. Then there's the other kind. The secrets that are kept for the preservation of sanity.

Jack has his own set of secrets that he thinks I don't know about. The ones that he thinks he keeps to protect me.

The only thing he's protecting is himself.

I don't have many secrets that I keep from him. Most days I don't even remember them; other days they weigh down on me until I feel like I'm buried so deep that I can't breathe anymore.

Today was one of those days.

My husband sleeps like the dead beside me—other than the snoring—while I toss and turn, unable to find rest. My secret weighs on me too heavily. But there's no release, no way out. Not that I can see.

With a tray of coffee and cinnamon buns in her hands, Megan tapped her toe on the slightly ajar door to Peter's study before nudging it open with her foot. A slow simmer of anger burned inside of her, but instead of confronting Peter right away with her accusations, she'd taken time to calm down by making coffee and calling Laurie.

Except she hadn't answered. Again.

"Hey." Peter barely glanced up at her as he sat hunched over his computer. There was a small ding, which Megan recognized as a chat notification.

"Talking to a client?" She put Peter's coffee in front of him before sitting down in one of the room's chairs.

His head jerked up, and he spilled the coffee he'd just grabbed. "What? No."

Megan's brows rose as she took a sip of her coffee and stared at her husband.

His message notification sounded again.

"I realize you're working from home this morning, but would you mind turning your sound off for a few minutes?"

Peter jabbed a button on his keyboard with his index finger, and then pushed himself away from his desk and stood up. Megan watched as he stretched his back, working the kinks out of his tired muscles.

"So if it wasn't a client, who was it?" Megan waited until he sat down in the opposite chair before she asked again. She had an idea who it was, but it would be nice if he told her himself.

Peter held the cup in his hands and stared into it. The silence in the room stretched until it wrapped itself around Megan like a suffocating blanket.

"Is there an issue?" As hard as she tried, she couldn't keep the anger out of her voice. Peter caught it when his head lifted, and he looked at her with tired eyes.

"No," Peter shook his head. "It was Sam. But it's not what you think . . . which is why I . . . you tend to overreact when it's her—"

"That's not an excuse," Megan interrupted him.

Peter leaned forward. "I know."

That was all he said. *I know.* As if that would make any difference.

She let the silence stretch between them. She wanted him to tell her on his own accord, without her fishing it out of him. She wanted the truth for once. Lately, that seemed too much to ask for.

"Figured you might want one of Jan's cinnamon buns." She indicated the plate on the tray.

She watched him take a few bites, savoring the pastry but refusing to look her in the eye.

"You'll never believe who I ran into at the bakery."

Peter took another bite of the bun and looked at her quizzically.

"Detective Riley." She watched as he struggled to swallow. "He wanted to make sure you got his message."

A pin could have dropped on Peter's desk and the neighbors would have heard. Megan wanted to wipe the shocked look off her husband's face with her cinnamon bun, but she liked Jan's baking too much to waste it like that.

As she took a bite of her own cinnamon bun, Peter struggled to clear his throat.

"Listen, I wanted . . ." Peter's struggle was obvious. "I didn't know . . ."

Megan had no sympathy as he struggled to explain himself to her. It was all she could do not to let her anger take over. Even Kathy would be proud of how she was handling herself right now.

"Just tell me the truth, Peter. That's all I ask."

Peter let out a deep breath. "The truth?"

"I deserve that much, don't I?" She angled her body toward him and waited. A tangle of emotions crossed Peter's face as he searched hers. What was he trying to find? Acceptance?

"He's an old man, Megan." Peter leaned forward. "He's lost everything, and I . . . just didn't think he was a threat to Emma. So I asked Detective Riley to drop the restraining order. It wasn't necessary."

Megan leaned back in her chair. "You didn't think to discuss this with me first?"

"No."

The impact from that one word hit her hard. It wasn't that he forgot, but that he purposely didn't want to talk to her about it first.

"Why not?"

Peter clasped his hands together and stared off into the distance. "Because you're not willing to let go and see past your own anger. All you concentrate on is keeping Emma safe from anyone and anything that could hurt her."

Megan's chest tingled as she stared at Peter and tried to wrap her head around his words.

"That's not fair," she whispered. "I'm trying, Peter. I'm really trying."

Peter blew out a puff of air. "I know. And you're right, I should have told you. I need you to trust me on this. He's not going to hurt her, not the way you're afraid of. Don't you see how much she misses him?"

Megan nodded. "I do see. And I hate it. I hate that he had the opportunity to mean so much to her. It's not fair."

"I'm sorry."

Megan wiped the tears away and looked up in surprise.

"For what?"

"For not trusting you enough. I should have told you."

Megan tilted her head. That was the problem, wasn't it. "Yes, you should have. But you didn't. Why? What aren't you telling me? You've seen him, haven't you? So has Emma. That's what you've been hiding from me, isn't it? That's why she wanted to make sure you'd take her on the date and why you had the restraining order lifted. Oh my God . . ." Megan covered her mouth with her hands. "And you didn't care about how I'd feel?"

"Stop!" Peter's eyes clenched tight as a grim look covered his face. "This is why I haven't said anything to you." He rubbed his face with his hands. The look on his face when he took his hands away alarmed Megan. His lips pinched together as his jaw clenched.

"I don't understand."

Peter shrugged. "What's not to understand? Emma's home, she's safe, she's happy, and yet you can't seem to accept it. It's as if you're waiting for the other shoe to drop, for something else to happen. You're in panic mode, Meg. All. The. Time. And it's exhausting. You're worn-out—we're worn-out."

Megan's anger deflated at his words. He was right. Of course, he was right. She rubbed her forehead and let his words sink in.

"Megan, I love you." He reached across and laid his hand on her knee and squeezed. "I need you to trust me, please?"

Megan lifted her hands, to get him to stop from saying whatever else he was going to say. He was asking a lot from her. Maybe too much. Her body hummed with tension as she struggled to take it all in. He didn't trust her. That hit her hard. He'd skirted the whole issue about Emma seeing *that man* and threw everything back at her as if it were all her fault. She slowly lowered her hands and clenched them at her sides. She couldn't look at him, not yet, so she stared blankly out the window instead.

"It's not fair for you to place all the blame on me," she whispered quietly. "It's not fair of you to want me to trust you when you obviously don't trust me." A heaviness settled in her heart. This was it. This was their breaking point. She'd failed in his eyes as a mother and most likely as a wife. She turned to look at him and wished she hadn't.

A grave look covered Peter's features moments before he stood. She wasn't sure she wanted to know what that look meant, but it looked like she didn't have a choice in the matter. He picked up a file, and the first thought that popped into Megan's head was that this was the moment she'd been dreading for the last year: In that file were divorce papers. He couldn't do it anymore. He couldn't handle her anymore—her insecurities, her stubbornness, her inability to look beyond their youngest daughter. All of Megan's fears were playing out right now, and she wasn't prepared.

Megan's hand shook as she reached for the folder he held out. Her chest was heavy and a threatening weight of fear gripped her shoulders. She bit her lip as she glanced at the plain brown folder.

"It's not what you think it is," Peter said before retaking his seat.

Megan moistened her dry lips as she set the folder in her lap and slowly opened it. Time stood still as she recognized what she was seeing. Her nostrils flared as her eyes widened in surprise.

"I don't understand." This didn't make sense. It wasn't possible.

Peter threaded his fingers through his hair before resting his elbows on his knees. He messed up his hair enough that it stood out all over the place. Megan wanted to reach across and smooth it back, but she resisted.

"I offered to buy Sam out of the company. She accepted." He twiddled his thumbs as she glanced back down at the papers in the folder.

"You what?" Megan was having a hard time wrapping her mind around this. One minute they were talking about the restraining order and her failure as a mother, and the next they were discussing a business deal?

"How can we afford to buy her out? She came in because we were struggling." None of it made sense. They didn't have the money to go on their own, let alone buy out Samantha's shares.

"But we're not now, Meg. I've managed to land some really good deals in the past year. We're okay."

Megan closed the file and sat back in the chair. She picked up her coffee and tried to think through the past year. So all those late nights, the meetings, the empty spot beside her in bed when she'd wake up in the middle of the night—it wasn't that Peter wanted to get away from her?

"Sam doesn't mean anything to me, Meg. She was only a business partner."

"But she . . ." Megan started.

"Has come between us," Peter finished for her. He stood up and reached for her hands. "I know things aren't perfect yet and that we have a long way to go, but losing you, our marriage, the kids . . . it's not worth it. Not to me. So we made a deal. She's moving away and wants to start up her own company." He pulled her in close and wrapped his arms around her.

Megan resisted, her body tense. All of this was too much, too soon. Too fast. She pushed herself away from Peter and sagged back into the chair.

"All this time, I thought you were getting ready to leave me. The texts, the late hours . . . I've just been waiting for you to tell me you've had enough."

"Never." Peter knelt down in front of her and took her hand.

Megan stared down at their hands. "Trust goes both ways, Peter. If you want me to trust you, then you need to do the same. Trust me when I tell you that it's not time to allow Jack into Emma's life. Not yet. Maybe someday, when she's older, when I know . . ." She stopped when she realized what she'd almost admitted. When she was ready to deal with having Jack in Emma's life. It all came back to her, didn't it? Peter was right.

"She is ready. She's been ready since the day we brought her home. She needs him, Meg." Peter's voice was raw with emotion and filled with a sense of certainty.

Her lips quivered as she leaned forward, keeping her gaze on their hands.

"But what if I'm not?"

CHAPTER TWENTY-FIVE

After yesterday's turmoil, Megan planned a nice quiet day where the girls could relax and Emma could rest up. She swatted at a bee as it buzzed around her hand before she dipped the watering can and sprinkled her flowers. She preferred to do it earlier in the day, before the sun got too hot.

"Knock, knock."

Megan turned to find Laurie standing at the patio doors, waving a small white flag.

"A little over-the-top, don't you think?" Megan set the can down on the grass and wiped her hands on her shorts.

Laurie shrugged her shoulders. "Just in case."

Beside Laurie, on the patio table, sat two coffee cups and a bag. Megan recognized the bag from Brewster's Bakery. "Peace offerings?"

She caught the uncertain look in her friend's eyes and the hesitation as Laurie's arms reached out. It had been two days since Alexis's birthday, and other than stopping by that evening to take Alexis to a late-night movie, she'd kept her distance.

Megan stepped forward and gave her friend the hug she needed even though her heart wasn't really in it. She'd be a liar if she didn't admit she was still feeling hurt from Laurie's silence. After a moment, they both sat down and reached for the coffee, neither one willing to break the silence between them.

Laurie fidgeted in her seat, crossing and then uncrossing her legs.

"I'm sorry I didn't come to Alexis's party. I was too much of a coward, not wanting to face you right away, but it's not an excuse."

Megan edged her feet out of the flip-flops she wore and curled them beneath her legs. "I had a feeling that's why you didn't show. But"—she shrugged—"a phone call would have been nice."

A flush grew across Laurie's face. "I know. I tried to make it up to her by taking her to the movie."

Megan blew a wisp of hair that tickled her cheek. "Yeah, I know. Alexis mentioned it was only part of her gift, though. You know you spoil that girl too much." She kept her voice light, trying to defuse some of the awkwardness between them.

Laurie visibly swallowed before she glanced toward the house. "I like to. She's like my mini me. I thought I'd take her out for a girls' day today. Maybe have Hannah tag along? I'd take them to the mall so that we could look at some school clothes, and then do dinner and dessert, nothing too fancy."

Megan smiled. "They'd both love that. Alexis mentioned this morning that she needs a complete wardrobe makeover, supposedly."

Laurie ran her hands through her hair. "Yeah, sorry about that. I kind of brought up the fact that my mom would always take me clothes shopping before school, and I'd end up with a new wardrobe."

Megan smiled. "Summer's not over yet, you know. But thanks for giving me a head start."

"Well, I hope this will help." Laurie cleared her throat and looked out at the yard. "How's Emma feeling? Peter mentioned she'd overdone it during the party."

Megan glanced toward the house. "She's better. Poor thing had heatstroke. She practically slept all day yesterday."

"Lexi said it was the best birthday ever. She loved her golf clubs."

Alexis had told her the same thing, but knowing she was bragging about it to Laurie felt good. Peter promised to take her out golfing this weekend, and the kid couldn't wait.

Megan took another sip of mocha and enjoyed the velvety chocolate taste as it slid down her throat. A gentle breeze played with her hair as Laurie continued to fidget in her seat.

There was a giant elephant standing on the table between them, but it seemed neither one of them was willing to acknowledge it. Megan had hoped Laurie would bring it up, but from the way her friend avoided her gaze, she was probably having as hard a time thinking of how to do that as Megan was.

"All right, we need to talk about this," Megan finally blurted.

"Oh, thank God! I wasn't sure . . ." Laurie played with the cup in her hand before glancing up.

"How to tell me you were dating Riley?"

Laurie nodded before quickly shaking her head. "We're not dating. Not really."

Megan gave her a look that said, *You've got to be kidding me.*

"I just don't understand why you wouldn't tell me. Seeing you guys kissing wasn't exactly . . . Well, let's just say I wasn't exactly prepared." Megan worked to keep her tone level, questioning instead of accusing.

Laurie closed her eyes and sighed. She leaned back in her chair, setting the coffee cup on the table, and folded her hands together.

"I didn't know how to tell you," Laurie hedged.

Megan leaned forward. "We don't keep secrets from each other. Even when it means hurting the other person. Remember?"

Laurie's gaze dropped to her hands. "Meg, I . . . I'm sorry. If it had been anyone but him . . ."

Megan sat back. "What does that mean?"

"I know you have feelings for him." Laurie lifted her head.

Megan shook her head. "Had. Had, Laurie. I was vulnerable, hurting, and I took the easy way out instead of turning to Peter. You were the one who called me on it, remember?" She'd never forget that day when Laurie confronted her about her growing feelings for Riley. It was Laurie who had forced Megan to see what she was doing, to realize that if she didn't stop looking to Riley for comfort, she was going to destroy her marriage. That was when their motto of "the truth, even if it hurts" had really come into existence.

"Still." Laurie shrugged.

Megan pushed to her feet. "There is no still. You can't use me as an excuse for not telling me." She leaned against the deck railing and stared at her friend. She watched a wide range of emotions play across her face, from disappointment to anger to understanding. She probably mirrored those same emotions on her own face. This was another perfect example of her seeing her own needs and not looking outward to others'. She should be happy for her friend. Megan knew Laurie had been lonely since Kris's death. And honestly, she couldn't have found anyone better than Riley. They would be a good match.

Megan leaned her head back and stared up into the clear blue sky. "I probably should have told you we were coming by instead of dropping in on you like we did."

"Yeah, that would have been nice."

Megan heard the smile in Laurie's voice.

"I like him, Meg."

Megan let the words sink in and was surprised to realize they didn't bother her.

"So are you dating or aren't you?"

A sheepish grin grew on Laurie's face, and she tilted her head to the side. "It's been a long time. I'm not sure I know how to do the whole dating thing."

Megan leaned forward and lightly touched Laurie's shoulder. She couldn't even begin to imagine the range of emotions Laurie was feeling. It would have been less awkward if perhaps she'd found someone other than Riley to date, but it was what it was. There was no going back. If there were, Megan would have done many things differently, including not leaning on someone who wasn't her husband. But mistakes happen, and this was her best friend, her family. They'd been there for each other through thick and thin, each held the bride's bouquet while the other said *I do*. Megan had held Laurie's hands after Kris's death, and Laurie stood beside Megan when she refused to give up on finding Emma. They'd once made a pledge, back when they were teenagers, that they'd never let a guy get in the middle of their friendship.

"Honestly, I wouldn't either." Megan smiled at the thought. "You always had a way with the guys, though, even in school. Kris never stood a chance; the poor guy was lost the moment he saw you. I'm sure you'll figure it out." She squeezed Laurie's shoulder.

"Kris would be okay with this, wouldn't he?" Laurie's voice broke.

Megan sank down to her knees and grabbed hold of Laurie's hands.

"Of course he would. He never wanted you to be alone; you know that. And Riley has such a big heart . . . Kris would like him." She chuckled quietly. "No doubt they would have been best friends if they'd ever met. This is exactly what he would want for you. To live life. To be happy."

Megan thought about her own marriage and the sacrifice Peter had made for her. It couldn't have been easy for him to ask Sam to sell her shares.

"Can I just ask for a small favor?" Megan leaned back and rested her hands on the railing behind her. "Put a sock on the door if he's there next time?" She winked.

Laurie's eyes widened, and her mouth dropped. "How about you just text me if you're coming by?"

Megan laughed. "I think I can do that." She reached for the ignored bag of goodies on the table, peered inside the bag, and almost groaned. She pulled out a chocolate croissant, inhaled its delectable sweet aroma, and blew a kiss at her friend.

"If this is your idea of a peace offering, we need to fight more often." Megan reached for the second croissant and handed it to Laurie. "So are you gonna tell me what happened, or should I get Jan to spill the beans? You know she was dying to when we were last there."

"Oh, I know. Trust me." Laurie groaned. "We happened to be at the shooting range together and struck up a conversation afterward. We talked a bit about Emma and how well she's been adjusting and then"—she shrugged—"the conversation just took off from there, and the next thing you know, we realized we had a lot in common."

Megan nodded. It figured Laurie would have met someone on the shooting range. That was where she'd had her first date with Kris.

"So what?" Megan found herself asking. "One thing led to another and . . ."

Laurie nodded. "Honestly, that's what happened. We met for coffee another time and talked a bit, but that's it. Nothing else. It was too awkward. Too . . . personal. I mean, he was such an important person in your . . . our lives when Emma first went missing, and it just seemed too . . . weird. But there was a connection there, and we both knew it. I've been so afraid to tell you. I wanted to see if anything was going to happen first."

Megan took in a deep breath. She could hear the concern in Laurie's voice. It bothered her that Laurie would have been so worried, when she shouldn't have been. And it hurt to know that Laurie's concerns were valid.

"Oh, honey. No man will come between us, remember?"

Megan swallowed hard and then laughed when she caught Laurie doing the same. Megan rose from her chair and went to hug Laurie. She smiled at Hannah, who stood at the patio door.

"Mom?"

It was the tone in Hannah's voice that wiped the smile from her face.

"What's wrong, Hannah?" Megan unwrapped her arms from around Laurie.

"Where's Emma?"

A cold, slithering sensation worked its way down Megan's spine at her daughter's words.

"She should be up in her room, honey. She was playing with her ponies last I checked."

Megan's heart stopped as Hannah gave a tight shake to her head.

Laurie laid a hand on Megan's arm. "What do you mean, Hannah?" she asked.

"I just went to check on her, but she's not there. I looked all over too."

Megan brushed past Laurie and raced into the house. "Emma?" she called out as she searched the downstairs rooms one by one.

"Did you lock the front door behind you?" Megan yelled over her shoulder to Laurie before she saw the answer for herself. The front door was slightly ajar.

Laurie nodded. "Of course I did."

"Then why is it open?" Flustered, Megan waved her hand in the air before gripping the staircase rail. "And why wasn't the alarm on? Hannah, did you open the front door?"

Hannah followed close behind. "No, Mom. I promise. It was like that before I went upstairs. Mom, where is she?"

Megan raced up the stairs, her heart pounding with each step she took. Emma's room was empty, her blankets a mess on her bed. The dress Megan had set out this morning on the chair was gone.

Megan pushed past Laurie, who stood in the doorway to Emma's room, and headed to her bedroom, where the nearest phone was. She dialed Peter's number.

"Peter, Emma's not here." She could feel the panic begin to overwhelm her.

"What do you mean, she's not there?"

Megan shook her head and spun on her heels. She ran down the stairs and out the front door. It was all happening again. Just like before.

"Megan, talk to me," Peter's calm voice soothed her.

"I was outside in the back with Laurie. She locked the door behind her. Emma was upstairs playing when I went outside. But now Hannah can't find her." She knew she wasn't making much sense, and wasn't even sure if Peter could understand what she was saying.

"Where is she, Peter? Where did Emma go?"

There was silence on the other line. Megan struggled to breathe, and she searched the street in both directions. There was nothing. Nothing to see. No Emma. *Oh God . . .*

"Is her bike there? Megan, go look in the garage."

Megan headed to the little side door on their garage and almost cried when the knob turned in her hand. It should have been locked. Why wasn't it locked? *Oh my God . . .* Megan almost collapsed when she remembered. She'd entered through this door to get her watering can earlier. She must have forgotten to lock it afterward. She opened the door, praying she'd find Emma in there, but the first thing Megan noticed was that the light was on. The second was that Emma's bike was missing.

If there was one thing Emma knew how to do well, it was ride her bike. It was the first thing Peter had bought her when she came home, and she took to it like a natural. It was one of her favorite things to do—ride up and down the sidewalks during the day with her sisters.

"Megan?" Peter's voice deepened.

"It's not here, Peter. Her bike is gone. It's all my fault. Again. I left the door open. Peter, I left the door open." Megan stepped back out of the garage and turned toward her house. Laurie stood there with her keys in hand. "She's on her bike. I'm going to go look for her."

Peter's voice stopped her. "No. I know where she is. I'm closer. I'll go get her."

Time stood still.

"Where is she, Peter?" She thought about Emma's insistence about going on the date this morning. Was that where she went? Did she go to the donut shop? Why? Why would her five-year-old leave without saying anything?

"Peter? Where is our daughter?"

CHAPTER TWENTY-SIX

J ack rubbed his eyes and looked out the window again. Surely he wasn't seeing things. That couldn't be his little Emmie riding her bike alone, was it?

He ignored the boys at the table, headed to the front door, threw it open, and then ran past the vehicles and down the sidewalk. He wanted to run to her but didn't want to alarm her. She was only a few feet away now, and the smile she beamed at him was contagious.

"Sweetheart, where is your daddy?" Jack held his arms open and waited for his little girl to run to him. She hopped off her bike, threw her arms around his legs, and started to cry.

Jack bent down and gathered her into his arms. He rubbed his hands in a circular motion on her heaving back as she sobbed hysterically against him.

"Shhh, honey, it's okay. I've got you. Em, sweetie, stop crying," Jack begged. He didn't know what was wrong, but he knew he couldn't handle seeing her this way.

"Jack?"

He angled his head so that his cheek rested against the top of her hair and watched Doug make his way toward him. Kenny stood in the doorway of the donut shop, concern etched on his face.

"Can you take Emmie's bike and put it in the back of my truck?" Jack lifted her into his arms. He smoothed the hair down her back and tucked her dress in tight around her legs. He was starting to get worried. He glanced down the street to see where her parents were but couldn't find them.

She wouldn't have run away, would she?

Em snuggled in tight against him as he headed back toward the donut shop, her little body jolting as she hiccupped.

"How about one of those strawberry-filled donuts? Those were Grandma's favorite. Remember?" All he wanted was for his little girl to calm down. He needed to find out what was wrong and why she was alone.

He sat her down in the chair beside his at the table and nodded to Doug, who went to get her a donut from the front counter. He caught the way she kept her head down. Jack grabbed a couple of napkins and laid them in her hands. Her sniffles broke his heart.

"Em, honey, where is your daddy?" Jack gently touched her cheek and forced her to look at him. He kept his voice even, with a hint of authority so that she'd answer him.

"At work," she whispered through trembling lips.

"And where is your mommy?"

Em's lips turned into a pout, and he caught the look of stubbornness in her eyes. She crossed her arms and stared at the ground. He wasn't going to let her avoid his questions. This was too serious. It was a fine line he walked between coddling and remaining stern.

"Princess, I need you to tell me. Please?"

She glanced out the window behind him before turning her gaze to him.

"She's at home, Papa."

Jack sighed. "Does she know where you are?"

She shook her head.

Jack groaned and sat back in his chair. "Oh, honey, you can't do that." He could only imagine the fear and panic her poor mother must be feeling. He glanced at his watch and tried to judge how long she'd been missing. He didn't know exactly where his little girl lived, but it couldn't be too far, since the five-year-old girl had ridden her bike. Doug carried a tray with a powdered donut and a small chocolate milk and set it down in front of Emmie.

"What are you going to do?" Doug sat down beside him. Kenny joined him but kept quiet.

Jack tightened his lips. "There's only one thing I can do. I have to take her home."

"Do you know where she lives?" Kenny asked.

Jack shook his head. No, but she should.

"This isn't going to go over well, you know." Doug shook his head. He heard the warning in his friend's voice.

"Eat your donut and drink your chocolate milk, sweetie. Then we'll hop in the truck, and I'll take you home, okay?" Jack glanced down at his girl before staring out the window. Cold fingers trailed down his spine as he thought about the next hour. He wouldn't blame her mother if she called the cops on him. He almost expected to see the flashing lights pull up into the parking lot.

Instead, what he saw was Peter pulling into the parking spot right across from where he sat. His eyes held a frantic look as he gazed inside. Jack lifted his arm in a wave, and Peter slammed his door shut and raced toward him. Jack pushed his chair back and stood, groaning at the ache in his knees from the sudden movement.

"Em, your dad is here, honey," Jack said when she looked at him.

Her eyes grew round and her back straightened as she slowly turned in her seat to face her father.

Jack was beyond thankful that it was Peter who now stood before him and not a police officer or Emmie's mother. But his first instinct was to protect his little girl from whatever punishment her dad was about to inflict. She was only five years old. She didn't need to be punished. So he was surprised when he noticed the tears in Peter's eyes as he knelt down beside her chair and rested his hand on her arm.

"You had us worried, pumpkin." There was a roughness to Peter's voice that Jack more than understood.

"I'm sorry, Daddy," Em whispered.

Peter stood up and placed a kiss on her head before turning his attention to Jack.

"Has she been here long?" There was a desperation in his voice that had Jack on edge.

"Only a couple of minutes." He needed—no, he wanted to soothe the man. "Her bike is in the back of my truck."

Peter closed his eyes for a split second before squatting down beside her again. "Honey, why did you sneak out of the house? Your mom is worried sick about you right now."

There was a look in Em's eyes that Jack knew all too well. He placed his hand on her shoulder and squeezed lightly.

"You left without me, and Papa was here waiting," she said before taking a bite of her donut. She gave the impression that she didn't understand what she'd done, but Jack knew otherwise. He'd seen the fear and worry in her eyes moments before she threw herself into his arms.

"Oh, honey." Jack sat back down in his chair and waited for her to look at him. "You know what you did, don't you?"

The donut dropped from her hand as she nodded.

"I think you owe your daddy an apology, don't you?"

She nodded and lowered her gaze before jumping at the sound of her name being called from across the small store.

❧

"Emma!"

Relief flooded through Megan's body the moment she saw her daughter. Once Peter had told her where Emma was, it was as if her whole world had exploded in front of her. She didn't want to believe him. She couldn't believe him. All his talk about trusting him flew out the window in that moment.

"Megan, wait." Megan almost yanked her arm out of Laurie's grasp but stopped. Thank God for Laurie being there. She'd driven to the donut shop after Megan managed to get their neighbor's eldest daughter to watch Hannah and Alexis.

The small donut shop was silent when she screamed her daughter's name. She looked around the space, took in the dozen small tables and the single waitress standing behind the counter, and noticed how all the people in the store stared at her.

She focused on the men who stood at the table where her daughter sat. Her husband and . . . Jack.

She took tentative steps toward the table, refusing to look at Peter or anyone else.

"Megan." Laurie reached her hand out and forced her to stop. "Try to calm yourself before you say or do anything, okay?"

Megan searched her best friend's eyes. All she read was concern. "I know," she whispered.

It wasn't hard to miss the sense of feeling overwhelmed on Emma's face when Megan reached the table. She sat down in the empty seat in front of Emma and lightly touched her daughter's knee.

"That was quite the ride you took this morning." Megan bit her lip as she kept her voice low and calm.

Emma's lips trembled as she met Megan's gaze.

"I was really worried, honey." Megan placed a gentle kiss on her daughter's forehead. She still felt a bit warm, just like earlier, and riding her bike for several blocks wouldn't have helped. She needed to be home, resting, drinking lots of fluids.

Megan looked up at Peter with accusation glaring in her eyes. This was his fault.

"I wanted to see Papa," Emma whispered.

Megan smoothed her daughter's hair and sighed. She glanced up at Jack, and from the look in his eyes, she knew the guilt he carried outweighed her own.

"I'm sorry, ma'am. I had no idea she would come by herself." The sound of *that* man's voice sparked a wave of fury she struggled to bury.

Megan's back was tight; her shoulders back as her breathing slowed. It took everything in her not to lash out at this man she so desperately wanted to hate. But she didn't. She lowered her voice instead. "No, but you knew she'd come with Peter." She looked away, unwilling to hold his gaze.

She was conflicted over what to do now. She could insist Emma leave with her and come home, but how much damage would that inflict on Emma, forcing her to leave Jack again? Or she could allow this visit to continue, leave with Laurie, and trust Peter to take care of the situation—or stay, and deal with the repercussions later with Peter.

"Megan." Laurie stood behind her. "Why don't we go get some coffee?"

With careful precision, Megan stood, her back rigid, as she stepped away from the chair. She leaned down, kissed Emma's cheek, and whispered, "I love you," into her ear before she stepped away. She angled her body enough not to touch Peter as she passed him. She was furious with him, and it took all her control not to lash out.

"I can't believe he did this behind my back," Megan hissed to Laurie as they walked toward the counter.

"Really, Meg? It's not like you gave him much choice." The look on Laurie's face had Megan's cheeks burning with shame. Laurie ordered two coffees and pulled out her wallet.

"That's not fair."

Laurie's brow rose. "What part?"

"Excuse me?" Disbelief laced Megan's tone.

Laurie took the coffee mugs and headed toward a table. Megan followed once she realized Laurie wasn't going to answer. She couldn't believe Laurie would side with Peter on this.

"What is your problem, Laurie? How can you say something like that?"

Laurie gazed across the room. "I can say that because Emma is the one who is hurting here, more than you and Peter combined."

Megan watched how her daughter's gaze flitted between Jack and Peter as if she was unsure of who she'd wronged more. That was when it hit her: Laurie was right.

Emma was caught in the middle.

Megan wanted to cry. It was her fault her daughter was in this predicament. Her fault that Emma thought she had to keep her visits with Jack a secret, that she couldn't trust her parents enough to be sure they would continue. It was why her little girl thought she'd had to come alone.

"It's not fair, Laurie. After everything she'd been through . . ." Megan pressed her lips tight.

Laurie reached out, and Megan held tight to her hand.

"No, it's not. But it's time to stop forcing Emma to forget the last two years of her life just because you can't forgive."

Laurie was right. And so was Peter. Was she the only one blind to what Emma was going through? Was she the only one not listening to what Emma had been saying all along?

"I don't know if I can, Laurie. How do I welcome her kidnapper into our lives? I shouldn't have to."

Laurie shook her head. "But you're not. That's her Papa she's sitting with, Meg. There's a difference."

Megan toyed with her coffee cup until she noticed Emma standing beside her.

"Hi." Megan twisted in her chair and helped Emma climb onto her lap. "Do you want to talk?" She kept her voice calm. All she wanted to do was hold Emma close and forget the rest of the world existed.

Emma nodded. Her eyes were wide and solemn, and she wrung her hands together in her lap.

"I'm sorry, Mommy," she whispered.

Megan wrapped her arms around her daughter and held tight.

"I'm just glad you're okay. I was scared, honey. I didn't know where you were."

Emma turned and placed both of her hands on Megan's face. "I was right here with Papa. I was safe."

Megan sighed. She reached for Emma's hands and planted kisses on her palms. "But I didn't know that, honey. It's not safe to leave the house without telling me, okay?"

Emma gazed over at Peter and then Jack. "You're not mad?"

Megan bit her lip. She was terrified. Worried she was making the wrong decision. Peter waited for a signal from her, a sign that all was okay. She couldn't give that. Not yet.

"Not at you, honey. Never at you."

How could she be angry with her five-year-old? Could she blame Emma for wanting to see her Papa? No. But she was furious with Peter for allowing it to happen.

A seed of doubt sprouted in her heart. As much as she wanted, she couldn't place all that blame on Peter either. Some of it, yes. He should have talked with her first. He should have told her, even if he knew how she'd respond.

She wanted to hate Jack. She wanted to erase him from every aspect of Emma's life even knowing that doing so made her look like a monster. But what she wanted to do and what she would do were two different things. They had to be.

"Mommy?" Emma's timid voice reached out and wrapped itself around Megan's heart. "Mommy, can I go and sit with Papa again?"

Megan's heart ached as she listened to the sliver of hope enter her daughter's voice. She opened her mouth and tried to think of an alternative to tempt Emma with. But her mind was blank.

All she could do was nod and watch her daughter walk away. It hurt, more than she wanted to admit. Megan looked away. She counted under her breath, trying to calm herself enough to sit and watch Emma with *that . . . that . . .* Megan sighed. With Jack. Even saying his name hurt.

"Megan," Laurie whispered to her. "Megan." Her voice, more insistent, had Megan glancing up. Laurie was staring beyond her shoulder. Megan half-turned in her seat to find Emma standing there, her hands clasped in front.

"What's up, honey?"

Something like a smile flitted across Emma's face. "I just wanted to say I love you." She lunged toward Megan and wrapped her tiny arms around Megan's neck.

The constricting band that was wrapped tight around Megan's heart loosened. As long as she had this, nothing else mattered. Nothing. Not her insecurities, not her fears, and not her anger.

As she wound her own arms around Emma and held her close, she caught Peter's gaze. A soft smile spread across his face as he watched her.

After today, their lives were never going to be the same and Megan wasn't sure how she felt about that.

CHAPTER TWENTY-SEVEN

Megan sat out on the back porch and waited for Peter to join her.

He'd wanted to come home to talk things over earlier in the day, but Megan needed time to process what had just happened. Her emotions were too fresh, and nothing would have been resolved.

But she didn't stew all day either.

Laurie ended up taking both Hannah and Alexis out on their girls' date, while Megan and Emma stayed home during the day. Things were quiet, with Emma playing in the backyard with Daisy while Megan cleaned the kitchen. Her cell phone continued to go off, first with phone calls from Peter and then text messages when he realized she wasn't going to answer. Eventually, he got the idea, and his last text was that he was sorry for not being honest with her and that he loved her.

Of that she had no doubt. He just had a funny way of showing it lately.

Her kitchen was now spotless, her fridge cleaned, her floors scrubbed, and her hands raw from the hot water they'd been immersed in while she worked out her anger. But she felt better now, calmer and more relaxed. Ready to discuss Emma sneaking away to visit Jack.

Just the thought of Emma riding her bike that far had Megan's hands shaking and her heartbeat racing. Sure, their street was relatively quiet, but she would have had to cross two major streets before reaching the donut shop. Anything could have happened to her. Megan brushed that thought away. She needed to calm herself down.

Before her cleaning spree, she'd asked Emma to help her make fruit salad for lunch and attempted to talk to her about what happened. At first, her daughter was quiet, not willing to offer much in the way of explanation, more concerned with whether Megan was still mad at her. How was she to explain to a five-year-old just how much danger she'd been in without scaring her too much? How did she confess her own fear of Jack being back in their lives when to Emma he was her Papa?

Laurie was right. When Megan had dropped Emma off for dinner and a sleepover with her sisters at Laurie's house an hour ago, she'd said as much. It was time for Megan to face her fears—and that meant dealing with this trust issue between her and Peter.

The evening was still young and the warm wind whispered against her skin. Megan leaned her head back as far as it could go, her hair hanging down, tickling her back and arms as it swayed in the breeze.

A door slammed and minutes later, soft music flowed from the open window and door to the kitchen. Ahh, soft jazz, her favorite. Megan suppressed a smile as the screen door opened and a chair was pulled back from the table.

She opened her eyes to see Peter beside her holding a bouquet of white roses. She smiled slightly as she took them from his hands and brought them up to her nose. They smelled divine.

"I'm sorry," Peter whispered. He stood and reached for her hands, pulling her up with him. He wrapped his arms around her and held tight.

"I know you are," she said against his chest. She rested her head against him and listened to the steady beat of his heart. She pulled away and stood by the railing, watching Peter as he realized she hadn't said she forgave him.

"You ask me to trust you, but then in the next breath you lie to me. I asked you point-blank if Emma had seen Jack, and you li—"

"I never lied." Peter hung his head.

"You never told me the truth either. Lie by omission. Isn't that the same thing?" It was a moot point, really. What's done was done. There was no turning back time, no wishing for things to be different.

Peter lifted his head, his Adam's apple bobbing as he swallowed. She read the conflicting emotions in his gaze, the desire to defend himself, the apology, and the grief. She looked away.

"I'm not sure I can apologize for placing our daughter's need first. Keeping it a secret from you, yes, I was wrong, and I'm so sorry for that. But I don't regret taking Emma to see her grandfather."

"He's not her grandfather." Megan wished she could take back those words the instant she said them. "I don't want him to be her grandfather." She blinked back the tears she hadn't wanted to cry all day.

When Peter pulled her back into his embrace, her body stiffened. She didn't want to give in. She didn't want to accept this.

"She's the only family he has left, Meg." Peter rested his chin against her head and stroked her hair. The tears fell harder as she thought about what he'd just said. What if it were her own father? What if he were all alone?

She lifted her face. "That's why this means so much to you, isn't it? Because he's a father who has been left alone."

Peter's gaze clouded over before he looked away.

"You see him as a father, don't you?"

Her husband shrugged. But she noticed he didn't deny it. Megan's soul sighed. How could she fight against that? Losing his father had devastated Peter in a way she could never understand. She loved her dad, but he was more of a distant father, showing his love by providing for his family rather than being there emotionally for them.

"He's dying, Megan. Emma's lost so much in such a short time. She's going to lose him, too, eventually." His arms dropped, leaving her feeling chilled. "We took him away from her once. I don't want to do it again." His face turned to stone as he said those words, his gaze determined. "I need you to trust me."

Even if Megan had wanted to fight him on this, she knew she wouldn't. She couldn't. She dropped down to rest on her heels and pulled out a box from beneath her seat.

She'd thought long and hard about doing this. It would have been very easy for her to destroy the box she'd hidden high in her closet, to shred the letters between Jack and Emma and pretend she'd never attempted to keep them apart. Except, if she was going to put Emma's needs first, then being honest with Peter about this was necessary. No more secrets.

"I was wrong to do that to her," she said as she handed the box to Peter.

He took the box from her hands and slowly opened the lid, his eyes widening when he realized what was inside.

She stepped closer and placed the palm of her hand against his cheek. His five-o'clock shadow tickled her sensitive skin.

"I do trust you," she whispered.

CHAPTER TWENTY-EIGHT

May 5
    Dear Jack,
    I love you. I hope when you eventually read this journal, you will remember that above all else.

    I've never remembered things with such clarity as today. It almost makes me wonder if this is my last good day. Will the rest go downhill from here? Will I forget who you are, Jack? Will I forget about Mary and our sweet precious Emmie?

    I hope not.

    But if I do, I want you to remember this: above all else, you are my heart.

    I haven't been the perfect wife, but I've been the best one I can be. I made mistakes raising Mary, but looking back, I made the best decisions I could at the time.

    How Emmie came to be with us—I don't think I can ever be forgiven for that. I don't believe it's a memory of something else that is confusing me or a nightmare I can't wake up from. It has to be the truth. I don't remember much about that day, but I do know that our Mary is dead, and I don't think she had a daughter. I don't know how I found our precious Emmie, but Jack . . . I need you to do the right thing. I can't. I don't trust myself anymore.

I will say this, to hear the laughter in your voice and to see the love in your eyes, I will cherish that forever. Our Emmie has been a miracle in our lives; she's given our old bones a reason to live.

I love you, Jack. I always will. Hold that close when things go dark.

Jack sat up in his room, his heart heavy as he held Dottie's journal in his hands.

Of everything he'd done since Dottie's death, reading this journal was the toughest yet. Going through her clothes, making room for the boys to come and stay with him, even packing up her knick-knacks hadn't hurt as much as this one small book.

He tried to wrap his head around what he'd just read. How had he not seen just how far Dottie's illness had taken her? So much heartache might have been averted if he'd only opened his eyes and seen what was happening to his girl.

She asked for love but not forgiveness. He would have given her both, no questions asked.

A heavy tread up the stairs alerted him that he'd soon have company.

"If we don't leave soon, we'll be late. Kenny's all in a panic." Doug edged Jack's bedroom door open and stood there.

"Tell the old man to keep his pants on. I'm coming."

Doug pointed to the journal in his lap. "You found another one?" His gaze strayed over to the bookshelf full of Dottie's journals.

Jack considered how much to tell Doug. He caught the worry in his friend's eyes and knew the time for secrets had passed.

"It's her last one."

Doug took a step into the room and sat down in the wicker chair beside the door.

"Did you read it?"

Jack nodded. "She was a stronger woman than I gave her credit for." He shuffled the book in his hands, not willing to part with the feel of it, for even a moment. It was the last thing she'd written, her last letter to him.

"Does she talk about Emmie?" Doug leaned forward, resting his elbows on his knees.

Jack shrugged.

"What are you going to do about it?" They'd had this discussion many times, about how Dottie found Emmie and brought her into their lives. They'd both tried to understand, to reckon how Dottie's mind must have been during that time.

"Nothing." Jack grunted. "It's time to leave things in the past. That girl is where she should be, with her family. Living in the past, having these questions hang over my head, and needing answers does nobody any good."

He pushed himself up off the bed and reached for a box he'd set behind him. He slid the journal beneath balls of yarn and lifted the box into his arms before turning around.

"I can hear Kenny whining. Let's go." He followed Doug out of the room and down the stairs. Kenny sat at the kitchen table, with the new oxygen tank at his side.

"Sure you want to go? It's only bingo." The old man needed to be back in bed, not traipsing about, especially in his condition. But there was a fire in Kenny's gaze and Jack knew bed was the last place he wanted to be. The nurse, after checking on Kenny earlier, had told Jack to let the man enjoy what little time he had left. So that's what he was going to do.

It was advice Jack meant to live by as well.

❧

The smell of roasted turkey wafted through the kitchen. Megan stood at her kitchen island, chopping sweet potatoes to make Peter's favorite dish—candied yams. Every element on her stove was in use, as well as her slow cooker and oven. Chaos reigned in her house, and she was loving every minute of it.

It was Thanksgiving, and she had so much to be thankful for this year. In the last few months, their family had grown closer; the rifts once so deeply entrenched now healing. Her relationship with Peter was stronger than it had ever been. They worked as a team in their marriage, in their home, and she was even working a few hours in the office during the day. It almost reminded her of the early years of their marriage.

The past couple of years Thanksgiving dinner had been held at her parents' house, but this year Megan wanted her home to be full of laughter, love, and family.

Sheila stood at the sink washing dishes, while Laurie sat at the kitchen table putting together a photo album with Emma and Hannah. Daisy was outside barking up a storm as she chased a squirrel around the yard.

"I can't believe it hasn't snowed yet," her mom muttered as she stared out the kitchen sink window. She smiled over her shoulder at Megan, who smiled back. So far, fingers crossed, there'd been no arguments, no nitpicking about the dishes. Hopefully, it would continue that way.

"Is there anything I can do?" Peter's arms snaked around her waist, and his lips left a lingering kiss against the pulse in her neck. Megan leaned into him and rested her head against his shoulder.

"Just cutting the last veggies. We should be ready in an hour." She slid the knife through the last half of the sweet potato and pushed down. These might be one of her favorite root vegetables, but she hated the effort it took to cut them.

"Want me to do that?" Peter reached his hand out for the knife. Megan relinquished her hold and stepped away to check on the pots on the stove.

"Megan, you look gorgeous here." Laurie held up a picture. Megan blushed. Peter had taken that last month when they'd gone for a walk down the boardwalk. The girls surrounded her, their arms all around her, while the wind blew her hair every which way. Her eyes sparkled and her cheeks were rosy from the nippy wind. She'd never been happier, and it showed.

"You should frame that one," Peter said as he peeked over her shoulder.

"Mom, when can we eat?" Hannah barreled into the room, almost tripping over her feet before Peter stopped her with his arm.

"Not yet, honey." Peter twisted her around by holding on to her shoulders and pushed her back in the direction she came. "You're supposed to be keeping Grandpa Dan company." Peter leaned closer to her ear. "Remember, we need to keep him out of the kitchen."

Megan winked at Peter once Hannah left. Her father knew nothing about cooking, but he thought everyone wanted his opinion. It was Hannah's job to keep him out, and so far she'd done a great job.

"Which one's your favorite, Alexis?" Megan stood behind her daughter and played with her hair. Alexis was hunched over the photos, shuffling them back and forth.

"I like this one." She pointed to a picture she'd taken herself of Emma playing in the backyard with Daisy. Daisy sat in her lap, a bone between her paws, while Emma stared at something in the distance, not shown in the picture. There was a peaceful look on her daughter's face. Megan could see why Alexis liked it so much.

"You take great pictures. Maybe you should add a camera to your Christmas list?" Megan thought about the new camera hidden away in the upstairs closet. She couldn't wait to give it to her and hear the excitement in her voice when she opened the gift.

"Thanks," Alexis mumbled. She lowered her head and tried to hide her face behind her hair as it swung forward.

The atmosphere in the kitchen was full of energy. Daniel and Hannah were shouting at the television in the other room, while Sheila was humming to herself at the counter. Emma kept checking the clock on the microwave while Laurie tried to distract her.

Megan poured herself a small glass of white wine and refilled both Laurie's and her mother's glasses as well. "Why don't you sit down for a few minutes, Mom?"

Sheila wiped her hands on her apron and reached for the glass. The doorbell rang at the same time.

"Do you want me to get that?" Peter asked.

Megan shook her head. "I've got it."

The doorbell rang again just as Megan grabbed the doorknob.

Jack stood on the other side, wearing his Sunday best, from what she could tell. He held a box, and from the way he shuffled it in his hands, he looked a bit nervous.

"Jack." Megan opened the screen door. Butterflies took off in a dizzying pattern in her stomach as she worked on keeping her smile in place.

Jack's fingers whitened as he tightened his grip on the box.

"Thanks for inviting me." He cleared his throat before his focus dropped to the box.

There was an awkward moment of silence. "Are Kenny and Doug okay being home alone today?"

Jack shrugged. "I dropped the boys off at the retirement home. There's a game of bingo playing, and Kenny wanted one last chance at winning the pot."

Last month, Doug and Kenny had moved in with Jack. Peter had mentioned to Megan one night that the only reason he'd held out for so long was due to their morning coffee dates. It didn't take a genius to figure out Jack felt he needed an excuse to continue seeing Emma, and he thought that was the only way—to be at the donut shop every morning. After a little bit of coaxing on Peter's part, Jack had invited his friends to move in.

She was about to look inside the open box, to see what was so important to him, but there was a look on his face that stopped her. "Is Kenny getting worse?"

Jack shrugged. "Not sure he'll make it to Christmas." She caught the bright sheen of tears in his eyes and knew it was time to change the subject.

"Jack." She needed to say this before anyone else came out, especially Emma. "I'm glad you could accept our invitation. This is Em's first Thanksgiving since she's come back, and it was important to her . . ." That didn't quite come out the way she wanted.

It had been a hard battle for Megan ever since that day when Emma had run away to the donut shop. The last thing she wanted to do was accept Jack as part of Emma's life. She'd been livid with Peter, and it had taken many counseling sessions before her anger had subsided.

Emma needed Jack in her life. He helped stabilize her, and his presence in her life created a sense of security. He was her grounding. As much as Megan hated it, she had to accept it. It would have been better if Peter hadn't gone over her head and allowed the relationship to grow, but in order to keep a solid front with the girls and to rebuild their marriage, Megan swallowed her pride and put her daughters' interests ahead of her own.

Emma and Peter continued their dates with Jack, and Megan tagged along a few times, until, at the urging of their counselor, they invited Jack to join the family for activities outside the donut shop. It started with trips to the beach and out for ice cream; then Peter invited Jack over to watch a football game; eventually, he began to come for Sunday dinners.

Whether she wanted it or not, Jack was now a part of their lives. And to be honest, he was growing on her. She kept her distance at first, not really interacting with him much other than the polite basics. But it was as if Emma knew her hesitation, and she did everything she could to bring them closer.

Jack shook his head. "Megan, I know inviting me wasn't your idea, but . . ." His voice choked up, and he didn't meet her gaze.

Megan reached out her arm. "No, it was. My suggestion."

Jack's head lifted, and she saw the surprise in his eyes. He held the box out for her.

"I, um, well, I was going through the house, and I found a few things. There's wool—not sure if anyone knits, but there's plenty in here for hats and scarves and whatnot. Plus, there's . . ."

Megan looked inside. Amid the colorful balls of wool was a book. It almost looked like a notepad or a journal. She reached for it but didn't open it.

"There's nothing I can say to explain what happened to my girl, to Dottie. I wish I could. I've wanted to give you a reason or something to help answer questions I know you have."

"It's okay."

Jack's eyes gleamed. "No. It's not. But I found Dottie's journal. She was meticulous about writing in that thing daily. For years. There's a bookshelf full of her diaries. But this one . . . she didn't write in it as much. It starts when Em . . . when she brought Em to our house, and it ends just before . . ." He cleared his throat a few times.

Megan held the journal close. "You're saying it's all in here? Everything from those two years?" She couldn't believe it.

Jack placed the box down on the ground. "Her mind was al-ready going, so she didn't write every day, but . . . I wanted . . . I thought it might help you get to know my Dottie . . . and why she thought Em was our granddaughter."

Megan's heart swelled as she read the honesty in Jack's gaze.

"Thank you," she whispered. She took a deep breath and tried to compose herself. The sound of a chair being pushed back on the tiled floor and bare feet running toward them forced her to be calm. "Thank you." She smiled as she held the journal close to her chest.

"Papa!" Emma launched herself into Jack's outstretched arms. "You're here!"

Megan watched the barrage of emotions sweep across Jack's face as he held her daughter tight in his arms. If anyone had asked her a few months ago whether she would have welcomed this man into her home like this, she would have laughed. Never in a million years. It had taken a lot of soul-searching before she realized this man wasn't the enemy.

"You're part of our family now." Megan placed her hand on Jack's arm and smiled. Peter met them in the foyer and shook Jack's hand in greeting before walking him into the family room where the football game was playing.

Megan sank down on the steps and opened the journal in her hands. There was a bookmark at the back, and it was where she went to first. She was curious as to why this spot in the book was marked. What she read would forever change her.

Dear Jack . . .

A NOTE FROM THE AUTHOR

I wrote this book specifically for those who fell in love with Emma's story in *Finding Emma*. Without your input, without your e-mails and your comments, I would have never created *Emma's Secret*. I hope you will fall in love with this story and feel drawn even closer to the characters, and that after you read the final page, you'll be able to put this book down with a sigh of satisfaction.

To my husband and family for encouraging me to write a story from my heart and for all your ideas on how to create a family worthy of this story. And to my girls of awesomeness, for standing by me, for believing in me when I didn't, and for just being awesome! This is just the beginning . . .

A special thank-you once again to Sherri Gall. Thank you for listening to me ramble, for reading and responding to my frantic text messages when I'm trying to figure out a plot point, and for all your ideas and suggestions on how to create a secret that only Emma could have.

To Jean Brewer and the Dachshund Group—there's a special spot in this story just for you. To Wendy Keel, Amy Schaubel, Lyn Campbell, and Alyssa Palmer—thank you for your keen eye, your suggestions, and your belief in me as a writer.

And, finally, to Carmen Johnson, my amazing editor who fell in love with Emma's story and also believed in me as a writer. One day, I'd love to share some chocolate with you and celebrate our success!

ABOUT THE AUTHOR

Steena Holmes is the author of two previous novels, *Chocolate Reality* and *Finding Emma*. Holmes enjoys writing stories that other mothers of young children can relate to. She currently lives in Calgary with her husband and three daughters.